P9-ECR-593

DRIVEN TO RAGE

By

Carol Sheldon

Copyright © 2013 by Carol Sheldon

All rights reserved. No part of this publication may be reproduced, distributed or transmitted in any form or by any means, including photocopying, recording, or other electronic or mechanical methods, without the prior written permission of the publisher, except in the case of brief quotations embodied in critical reviews and certain other noncommercial uses permitted by copyright law. For permission requests, write to the publisher at the address below.

Published by Houghton
215 Main Street, #105
Sausalito, CA 94965

Website/blog: www.carolsheldon.com

Most of the characters are entirely fictitious. Real names of the times have been changed, except for Big Annie Clemenc, her husband Joseph, Frank Stavs and Governor Ferris.

Ordering Information:
Best way: order directly from author at blog: www.carolsheldon.com
Special discounts are available on quantity purchases by schools, associations, and others. For details, contact the address above.

Book Layout ©2013 BookDesignTemplates.com

ISBN - 13: 978 – 1490350646
ISBN - 10: 1490350640

Photo Credits: Big Annie, Miner, Quincy No. 6-- courtesy of MTU Archives; couple--Dreamstime

DEDICATION

This book is dedicated to the memory of Big Annie, to all those who supported fair labor practices in the past, and to those who do today.

ACKNOWLEDGEMENTS

There are many who helped bring this book to fruition: Crys Rourke, my editor, who tempered her criticisms by sprinkling them with remarks like "This scene rocks!" Her wisdom helped to make many improvements to the original text. Teresa LeYung Ryan gave me much to think about with her in-depth editing, facilitating a richer book. Several other readers found the inevitable typos and gave valuable comments: Marilyn Bentley, Stuart Chappell, Sandi Rubay and Allison Pratt. In addition Allison provided invaluable assistance in first helping me with tech issues on my new computer, then downloading the manuscript into the template, and countless other tasks. Her patience and generosity have been remarkable.

Josephine Biasi created the wonderful cover with photos that aid in defining the story's content. I thank Joel Friedlander and Tracy Atkins for the creation of their marvelous templates, and prompt response to questions and fixes. Geoff Kidd came to the rescue finding roguish punctuation marks with a magic tool. The organization which continues to give me priceless help is the Bay Area Independent Publishing Association.

Lastly, I couldn't have envisioned this book without the historical facts in their books by Emeritus Professor Larry Lankton , Arthur Turner and others.. (See reference books at back of book.) If there are historical mistakes in the text, they are most likely mine.

AUTHOR'S NOTE

After the publication of my previous book, *Mother Lode*, I was asked by people in the Upper Peninsula to write a story about the "Italian Hall Tragedy", which occurred in 1913, and Big Annie, who organized and led parades for the strike that year. This is that story, built around historical accounts of the mine workers, the union, and the strike.

Driven to Rage follows a family who are caught in the center of one of the longest running ideological clashes in history; the conflict wrenches them apart.

There are heroes and scoundrels, murder and mystery, lovers and secrets. Like any novel worth its weight, let's hope this is a tale to capture your interest. So dive down the shafts, and explore the tunnels with the miners of 1913.

Most of the characters are entirely fictitious. Real names of the times have been changed, except for Big Annie Clemenc, her husband Joseph, Frank Stavs and Governor Ferris.

I have tried to be historically accurate in setting the stage with verifiable facts in describing the people, the provocations, the rebellion of the workers, and management's position. The conflict is real, and still rages today.

CHAPTER ONE

There was a whooshing sound, a blast of air, and a terrible thunderous crashing. Calvin Willis stood absolutely still while the noise reverberated all through the mine.

My God! Not another cave-in!

It was the sound all miners feared— being struck dead by falling rock, or worse yet, buried alive deep in the bowels of the earth, while the walls of the shaft collapsed, roared and echoed above and around them.

There would be warning sounds— first the cracking and dust falling from the walls. Sometimes that would be enough to speed the men to safety. Sometimes it was not.

Calvin would have to climb down the old stationary ladder, with no light but the small carbide lamp on his helmet. The man-car would be readying to take men from the stricken level to the top. It was difficult to see. He stumbled toward the ladder, reached it, and fairly skipped down the rungs.

Halfway down he heard the second blast. The ladder wobbled, twisted and threw its rider. Calvin dropped a few feet, his hands strumming over the rungs, but falling too fast to grab on.

Twisting to the side, he managed to jam a foot between the steps, and hook the vertical bar with his right arm.

The wobbling finally stopped. The silence was almost as frightening as the previous thunder. Stifling fear and pain, he continued to place one foot carefully below the other, descending into darkness and dust.

The Keweenaw Peninsula in Northern Michigan is an icy finger that slices into the cold waters of Lakes Superior. Many copper mines dot this small strip of land. The Keweenaw was the largest. It was in one of its shafts that Calvin Willis found himself in a cave-in.

"Will there be anything else, Mrs. Willis?" Patty asked her mistress.

Patty was a loyal housemaid, a good-natured Irish woman, and Betsy Willis was fond of her. She was peppy and jolly, and Betsy enjoyed her company.

"No, Dear. You've done a fine day's work, and your meat pie smells delicious. Oh, wait. If you could just put these pins in my hair. You do it so much better than I."

Betsy was still beautiful, at forty-three, without a line in her face. Patty finished fastening her mistress's flaxen hair in a bun. Betsy liked it better down, but it wasn't considered seemly for a married woman to let it hang loose, untamed.

I'll be off now," her housekeeper replied.

Betsy Willis waited eagerly for the post. Her husband knew nothing of her letters to the editor. He would be enraged. She made a point of being sure to intercept the mail each day before he returned from work. Most days there was nothing, but she had to be alert every day.

Thus far, the *Mining Chronicle* in Houghton, which served the whole Copper Mining Community, had refused to publish a single one of her letters.

"They are so biased!" she complained to her friend, Rose. "They always take the side of Management, never the miners."

"Why don't you try the papers outside of Houghton?" her friend suggested.

Betsy found favor farther away. Some small presses around Marquette, and further south near Detroit and Chicago printed her letters. They were kind enough to send her copies, and even some of the controversial responses.

She dared not write under her real name. She took on the assumed name of B. T. Wilkins. She would have preferred to write as a woman, but feared her words would find even fewer ears.

She was incensed that the management of the Keweenaw Mining Company was so arrogant, standing, as it did, as the irrefutable lord and master over all it owned and all those it employed. What were they doing for their poor workers?

Betsy was married to a man who stood for management. He owned a profitable general store on Company land. Their two sons worked for the Company— Roy as a shaft supervisor, and Calvin as a shift captain under his brother. She didn't expect any support from this triumvirate of male power, all on the side of Management.

She stepped out on the veranda. Where was the postman? Late again. She sat on the swing in this hot and humid July, while mosquitoes buzzed about her. They were so large some joked they were the state bird.

She tried to focus on the garden, so lovely and fragrant this time of year. The lilacs were gone, but the roses, forget-me-nots and the spreading-pea were profuse and colorful.

She heard his buggy— Jeremy home already? Oh, my God, and the post not yet here.

"Smitty's trying to make up time he lost when he had influenza," Jeremy said as way of explanation. "Didn't see any point in both of us staying on."

Jeremy approached the porch. A stout and strong man, he looked older than he was, which was fifty-three. He strode through the house, but his wife remained on the porch.

He called from within. "Betsy, get me something cool to drink, will you?"

Reluctantly she went to the kitchen and poured two glasses of lemonade made earlier in the day. Anxiously, she jabbed at the big block in the ice-box with the ice pick, sending bits flying across the room.

When she returned to the parlor, Jeremy was holding the mail! Betsy held her breath. She could feel her hands shaking, and the ice tinkle against the glasses. She set the drinks on the table. Jeremy was riffling through the mail.

"Bills, bills," he was saying. "Oh, what's this?" He turned the letter over. "From the *Flint Gazette*. July 20, 1912. Addressed to a B.T. Wilkins. Do you know any Wilkins?" He didn't wait for an answer. "Wrong address."

He tossed the letter aside, and took the others to his desk. She took a deep breath. Dare she pick up the discarded missive?

A piercing whistle sounded through the town.

"The whistle—"

"What about it?"

It was such a frequent trumpet Jeremy seldom paid attention to it.

"That's not the whistle for the end of the shift," Betsy said. "It's too soon. I wonder if there's been trouble—"

"Betsy, you're a worry-wart."

They sat sipping their lemonade, while Jeremy regaled her with tales of the day— when some heavy man sat on the chair near the flour barrel, and it broke landing the poor man on the floor, and how two urchins had run off with a couple of apples each. Betsy wasn't listening.

"And what do you think about that, my dear?"

"I'm sorry. About what?"

"Pay attention, Betsy. About rampant theft."

"It's against the law."

"Of course it's against the law," he continued. "What's the law doing about it? Our friend, Sheriff Foster is getting lax, I fear."

As usual, whenever Jeremy got excited or angry, the color rose in his face.

"I'm sure he's dealing with more important things than a few stolen apples."

The ring of the telephone invaded their silence. Betsy still had not gotten used to this intrusion in their home.

She rose to answer it. What she heard was a lot of cackling, cracking noises, and no voice.

"Hello, hello," she kept saying over and over.

But only the annoying sound continued. Finally, she hung up.

"I don't know who it was," she told her husband. "Nothing but noise. You don't suppose it had something to do with that early whistle—"

Jeremy snored with irritation. He stood and made way for the newly installed water closet, attached to the back of the house.

Betsy waited for him to be out of sight before darting for the dispatch. Just then he returned.

"Curious about that letter," he said, picking it up.

He looked at the envelope. "July 20, 1912." He tore it open and looked at the contents.

Betsy was sure all color had drained from her face.

"Some nut-case trying to foment trouble for mining companies. Listen to this. '*Dear Editor, I write this in the hope that those of your readers with open minds will understand what our poor miners in the copper pits must endure. The safety conditions are such, that a wife never knows when she hands his lunch pail to her husband if she'll ever see him again. Cave-ins are not uncommon. Insufficient supports---*'" Jeremy tossed the dispatch back on the table.

"Crackpot."

The telephone rang again. Jeremy answered it.

"What!"

Betsy listened to a long silence.

Jeremy's face turned ashen. "When did it happen?"

Silence.

"How is he now?

Betsy knew something terrible had happened. But what? And to whom? Finally Jeremy got off the telephone.

"That was Roy. There's been a cave-in in his shaft."

"Is he hurt?"

"No. He wasn't there at the time. But Calvin was."

Betsy sucked in her breath. "Cal? Is he— ?"

"Roy is headed for the shaft now."

Betsy sucked in her breath. "Oh, my God! Is Cal . . ?"

Jeremy was out the door before Betsy could finish her question.

Cal couldn't give in to fear. He somehow managed to get to the shattered level. Clouds of dust were so thick he could barely see where he was going, but the shouts of men led him to the collapse.

His helmet lamp flickered, came up brightly, flickered again, and went out. Cal stopped for a moment and took a deep breath. Choking on the dust, he tied his kerchief over his nose and mouth and forged ahead in total darkness.

His left foot was shooting up tremendous bolts of pain. But he couldn't think about that now. He had to get to the men.

As if coming from another level, the first words he heard were, "He's dead."

"Who?" Cal called out.

"Fritz Rosenberg," someone shouted back— and then the echo, "Fritz Rosenberg."

"Anybody else?"

"Dunno yet."

Cal got as near as he could. A mountain of rubble lay between him and his stricken crew, filling the narrow drift wall to wall.

He heard, "Carl's bleeding a lot."

Cal coughed out, "Rip up somebody's shirt. Tie it around the wound— tight."

Then he realized he didn't even know where the man's injury was.

Damn. He couldn't get near his men. How the hell was he supposed to direct them?

He could see that there was a small space— about twelve inches between the top of the rubble and the ceiling. Maybe he could squeeze through.

He began the torturous climb over the mountain of rock— stumbled and fell. Rocks, dislocated for the second time, tumbled around him.

Two rays from the helmet lamps shone above him, lighting the dust like thousands of galaxies. The miners were clambering to the pinnacle of the rubble. Finally, they got over the top, and started slipping down.

"Give us a hand, sir, we'll help you over."

Gratefully, Cal accepted. Excruciating pain shot up to his thigh, as he placed his throbbing foot on one unsteady rock after another. He felt faint, and fought back nausea.

"You're hurt, sir," remarked a man called Tory.

"How many injured?" Cal said.

"Three, maybe four. Not sure if they'll all survive."

The hours ticked on— five o'clock, six o'clock. Betsy's daughter AnnaBeth was still upstairs. Betsy saw no need to alarm her, and didn't call her down. She paced the floor. When would she hear what was happening? Jeremy had gone to the mine hours ago. He had not called. No one had.

AnnaBeth, her eldest, finally came downstairs. She'd been reading *Gone with the Wind.*

"Where is everyone?"

When Betsy told her, the young woman turned white.

"Why didn't someone tell me?" AnnaBeth said.

Betsy squeezed her hand.

"What if something's happened to Cal?" she asked, eyes widened with fear.

"We'll pray that nothing has," Betsy said.

But AnnaBeth could see that her mother was upset. She sat beside her and pulled her mother's head down on her shoulder.

Finally, Jeremy came home. Betsy waited for him to speak.

"Pour me a glass of whiskey," he commanded.

"Get on with it!" She screamed silently.

Jeremy gulped the whiskey.

"Roy is in the shaft helping out. Two dead, four injured— one seriously."

"And Cal?"

"He's on top now, too."

"Is he hurt?"

While Betsy stopped breathing, Jeremy chewed on a piece of ice.

Finally, he answered. "A sprained ankle, he thinks."

Betsy released a great sigh of relief— and sent up a prayer.

Everyone was out of the shaft now— the healthy, the injured, the dead. The injured were taken to the hospital, the dead to the morgue.

Tears were running down Cal's face.

"Come on, Cal," his brother tried to soothe. "It happens sometimes. It's terrible. But it's not your fault. You did everything you could."

"Those guys were my friends, Roy. I've known Carl all my life."

"I know."

The brothers could be mistaken for twins, they looked so much alike— except Cal, who was a year younger than his brother, had brown eyes like his father, and Roy's were blue as his mother's. Both were sturdy lads, about five feet eleven and weighing around one hundred ninety pounds.

Earl Foster had arrived on the scene of the cave-in some time before. He had held the position of sheriff in Houghton County for seventeen years. Robust and kind, he was well-liked by almost everyone.

"Anything else I need to be involved with here?" Earl asked. "I've finished my preliminary report. That's about all I can do for now."

"Not unless you want to sue the company for not installing enough stulls," Cal burst out. "Those walls need more supporting!"

"Be quiet," Roy commanded. "You're on management's side now, brother. Be careful what you say."

"I'm not going to quote you, son," the sheriff said with compassion. "Anything I can do to help?"

"Maybe a lift, for my injured brother."

"Will do."

Although there were many automobiles in this progressive town, Earl Foster didn't own one. They helped Cal into the sheriff's buggy.

At home, Roy and Earl Foster got Cal into the house.

Roy helped his brother into the bath. Betsy prepared an ice-pack for his ankle.

"If it isn't better in the morning," Roy said, "you should see a doctor."

He returned to the parlor to talk to his father. The sheriff was gone.

"That was the third accident at the Keweenaw in as many months that's killed someone," Roy said. "Some of them weren't even twenty years old!"

"Risks come with the job," Jeremy Willis said.

"Much too often!"

Roy was stamping back and forth across the floor. "The Company should take better safety precautions!"

"I'm sure they do what they can," their father replied.

Roy fairly shouted, "Even when they don't shore up the walls where they're busting out rock?"

For a week, Cal lay in pain on the sofa, while Betsy and AnnaBeth hovered over him. AnnaBeth read to him, she sang to him. Sometimes she lay on floor beside the sofa dozing. But she was nearby, in case he needed something.

In the parlor, a week later, Roy sat next to his brother.

"Stay off that ankle," Roy cautioned. "Give it time to heal."

"But I've got to get to my shift! I can't be a lay-about forever."

"I'm covering for you."

"Roy—"

"For at least two more weeks. Then we'll see."

Cal sighed. "How many levels have been closed?"

"Three. One above, and one below Level Eight. I can't open those until we determine how safe they are."

Carefully, Roy elevated Cal's leg and placed another pillow under it.

"You sure you wouldn't rather be upstairs?"

"No. I'm fine here. Closer to the commode."

"Well, if you don't need anything else, I'll be off to work."

"Go," Cal said. "And thanks for everything."

"What are brothers for?"

It took a month before Cal's ankle was healed enough to let him return to work. The collapsed level was still closed, but all other levels were open.

On his third day back he said to his brother, "I want to see Level Eight."

"Cal—"

"*You've* seen it."

"Yes." Roy sighed. "All right, but I'm going with you. It's a mess. You can't go hobbling over all the rubble with—"

"I know. I know."

They rode the man-car down, bringing extra lamps with them. The dust had settled as he knew it would, so it was at least possible to see the shape of things. It was an eerie sight. Light cast against the irregular walls created ghostly shapes and shadows.

"I can't have this rock trammed out until we know it's safe to go in there," Roy said.

They cast their lights around the rubble, and passed them across the walls.

They stood at the opening of the drift for some time. Roy had experienced more accidents than Cal, and he respected his brother's silence.

"Well, have you seen enough?" Roy finally asked.

"Wait!" Cal cried out.

"What?"

Cal threw his light on the wall just the other side of the rubble. "Do you see that?"

Roy directed his lamps on the spot where Cal was focused.

"What is it?"

"Look closely. There are carvings."

Roy looked. "Oh, I see them now."

"Is that a star of David?"

"Yes! For Fritz."

"And a cross— for Carl."

They had attended both funerals, but nothing touched Cal like this.

A lump swelled up in his throat. If he'd been alone he might have cried. Roy put his arm around his brother's shoulder.

The miners, mainly immigrants from many different countries, were very clannish and loyal to their ethnic groups. But when it came to disaster, they were a brotherhood.

As if branded on his brain, Cal would never forget the cross and star the men had carved in the wall before they'd been rescued.

James McNeary caressed the five pound chunk of pure copper that lay on his desk. He was the general manager of the Keweenaw Mine, and mightily satisfied with what he'd accomplished for the stockholders back east, and the community he reigned over. This town of thirty-five thousand, unlike other communities its size, had completely paved streets, electric lighting, streetcars that ran twenty-four hours a day. Telephones were common too. James McNeary had put Red Jacket and the Keweenaw Peninsula on the map. Of course there were several other mines about, but none as large and progressive as the Keweenaw.

Red Jacket was on the big-time circuit of entertainment along with New York, San Francisco and Chicago, bringing in the likes of Enrico Caruso and Douglas Fairbanks. James McNeary was proud of what he'd accomplished in this frozen finger of the north. Along with other towns, the population was approaching one hundred thousand. Life was good.

CHAPTER TWO

For Roy, it was a good time except for the accidents. The work at the mine challenged him. He enjoyed the frequent carousing after work at The Red Nugget with his mates. Sometimes in the evenings he played Poker with Cal and Pa. Once in a while a few of the neighbor men would join them. Then the stakes would go up, the betting turn more reckless and the shouts more raucous. Betsy and AnnaBeth found it difficult to sleep.

That is— until this summer. At twenty-four, Roy was in love. Jenny Foster, the daughter of Tobias Foster, and niece of Sheriff Foster, was the finest gal Roy had ever known. He had noticed her singing at the Methodist Church for a long time. It was his single motive for attending services. He had finally gotten up the courage to speak to her.

Tall and slim, she was very shapely. Roy knew he couldn't do better than to win the hand of this lovely girl, whose disposition was as sweet as her features. He meant to make her his bride.

More and more poker nights gave way to visits at Jenny's home. This meant giving up The Red Nugget after work in exchange for a good bath.

And while he was soaking, Roy could just imagine what pleasures the night would bring. He didn't mind the razzing that went along with his new habits. It was all part of the scene that made up that magic time in a young man's life when he was smitten with love. Warm evenings were spent with his sweetheart strolling down Fifth Street to the ice-cream parlor, and then out toward the edge of town, away from prying eyes.

But Roy didn't much like it that her father, as well as his own parents, expected them to wait a couple of years to consummate their intentions. She was too young, they said.

He wanted her now.

Often in their evenings, Jenny brought out her violin and entertained Roy and her father with melodious music while the men enjoyed a glass of port and a cigar. At some point Tobias would excuse himself, leaving the young people alone in the parlor, while he retired to his bedroom to read.

Roy had a very hearty sexual appetite and much of their time was spent with Jenny dissuading him from going too far. Endless arguments ensued.

"Please, Sweetheart. You know I love you."

"Then we can wait. . ."

"Jenny, I can't stand it. I love you."

"I love you too, and that makes it worth waiting for. Doesn't it?"

Roy groaned. "Yes, but what are you worried about?"

"You know. I might . . ."

"Then we'll get married."

"I don't want it that way."

And a replay of this time-immemorial dialogue would go on night after night. In truth Roy understood Jenny's position perfectly, and respected her for it, but he was getting so randy he could hardly bear it, and two years seemed a lifetime.

As he approached the front door, Roy could hear his parents arguing. He waited on the porch. But even from there he could hear the disagreement.

"Jeremy Willis, I cannot leave it alone. Those poor people—"

"It's not our business, Betsy."

"It *is* our business! I have to find Patty."

Calvin came up the steps. Roy motioned him to be still and sit beside him on the swing.

"They're having a row," he whispered to his brother.

Betsy continued. "But where have they gone? And why haven't I heard from her?"

"If it's the house cleaning you're worried about, there are plenty others—"

"It's not that, Jeremy. I care about Patty."

Jeremy put his head in the newspaper, and Betsy knew the conversation was over.

There were seasons of affection, as she called them— times when, if she did not contradict him, or worse yet, disagree with him in public, Jeremy could be quite kind and generous. But if she dared cross him, he was harsh indeed.

His position and reputation were everything to him. Just a few months ago he had been appointed to the Board of Supervisors and he felt much honored. He was one of only two "members at large" from the community. All others had administrative positions in the Keweenaw Company. He knew his role was subordinate. He was allowed to vote, but it was understood that he would follow suit, would defer to his seniors in all matters discussed, and would not make new proposals. Still, he swelled with pride at his new standing.

He felt established enough to buy a motor car. Not one of those tin Lizzies. Henry Ford had said you could have a Model T in any color you wanted, as long as it was black. No, he'd get an Oldsmobile, in a wine color if he could, or maybe dark blue. Yes, he would do that.

Two days later Betsy said to her daughter, "You'd think Patty could have sent word."

Finally, in frustration, she decided to go to that part of town set aside by the Keweenaw for their workers.

"I'll go with you, Mother," AnnaBeth said.

"No, Dear, I wouldn't want you to see such sights as I'm likely to encounter."

"But you shouldn't go alone."

"I'll be fine. You start supper, will you? You can warm up the ham and parsnips, if I'm not home."

Betsy didn't have an address, but counted on her inquiries directing her to the right place. She walked along Elm, and back up to the main road, past the mine. She continued on flat ground for half a mile, where she could see the tiny plots of land and houses leased to the employees of the Keweenaw. The miners' houses sat all in a straight row, and for the most part looked much the same.

Betsy thought the whole village looked forlorn. Each modest house had an outhouse and a fence separating it from its neighbors. The place was almost treeless, save for a few young saplings struggling to survive in the sun-baked clay. Nonetheless, some tidy gardens displayed their vegetables. Here and there she saw a cow or a bleating goat.

She walked along the dirt road until she caught sight of a woman tending her potato patch.

"Excuse me, please," Betsy waited for the woman to look up.

Seeing Betsy's finery, the woman stared at her. "No Inglis," she said, and turned away.

Betsy nodded and continued down the road hoping to see someone else. She would rather avoid knocking on doors if possible. In a few blocks she encountered another woman rounding the corner with her shopping basket. Betsy stopped her.

"Could you direct me to the home of Patty and Michael Riley, please?"

"Riley, is it? I've not heard of them." The woman looked puzzled. "But you've come to the right part. This is the Irish section it is, and by the name, I'd say you're lookin' for Irish."

"Yes."

"Well, ma'am, I know all the Irish here, and there's none called by that name. What kinda work does your man do?"

"Mr. Riley is a trammer for the Keweenaw."

"Oh, there's your answer then! The trammers don't live here. These houses are for miners."

"Where are the trammers' houses?"

The young woman raised her head. "Why ma'am, the trammers are simple laborers, not skilled at anythin'. It's mucking out the rock they do, after the miners have found the veins of copper. The miners, like my husband, has to choose where to drill and where to set explosives, a job that takes—"

"Where do the trammers live?"

The young woman shrugged. "Wherever they can find, here and there, is my guess. But not on company property, I can tell you that. Try the west end, past the sawmill."

"Thank you and good day, then."

Betsy strode away, upset that she'd come so far for nothing, and smarting that she'd had to be schooled by a simple miner's wife. Well, of course she knew the difference between the work of a miner and a trammer. But it shocked her that while the miner was provided with home and garden, the trammer was offered no accommodation at all.

She increased her pace. Well, certainly the Company would have the addresses of their employees. As long as she was near the mine, she decided to stop and get the information.

On the grounds, she strode directly to the building on which hung a sign that read "Employment." Under it was written in smaller print, "Reliable, Sober Men Wanted. Good wages. Apply within". She was shown into a small cubicle, the office of the chief clerk. Everything in it was covered with dust. Several dirty coffee cups lay about the desk and the nearby cabinet. As he motioned to Betsy to sit down, Mr. Copley waved at the flies that buzzed about his partially eaten meal.

A plume of dust rose to greet her nostrils as the man dropped a large ledger on the desk. Betsy reached for her handkerchief.

Betsy looked down at the book. As the clerk turned the pages, she could see that many names had been crossed out, and others added. They were all in heavy black ink, in a hand she recognized as being from the old country.

"Would you be knowin' when he began employment with us?" Mr. Copley asked. "The names are entered by date, so that's the only way we have of findin' them."

"I believe it's was about six years ago. They'd just arrived when his missus came to work for me."

"Oh, that long ago?"

Mr. Copley dropped a second ledger on the desk. Another plume of dust caught the slender ray of light through the grimy window.

He turned the pages and after some time declared, "Ah, here we have it." He copied the address down on a piece of paper. "This is where he lives, unless they've moved. They're supposed to let us know when they change their whereabouts, but they don't always."

Betsy thanked him and took her leave. She was angry as she marched along the road. She was appalled at what she'd learned.

Approaching an unfamiliar part of town, she debated whether to turn back or to go the other way and try to find the home of the Rileys. She was hungry and tired, but she didn't want to give up now.

She hadn't gone this far on foot in a very long time. Her feet ached. She felt hot and dirty. The August winds whipped up the dust in the streets and blew it in her face. By nine o'clock the heat had burned the dew off the flowers and grass. It was going to be a very hot day.

She followed the directions to a neighborhood so filthy that she had to pick up her skirts to avoid dragging them in the dirt and the litter. Horse droppings were thick with flies as big as nickels. The stench of manure invaded her nostrils. Betsy felt she could taste it in the dust that pervaded every pore. She heard a splash and turned abruptly. The contents of a chamber pot emptied from the window above had just missed her. Betsy choked back her nausea.

As she turned the corner two scrawny half-starved cats rubbed against her legs and meowed. A naked toddler sat banging two stones together on a stoop. This was the street she was looking for— now to find the right building.

Betsy could find no numbers on the houses. She was about to inquire of a man approaching her, when he shot a wad of tobacco so close to her she had to jump to escape it. When the next person came near she screwed her courage in place and approached him.

"I am looking for number fourteen. Would you know which door that might be?"

"Sorry, mum. I don't live on this street. You'll have to ask within."

Well, she supposed, she should have done that in the first place. She knocked on the nearest door. A woman heavy with child, and another under her arm came to the door.

She would have been pretty, Betsy thought, a few years ago, or under other circumstances. Time and hard work had taken its toll. The woman pushed loose strands of pale hair away from her face, and wiped spit-up from the baby's mouth.

"Yah, das is number fourteen, and dere are four families here, but none by name Riley."

"Perhaps I'm in the wrong section, then. Where do the Irish live?" Betsy inquired.

The woman laughed. "Yer thinkin' of miners' houses. There's no sections here."

"You're sure you don't know the Rileys?'

"If he vasn't German, I vouldn't know."

As Betsy turned to go the woman said, "You might try askin' at de Irish saloons. That'd be vhere his friends vould be. But be sure it's Irish vhere you do your askin'. De others vouldn't know."

Betsy could hear a man singing a German love song in the next room. Now he came up to them and caught the last of what his wife was saying. "De lady von't go in de beer hall." He put his arm around his wife. "Who's it yer lookin' for?"

"Riley. Michael and Patty Riley."

The man shook his head. "Must verk on de day shift. I verk on de night shift. If he verked on de night shift I mighta heard of him."

She turned to the man. "Could you make the inquiries? I would pay you."

"Ach! I vould get torn to pieces in an Irish bar."

"I don't understand."

"Ah, vell das de vay it is. And if de Irish vas to come in Deutch bar? De same. Yah, de saloons are separate, for Slavs, Norvegians—everybody. It's bad 'nuf ve haf to verk togeder. Ve sure don't vant to drink togeder!" He laughed and pulled his wife toward him, looked at her with adoration, Betsy thought.

Again she turned to leave, but the man continued, "If you go up on Clancy Street, dats vere you find most de Irish. Dey vont boder you, Lady, not if you go in the daytime. Ask some fellow dere to help you find 'im. Yah, dat vould be goot."

Betsy had never been to this part of town. Street after street was lined with saloons. Finally she found Clancy. It was difficult for Betsy to navigate in her laced up leather shoes with the French heel. By now she was limping. The sights and smells were no better than she'd experienced in the rest of town. She passed people speaking in foreign tongues and bars with strange sounding names. No one and nothing looked remotely Irish. Occasionally, a door would open and Betsy would catch the boisterous clamor from within.

She began to feel queasy.

Her dress was much too warm for the afternoon. Comfortable when the sun had first shown itself in the sky, Betsy felt it must now be in the eighties. Her long skirts and petticoats held the heat; the tightness around her collar and wrists trapped it.

She began to feel weak. She remembered she'd been on her feet for hours and hadn't eaten since early morning. Suddenly she felt as if everything was whirling around her.

As she came to, the first thing she knew was that she was lying on something hard in a dark place. Groping beneath her, she thought it must be a table. Sensing a strong smell of beer and chewing tobacco, she strained to make out dim shapes. A dull thud was coming from nearby, but she couldn't place it. She tried to sit up. A sharp pain on the side of her head caused her to wince.

A man hurried up to her with a wet cloth.

"Don't try to get up, Mum. Here, put this to your face."

He tried to apply the cloth to her forehead, but Betsy pushed it away. "Where am I?"

"You're in a pub."

"What happened?"

"You fainted on the street, Mum. A hot day it is, too, and no wonder you went down."

Betsy felt her head. "How did I get in here?" She climbed off the table, and the barkeep helped her sit on a chair.

"Carried in by the first to see you, you were. And you are now speakin' to the owner of the establishment, Sean Sullivan. At your service, mum." He made a slight bow.

She could hear the sound of men's voices in the room. "I have to get out of here," she said.

"You'd best rest a bit first. Have you had anythin' to eat, Mum?"

Betsy shook her head.

Sean Sullivan motioned to someone. "Bring the lady a bit of steak and kidney pie."

"Oh, I can't." She tried to get up. "I must get home."

"It's hurt, you are, and faint with hunger. I wouldn't be decent if I let you go now, would I, Mum?"

Betsy's head throbbed, her stomach growled, and in truth the coolness of this dark den was comforting. She looked into the concerned blue eyes of the man watching over her.

"Did you say steak and kidney pie?"

"That I did."

She looked around her. "This must be a British pub."

"Irish, it is."

"At last," she mumbled.

Her eyes had adjusted to the dim light, and she could see a dart board. This was the cause of the thuds she'd heard.

The food arrived with a glass of beer. Betsy devoured the pie. She couldn't think of drinking beer and she didn't trust the water.

While she was eating, Betsy was entertained by a few of the men, including Sean. They were singing along with the piano player, who was banging out some Irish ditties on an old instrument. Betsy had the feeling they were showing off just for her. She was amused, and for a few minutes forgot how tired she was.

"The pie is as good as ever I've had," she declared, and meant it. "And I enjoyed the singing. I'm sorry, I've no money to pay for the food. I'll have to get it to you later."

"I wouldn't take anything anyway. It's not every day I get to serve a lady such as yourself. It's honored I am."

"You're very kind."

"If you don't mind my askin', what were you doin' on Clancy Street, all on yer own?"

Betsy colored. Normally she wouldn't be explaining herself to anyone except her husband, and not always to him. But this was not a normal time. "I've been everywhere looking for someone. His wife works for me but she hasn't come by for over a week. I don't know where they live."

"And who might that be?"

"His name's Riley."

"Michael?"

"Do you know him?" It was the first ray of hope she'd had all day.

The man put his fingers to his mouth and made a loud whistle. "Michael, get yerself over here! Look sharp, there's a lady here to see you."

Betsy couldn't believe her ears. A man, slight in build with a huge head of hair, approached the table.

The man looked puzzled. "You want me?"

"I am Mrs. Willis. It's your wife I want, actually. I was trying to find the correct address."

"Pleased to meet you, mum." The man removed his cap. "We had to move. Livin' with my brother-in-law, now we are. Duffy by name, over on Livery Road."

As if reading her mind Riley said, "My missus has a bad infection, mum. So weak she can't get to the chamber pot."

She wondered what in the world he was doing in a pub with a wife sick at home.

"I'll be going home now, anyway, if you like I can show you where we're lodgin'."

The barkeep spoke up. "The lady won't do any more trudgin' about today. I'll take you both in the wagon. That is, if the lady's feelin' spry enough to go."

The ride in the saloonkeeper's buckboard offered more unsavory views of the seamier side of town.

While they jogged along, Betsy said, "Why did you move, Mr. Riley?"

"I lost m'job, ma'am."

"Tell her what happened, Michael," Sean interjected.

"Well, you see . . ." Michael twisted his mouth in tandem with the cap in his hand.

"Go ahead, tell her. The lady won't bite."

"You see, I had— spells for quite some time, at home. But never on the job."

"What do you mean— "spells?""

"I'd pass out for a time, I would. Not for long. And then when I woke up, I'd be, confused, you might say. For a little while."

"I see."

"Nobody at the mine knew. But then it happened there Friday last. The captain he said, I was a l'ability to meself and others."

"I'm so sorry to hear this, Mr. Riley."

"It happened down below," Michael continued, "but the captain said it could happen goin' down the shaft or comin' up, and then I might fall off the man-car— maybe take one or two others with me."

"What will you do?"

"Dunno."

"Try the Miners' Fund," Betsy said. "Perhaps they'd help you, under the circumstances."

Dismally, Michael nodded.

"You were a good worker, weren't you?"

"Oh, yes, ma'am."

When they arrived at their destination, the barkeep spoke. "Here y'are then, Michael Riley. Don't be away from us too long."

Michael jumped down off the buckboard and offered Betsy his arm. She accepted it gratefully. It was a long way to the ground.

Once down, she turned and thanked her benefactor.

Sean Sullivan called after her, "It's here I'll be waitin' for you, mum, when you come out, to take you home."

"Oh, that will not be necessary, Mr. Sullivan."

"Oh, will it not, then? I'll be here anyway."

Before they entered, Betsy touched the arm. "How serious is your wife's condition? What does the doctor say?"

Michael shook his head. "I've no money for a doctor, mum."

"But the Company doctor—"

"There's no company doctor for us trammers. No, that there isn't."

Inside, Betsy's eyes didn't immediately adjust to the darkness. The only source of light came from one small window on the north side of the room they occupied. She was about to ask why no lamps were lit when she remembered that oil cost money too.

Betsy thought her nostrils had been assaulted enough for the day, but new obnoxious odors arose to insult them further. She found Patty in bed, her sheets soiled, the stench of feces and urine filling the room.

Patty opened her eyes, but otherwise showed little sign of life. Betsy felt her forehead.

"She has a high fever."

Michael nodded.

"What have you been doing for her?"

The man looked embarrassed. "Well, I bring her water, empty the pot . . . She won't take food."

"How long has she been like this?"

"She's been sick 'bout a week. The fever— two days."

"Try to get her to take some broth. And place cold wet cloths on her forehead. Change them often."

"Yes, mum."

"I'll send a doctor to her tomorrow."

"I have no money for the doctor."

"Never mind. I'll take care of it."

"I'm much obliged, ma'am."

Betsy turned toward the door. "Stay home and take care of her. You should be ashamed, hanging around the saloon with your wife so ill."

Michael hung his head, and mumbled, "Yes, mum."

"Why do you do it?"

She didn't wait for an answer. Sean Sullivan was outside waiting for her, and Betsy was glad for it.

"Climb in, it's takin' you home now, I'll be doin'."

"Yes, thank you."

"Was she bad?" he asked as they wound their way through the grimy streets.

Betsy nodded. "Why was he at the pub when his wife is so sick?"

"Ah, a man's got to get out now and then. It was only for a couple of hours."

"And how does he pay for his drinks?" Betsy bristled.

"They're on the house, mum. Or others buy 'em. We've all been sorry for his losin' his job."

"I see. I have to get his wife help. Apparently the Company won't do anything for them."

"Same with all of the trammers. If the Keweenaw feels like it, they'll do for the miner, providin' he's been with 'em quite a while, has a family to support, and not been out sick too much in the past. All the companies are happy to get the good skilled miner."

They rode through and out of the seamier end of town, and were on even ground now as they traversed paved streets.

"Those that knows his trade is worth somethin'." Sean Sullivan chuckled. "And they can get pretty high and mighty sometimes, lordin' it over the trammers."

"That's sad."

"The trammers get nothin'."

"Why is that?"

"With boatloads of immigrants comin' from all over the world, they're as disposable as sawdust on a butcher's floor. Sweep 'em up and throw 'em out. That's their feeling."

"My God."

"One mine worker dies a week in the mines on the peninsula, and two are crippled for life."

Betsy gasped in dismay.

"I reckon," Sean continued, "that it's the mines that reduce the average life expectancy to forty-seven years old."

"Forty-seven!"

"That's the county's average."

"But there are many old people about."

"And as many died before thirty in the mine."

"I didn't know it was that bad."

Betsy was quiet, and they sat in silence for a few minutes.

The next day Betsy arranged with a private doctor to see Patty, and to call and give her a report.

"What's wrong with her?"

"She has dysentery. I've given her some medicine, but I doubt it will do much good. It's advanced."

"Is there nothing can be done for her?"

"It's in God's hands now."

She didn't believe he'd be so indifferent if his patient had money and social standing.

Betsy wrote another letter to the editors:

I have long been aware of the poverty of the miners. Imagine my shock and dismay to discover that of the trammers! Living in ghastly conditions in the worst part of town, these poor people can hardly keep body and soul together. When they are injured or infirmed they are offered no assistance from the mining companies. It appears that management believes if they are unable to work they are of no use to the company. B.T. Wilkins

But she was still concerned about Patty. She had another idea.

"Roy, I want you to go out to Carlene's, the half-breed's place. She sells herbs. Sometimes she can heal people when doctors fail. Give her this message." Betsy explained to her son what to say, and how Carlene could find Patty.

Following the directions his mother had given him, Roy rode his horse out to the cabin south of town. He almost passed it, so hidden from view it was. But for the smoke he smelled coming from the chimney, he would have missed it.

"I had an omen someone would be calling for me," the woman said to him.

He gave the woman some money and a basket of food to take to the Rileys'. She gave him a pleasant smile, and he returned it with his own.

Roy described Patty's problem to this strange woman. He found her attractive in an unusual way, with eyes that went all the way through him. She was large, full busted, with an inviting red mouth.

"Is there anything you can do for her?" Roy asked.

The woman looked intently at him. "I might be able to save her."

This half Indian woman of the Ojibwa tribe had a compelling presence that puzzled Roy. It mesmerized him and made him uneasy at the same time.

Carlene invited him to come in for a cup of tea. Roy hesitated.

With a pleasant authority she said, "You can't ride all the way out here, and all the way back without a drop to quench your thirst."

Roy accepted.

Three days later, word got to Betsy that Patty Riley would be staying among the living.

CHAPTER THREE

Carlene lifted her heavy black hair, propped herself on one elbow and looked down at the man's strong build and ruddy features.

He had fallen asleep for a short time after he'd climaxed. Finally her gaze penetrated his consciousness and he blinked a few times, getting his bearings.

He had been here three times and it still took him a few moments to take in his surroundings. He lowered the bearskin that covered their bodies and looked at her until his loins responded again. Pulling her toward him by her great shank of black hair, he brought her wide red mouth to his.

"Come here, woman."

She pulled back. "Why you call me `woman'?"

"That's what you are. Otherwise, you sure got me fooled."

"I don't mean that—"

"You woman, me man."

"My name is Carlene."

"I'll try to remember that."

"You don't call her `woman', do you?"

His face turned an angry red. "You leave her out of this. Hear?"

She was quiet. In a few minutes he heard a sound— almost like purring. He listened for a few moments. The way she was breathing returned them both to a vein of tranquility.

On his twenty-fourth birthday Roy couldn't have been more excited. Ma had fixed a special dinner. As they gathered around the table, he couldn't wait.

Putting his arm around Jenny, he announced with a big grin, "Jenny and me are going to get married. It's official." He slipped a little ring on her finger and gave her a kiss.

"Congratulations," Pa said.

"When's the happy day, Roy?" Calvin asked.

Roy looked at his fiancée. "You'll have to ask the lady here."

Jenny looked at her father, who'd been invited for this special occasion. "Father thinks we should wait, a year or two."

"Wise choice," Jeremy concurred.

The announcement was not a great bolt of surprise to anyone, but still it added to the cheer that night. Pa broke out a bottle of champagne. When he popped the cork, it rocketed upwards. With an agile leap Roy caught it. Everyone clapped and toasted the young couple. Roy reveled in the attention they were getting. Pa produced two bottles of wine to go with dinner— not his home brew, but some good stuff he'd bought uptown.

Jenny kissed him and gave him a handsome linen handkerchief she'd made herself. She'd embroidered his initials in the corner.

"I shall cherish this forever," he said, pressing it against his cheek.

When he walked Jenny home later that night, he was the happiest he could ever remember being.

"Oh, Jenny, it's all so grand. We're going to be married! How many children do you want?" He picked her up and swung her around.

She laughed and said, "Enough to make you happy."

"How about a dozen?"

"Oh, not that many! Roy, are you serious?"

"Course not. A couple will do. Whatever you want, Sweetheart."

Suddenly he turned to her seriously, and lifted her chin under the streetlamp. "You know there isn't anything I wouldn't do for you."

She hugged him, right there on Walker Street.

When they were seated in her parlor, Roy's amorous demonstrations showed more restraint than usual.

As he was leaving she said, "I knew you'd see reason."

Roy smiled. He'd found a solution.

She held him close. "When we're married I'll give myself to you with all my heart," she promised.

"I know you will, Precious."

And Roy felt good inside every time he thought of Jenny, of their perfect future together.

The construction of the beautiful new Opera House in Red Jacket was talked about everywhere.

"Can you imagine— there's to be individual heating controls for each seat?" her friend Rose told Betsy.

"Impossible! How would that work?"

"Foot warmers, for each theatre patron. With a little lever, you can adjust the heat."

"Isn't it marvelous! I doubt if Broadway has such an invention as that."

"We're certainly getting modern."

"And guess who's engaged to perform for the gala opening?"

"Who?"

"The great Sarah Bernhardt."

"How splendid!"

Even Patty, who'd returned to work was interested. "Will you and the mister be going to it?"

"Oh, yes, I wouldn't miss it for anything."

"What's the name of the play, mum?"

"The Curse of the Aching Heart."

Betsy was on a committee to plan the dinner that would follow the performance. Cases of real French champagne were brought in, smoked salmon and caviar all the way from Norway.

The dinner went well, with everyone in high spirits from the good food and libations.

"If only I could write that way," she sighed to Rose after the performance.

"What about the performing— would you like to act, like Miss Bernhardt?"

"Oh, I couldn't!" she laughed. "Did you notice, Rose, how she held the audience, as if in her hand?"

"She was very captivating."

The next morning as Betsy was sitting at her dresser, Patty wanted to hear about the evening. She was hanging up the gown Betsy had worn the night before.

"Did you enjoy the show, mum? Was she as great as they say?"

"She was indeed, Patty."

"It must have been wonderful, sure!" She paused, and offered shyly, "My Michael likes the stage. Wouldn't he have loved to see that, now."

"Oh, yes?" Betsy was putting pins in her hair.

"He was in the musical hall business back home. Made his living at it for a while before I met him, that he did."

"I didn't know that."

"Tell you the truth that's what he'd rather be doin' now, if he had his way."

"But you wouldn't like that kind of life, would you?"

"Ah, no, mum. I made him quit that foolishness before I'd marry him. I told him I wouldn't go on the road with him— I wanted to settle, and have a family. And I wouldn't have him goin' off without me, either."

Betsy was putting the finishing touches on her hair. "I suppose not."

"But he plays around with a little group here just for the pleasure o' it. Mostly singin' they do, ole Irish songs in the pub, and sometimes the odd skit. Dirty humor it is too." She shook her head. "He misses the musical hall, that he does."

Patty laughed as she raised the window shade and made the bed up. "When he gets mad at me he threatens to run off with the next travelin' company that comes through town."

"He doesn't mean it, Patty."

"Was there dancin' and songs as well, mum?"

"No. It wasn't that kind of show."

In the evening Jeremy smiled. "You'll enjoy this, Betsy. The great Miss Bernhardt wishes to go down in the mine!"

"What!" Betsy laughed. "You are in jest!"

"I am not. She put the word out that she'd like to see the inside of a mine, and our Roy stepped forward and offered to accommodate her. Fancy that."

"Is she really going to do it?" Betsy was beside herself with excitement.

"She is, tomorrow. Roy suggested the No. 6, because it doesn't smell as bad as the others." He laughed. "Better ventilation. Still, the men had orders to clean the place up today."

"Jeremy," Betsy said thoughtfully, "What do the men use for a privy?"

"That's just it. Old dynamite boxes, if that."

"How horrid!"

"It's no place for a woman. Still, Parker was flattered that she'd want to see the mine. He figures it will be good publicity, and won't hurt the purchase of shares in the Company."

"And Roy is going to accompany her?"

"Yes, tough job— that," he laughed.

AnnaBeth had been listening. "Who's Sarah Bernhardt?"

"Just about the most famous actress in the country," Jeremy said. "Shouldn't you be washing up in the kitchen, eh?"

AnnaBeth looked puzzled.

"Jeremy," Betsy replied, "she finished the dishes an hour ago."

He turned to AnnaBeth. "Then you can go study. We can all improve ourselves by studying. For our whole lives."

AnnaBeth looked aghast.

"Why do you think I read books, and the newspaper?" Jeremy inquired.

She twisted her mouth. "I don't know, Father."

"To learn, girl— learn!"

"Jeremy," Betsy reprimanded, when AnnaBeth had left the room, "that was unkind."

"She's twenty-five years old, for God's sake. She's—" He hunted for the word he was looking for. "She's backward."

Betsy gasped. "Oh, don't say that."

"It's true. She's an embarrassment in public."

"How do you mean?" The color rose to her neck and face.

"She can't answer simple questions put to her. She stares."

Betsy would never look at her beloved AnnaBeth that way. "She's just shy."

"She'll always be a spinster. You know that, don't you?"

Betsy bit her tongue. Jeremy had driven away the only man who'd shown an interest in her daughter.

Plain, but not unattractive, AnnaBeth did not possess the charms of some young ladies. She was as sweet, as compassionate and loving as any young girl could be. If she wasn't witty and beguiling, Betsy loved her all the more.

Roy was excited to tell Jenny about the diva coming.

She put on her prettiest smile. "Perhaps I should go too, so she won't feel uncomfortable, being the only woman. And we could talk— woman to woman."

"Not on your life. I will not allow a fiancée of mine down there. Nothing about that place was designed for the tender sensibilities of a woman," he said, chucking her under the chin.

"I must say, you are a spoil-sport. It might be great fun, and something I'd remember the rest of my life."

"No doubt. But the answer is 'no'."

Jenny had to be content, but couldn't wait to ask Roy that evening if the great Miss Bernhardt really did go down, and what she thought of it.

"She said she enjoyed it tremendously, and the men should all be very proud of the hard and dangerous work they do."

"What did she wear?"

"I gave her one of my white coats to cover her dress." Roy seemed to have no more to say.

"And that's all?" Jenny felt a sense of disappointment.

"What did you expect, my dear?"

"Wasn't she frightened, going so deep into the bowels of the earth? Did she panic in the dark, and grab onto you, or scream?"

Roy laughed. "Not at all. I must say she conducted herself as well as a man. She showed no fear, which we all thought she would— though every man was prepared to catch her, should she faint."

"But Roy, the man-car is practically a vertical ladder, you've told me, with men crowded together, three on each step. You've told me they've fallen to their death, often a mile or more, if they so much as lean forward." She turned away. "I think I should have fainted."

"That's why you weren't allowed to go."

Jenny gave him a look, but he only smiled.

"Is she pretty off-stage?"

"It was hard to tell in the dark."

"Oh, Roy, don't tease."

"It's true—it's totally dark in the mine, except for the men's helmet lamps."

"You sat next to her?"

"Yes, Jenny, I did."

"And held her so she wouldn't tip?"

"And had my way with her all the way down."

"Roy Willis!" Playfully, Jenny started beating him on the chest. "You're terrible. You're deliberately provoking me!"

Roy only laughed as he caught her wrists. "You're making yourself miserable, Jenny, with all your questions. Her deportment was admirable, and so was mine. Now be satisfied. She's at least sixty, if not seventy years old!"

"Never! Why didn't you say so in the first place?"

Betsy made another visit to the employment office.

"Riley. Yes, I remember the man, don't I? Got the axe when he passed out on Friday last. Or was it the week before?"

Betsy brushed the flies away from her face. She watched one stick to a crumb on Mr. Copley's beard. It didn't seem to bother him. "Two weeks ago."

"It's a pity, but can't have somebody on the man-car might pass out and push a bunch of 'em off with him, like dominoes." Mr. Copley added gestures to illustrate his point.

"Is the Company doing anything for him?"

"They seldom do for the miners. The trammers are strictly on their own."

"How are they supposed to get on, then?"

Copley's dark eyes twinkled. "Say their prayers and tighten their belts, I 'spect."

She was seething by the time she got home. That evening she said to her husband, "Did you know Keweenaw isn't doing anything for Patty's husband?"

"It is not the Company's responsibility to take care of these men for life."

"But Jeremy— "

"It's dangerous work. They know that when they sign on."

"But when they're hurt or killed—"

"There are charities, and a fund for emergencies."

There was a bite to his voice, but she forged ahead.

"What's the fund called?"

"Are you questioning me, Betsy?"

"I had thought you had more compassion for the poor. You used to say—"

"I don't have to answer to you, Betsy. For that matter, I don't make the rules."

"Will you speak to someone on the board of supervisors about helping Michael Riley?"

"I will not! That is not my province, and I will not interfere."

But you have influence, Jeremy. You're on the board of supervisors!"

"Influence! It's a token position—a shop owner or two, to make it all seem so democratic."

Earl Foster was just sitting down to dinner with his wife, Cora, when he got an emergency call from a shaft supervisor at the mine. As sheriff, he had to go.

"Some crackpot set fire in the mine," he told his wife as he got his coat. It was August, but the evenings were chilly.

"What!"

He rode his buggy, with his old mare still at the helm. Bigot was bad-tempered at being made to go out at night.

"Getting tetchy, are we, old girl?"

As he bumped along through the darkness, Earl sang, *The old grey mare she ain't what she used to be.*

Then his thoughts turned to running through what facts he had on this case. He'd never heard of such a thing before. There were fires in the mines all right, when the huge, dry timbers that supported the walls started to blaze. None he'd heard of were set on purpose. Usually they were caused by sparks from a fuse set for a dynamite explosion. And the men were lucky to get out alive. Sometimes they didn't.

So it was some surprise when the shaft supervisor called Foster with this charge and asked for an immediate arrest.

Lights ahead signaled they were nearing their destination. There loomed the enormous Keweenaw Mine, holding irrefutable sovereignty over all it surveyed. There was an impressive spread of buildings above ground, but it was only the tip of the iceberg; a warren of shafts and drifts lay underground. The peninsula was dotted with copper mines, but the Keweenaw had no peer in this realm.

"How do you know he did it on purpose?" the sheriff asked Krause, the shaft supervisor.

"The nitwit confessed, practically bragged about it."

"Why would anyone set a fire in the hole?"

- "Don't know. But got my 'spicions."

"Which are?"

"He's an agitator. Not satisfied with working conditions."

"How did he figure on changing things that way?"

The other man shrugged. "Wants to make a point— get back at the Company."

"Damned dangerous way to do it. How serious is the fire?"

"Well, his partner put it out before it could do much damage, and they managed to get out of there unhurt."

"What's his name?"

"They call him Twister—Twister Trewella."

Earl arrested Trewella, who was being held at the Company office. They rode south through groves of birches, aspen and beech. They passed the church that Earl had always thought was too big for the hill it stood on.

On the long buggy ride, the culprit sat next to him in handcuffs. With his huge crop of red hair and no beard it was hard not to think of him as a boy. The lad said he was twenty years old, and had worked at the Keweenaw since he was fourteen.

"I can't take h'it no more," the youth told the sheriff, as his left knee bounced up and down.

"How's that?"

Earl Foster strained to decipher the Cornish accent.

"I got passed h'up, for learning the minin' trade. They must think I wanted to pick h'up and dump rock my whole life. Now Fred, 'e's my brother, and 'e's been a miner h'ever so long. So 'as h'other blokes."

"Did you think you could change the course of events by starting a fire down below?"

"I 'ad to do somethin'. Nobody h'ever listens. Trammers work harder than miners, h'and get less pay. 'Ad to do somethin' to get their 'tention."

"I don't think you realize what a serious offense this is. What if the whole shaft had caught on fire? It could cost the Company thousands of dollars—"

"I don't care h'about the Company."

"—And you could have lost your life. Did you think about that?"

As if to emphasize his point, the right wheel of the buggy dove into a pothole that jolted them both. Trewella cried out. Earl cursed himself for not keeping a better eye on the road.

The young man turned his head to the side and bit his fingernail—by necessity raising both cuffed arms.

"How many others feel the way you do?"

"Lots. We hain't 'ad a raise h'in a 'coon's age. I'm tryin' to stir h'up some h'action."

"I think you picked the wrong way to go about it, boy."

Earl was well aware that miners and trammers alike were not satisfied. The long day, poor wages and safety precautions were breeding discontent in all quarters. Every few years the matter would bubble up and burst, sometimes causing a strike among the men. But most of them knew that that path only led to empty bellies.

They came to Lake Portage. Nature had designed it to look like a polliwog—round on the east end, and narrow as an ordinary river where Houghton and Hancock faced each other. A bridge spanned the lake between the two cities. They crossed the bridge and drove up to the jail which was housed in the basement of the courthouse in Houghton. The jailkeep escorted them to a cell in the basement.

"I'll have to keep you here," Earl said. "You won't be earning any wages at all in jail. You married, son? Have any kids?"

"No."

"Well, that's good news, then." He started for the door. "You'll get a hearing in a few days."

When he left, he could hear Trewella sniffling. He wasn't at all sure the lad's train was on its track.

Even though Cora had warmed his supper up he didn't feel like eating any more. He was sorry for this Twister fellow, and he knew that was his greatest weakness as a law officer.

CHAPTER FOUR

In the early fall, when she heard that the Keweenaw Society was putting on a Benefit Ball, Betsy approached the chairman.

"For whom is the money being raised?"

"The proceeds will go to the Miners' Fund."

Betsy knew Red Jacket's finest would attend this annual festivity, as she had herself in years past, and she wanted to be involved. When she offered to help with entertainment, she was placed in charge. They knew her from the piano recitals and church pageants she'd performed in. The committee was grateful. With many other aspects to tend to, they left Betsy to prepare the skit she promised to produce.

"I'm sure whatever you do will be wonderful."

Betsy's head was in a whirl, but thinking she might do something to stir up some concern for the poor miners and trammers made her heart beat a little faster.

Patty recovered, but Betsy was not satisfied to leave things as they were. If Jeremy would not speak up for the poor workers, she would find someone who could.

Tales had spread around Red Jacket about a woman who was as gentle as a babe and fierce as a boxer. She was supposed to be tall— over six feet, and outspoken about her notions concerning the shameful distress a large portion of their community was living in. Some of the stories got so wild, such as her shouting out from roof tops, that Betsy wondered if this person was real. Perhaps, like the tales of Paul Bunyan, she was just a fable that got bigger each time with the telling of it.

She decided to ask around her neighborhood. The business people of Red Jacket lived in the better part of town. The homes here were well kept, with spacious lawns, large porches, towering conifers and deciduous trees. Betsy conferred with several neighbors. Yes, this woman really did exist, they testified.

"A trouble-maker she is. Sowing seeds of discontent among the miners. Trying to get them all riled up about their circumstances."

"As if the Company didn't do enough—providing schools for their young, all kinds of churches, and so on."

"What's her name?"

"Annie Clemenc. They call her Big Annie."

"Where does she live?"

"In the miners' section—Croatian part. Provided, mind you, by the mining company. Anybody over there can give you her address."

It was several days before Betsy drew up the courage to go to that part of town and seek out Big Annie. Finally, she put on her best bonnet, thought better of it, changed it for an everyday one, and set out to find this Annie Clemenc.

Annie Clemenc was neither an apparition nor a fable. She was real live flesh and blood, married to a miner, Joseph Clemenc. Although taller than she, he was in many ways a small man. Quiet and soft-spoken, he was the opposite of Annie, who was high-spirited, out-spoken and all the things he was not.

She had married Joseph because her parents were insistent. Although very attractive, at six foot two inches she had not engaged the attention of any other young men.

"Then I won't get married," she told her parents.

"And who will take care of you, eh?" her mother asked.

"I can take care of myself."

"And be a spinster like your Aunt Sophie? Forever living off the kindness and resentment of relatives?"

To Croatian immigrants, the lot of a spinster was a frightening specter, as it was to most folks.

Annie could see that her parents were afraid she'd be a burden to them.

Finally, she agreed to marry Joseph Clemenc. She felt she barely knew him.

She could not interest him in the subjects of the day, nor arouse his interest in much of anything. Each day with him was the same as the next. He'd come home exhausted from work, have his pint, and lie down for a rest until the evening meal was set. At the table he talked little.

"How was it down below today?" she'd ask.

"Same."

"Have they replaced the men who died in the cave-in?"

Dunno."

Working all day with the cooking, taking in other people's laundry, cleaning and trying to make a few vegetables grow in the poor soil, Annie fairly seethed with another kind of energy. All around she could see how little her neighbors profited from the hard labors they endured. They were no better off than their parents or grandparents had been. Year after year they struggled just to keep mouths fed. The men who worked the mines were not treated fairly. Oh, the companies said they'll take care of you:

"Look, we have parks, doctors, all kinds of shops and businesses right here on company property. Be happy."

But many were not.

Just this morning, Joseph had complained that he hadn't had a good breakfast with eggs and bacon for two weeks.

"I'm tired of porridge."

"The chickens aren't laying, and it would cost ten cents to buy eggs. We can't afford it."

It was true Annie'd been outspoken about the miners' lot, though she had not screamed from the roof-tops.

One day when she was working in her patch of cabbage and tomatoes, a woman came around the house, and called to her.

"Are you Annie Clemenc?"

"Yes."

"Could I speak to you, please? My name is Betsy Willis. I've come to talk to you about the unfortunate situation of those who work in the mine."

Annie was astonished. This wealthy lady with her fine clothes had come to her, and wanted to help the poor? It was hard to believe. For a moment she just stared.

"Oh, come in, and sit down. I'll fix some tea."

"I'd be grateful for just a glass of water."

"Yes, of course."

Annie brushed strands of hair out of her eyes, and took a cloth to her face.

When they were seated at the table, Betsy poured out her story to Annie, explaining graphically what she'd witnessed in the slums of Red Jacket, the squalor she'd observed and smelled. And she told Annie her experience at Sean Sullivan's pub, the one sweet note of the day.

"Is there anything we can do? Anything at all to help those poor trammers?"

They talked for an hour and a half, both of them getting aroused by the possibilities that occurred to them.

The next time they met, Annie said to Betsy, "Didn't you tell me some of these men did a little show business?"

"So my Patty tells me."

"And you have something to do with putting on entertainment at the upcoming Miners' Ball."

"Yes," Betsy said.

"Let's see if we can work the two things together."

Betsy blanched. This woman was reading her mind. "Go on."

"Use these men to put their case before the audience. In a skit."

Betsy swallowed. "Would we dare?"

"How better to get the message across than to perform at a fundraiser for the miners?" Annie produced a mischievous smile. "Remember, these good folks have already been softened by a few libations."

Betsy blinked a few times. Her heart was beating too fast.

"Do you have a better idea, Mrs. Willis?"

"No. No, I haven't."

"Then I think we should make a visit to your friend's pub."

"He's not my friend," Betsy protested. "And I dare not go there again."

"No, I see. Then arrange an introduction for me. And I'll take care of it."

How could she refuse? "If you think you can work with these people, Mrs. Clemenc, then I could do some writing for the program—from home".

"You'd be willing for us to work together?"

"Oh, yes, I would."

"It might be difficult, coming 'round to your home, Mrs. Willis. I have to work, and it might look strange, my making visits to someone like you."

"Would you like to work for me, Annie? Maybe once or twice a week? Patty only comes twice a week. I could use more help. And I'm sure Patty will be glad to help with the skit."

Annie smiled. "That would be the solution. And we could use the extra money."

Betsy queried Patty about her husband's theatrical talents.

"You said he did song and dance on the stage. He can act, as well?"

Patty laughed. "Oh yes, mum."

"Has he friends who do the same?"

"Aye, the lot of them get together and sing tunes from the old country."

"Where do they perform?"

"In the pub, if you call that performin'."

"Mr. Sullivan's."

"Sean hisself be the best of 'em all. You should hear him sing." Patty looked at her quizzically. "Why are you askin', mum, if you don't mind?"

Betsy introduced Patty to Annie when they both came to work the next day, and let Patty tell this woman about the men and their singing.

Annie was intrigued. "I'd like to hear them sing, see if they can learn new pieces and take direction."

Patty got excited. "Ah, pleased they'll be! It'll go to their heads, it will— gettin' to act up for the high class."

"We'd have to work out a time and place to practice, if they agree to do it." Annie said.

"I'm sure Sean would let you use the pub," Patty said.

Betsy wrote a note that Patty carried home for Michael to give to Sean Sullivan.

It didn't take long for word to get round to the singers, and back to Betsy and Annie. They would be honored, Patty said.

Betsy set to work writing the skit, and composing new words to familiar songs. The Benefit Ball was only four weeks away, and the men would need as much time as possible to rehearse the material. She wrote feverishly, and sat at the piano, trying out her new lyrics.

"Come in here, Patty. Tell me what you think of this."

"If you don't mind my sayin', mum, it might sound more like the men if you was to word it a bit differently."

"What do you suggest?"

"If you don't think it would upset their sensibilities too much, maybe you could say . . ."

"Go on."

"Instead of 'the wretched man' maybe you could say 'the bloody bloke.'

"Ah! That's it exactly." She turned to her servant. "Patty, would you be willing to take part in the skit, as well?"

"Oh, mum! I've never done nothin' like that!" She covered her face with her hands.

"We need at least one woman. Annie says it would be better to have two."

"Oh, I don't know, mum." She hid her smile behind her hand.

"It would be a small part."

"Well, if it's just a bit."

On the first Sunday that she was to meet the men at the pub Annie told Joseph she was going to church, and that she'd be late getting home. Afterwards she'd be practicing the skit for the Benefit Ball.

Joseph did not question her as to where the rehearsal would take place. No doubt he supposed they would be working at the church.

All during the service Annie's mind was on the pub and the men she'd be working with. For the first time she wondered if she was crazy to embark on this project. Would it do any good? More importantly, how much harm could it cause? She pulled her mind away from that thought. She had put her oar in the water and would not take it out now.

She strode the mile and a half to Sullivan's Pub. Sean greeted her at the door warmly, and took her to a seat by the fire. The place was empty except for two old men who sat in the far corner.

"It's good to meet you, mum. Mrs. Willis sent word about you. And I want you to know I think what you and her are doing is a real Worthy Cause. We was all very touched by just the idea of it."

She thought she saw a tear in his eye. But then the Irish were a sentimental lot, she told herself.

He brought her a plate of corned beef and cabbage. "It's the best in town," he announced.

"Thank you." She hadn't had such a good meal since Christmas last.

While she was eating she asked, "Are the men coming?"

"Oh, yes, mum. I told 'em one o'clock, about twenty minutes from now."

By the time she'd finished her lunch two of them had arrived. The first was introduced to her as Pat Keller. He took off his cap, wiped his hand on his backside, and shyly took her hand. He couldn't know that Annie was as uncomfortable as he. Soon Michael and Patty Riley joined them, followed by the man they called Pokey.

"As soon the piana player gets here, we can begin."

When Johnny arrived, Sean broke the ice by asking if she'd like to hear them sing a couple of the old country songs.

"Just to warm up, you know."

"Yes, that would be lovely."

Johnny took his seat at the piano and the others crossed to the little platform, conscious of their position and who stood next to whom. No doubt embarrassed by her presence, they sang in a stilted manner, with their hands at their sides. As to their voices, Annie wasn't sure what to expect, but the fine Irish tenor that Sean presented was beyond anything she'd dared hope for. And whatever the others lacked in sonority they made up for in volume.

Sean turned to them. "Now come, boys. I'm sure the lady doesn't want to watch a quartet of statues, as the likes of us present. It's a little action she'd like to see, if I'm not mistaken."

Annie nodded, and they began again. This time, encouraged by their leader, they put more into it, and convinced Annie they would be quite capable performers.

Annie knew she could only work with them once a week. She decided it would be best if they improvised, rather than try to memorize the lines. She described the plot for them.

Sober and respectful, they remained quiet, though dumbfounded that she wanted to put this story before an audience. But after Annie had taken them through it a couple of times, and taught them new lyrics to a familiar song, they loosened up a bit.

"It's very darin', it is."

"They'll put us all in the hoosegow, they will."

"Get the boot, that's what," said Pokey.

Sean tried to quiet them. "Now boys, calm down. It's a great thing Annie and Mrs. Willis are doin' for ye. Are ye goin' to turn cowards on them?"

"You don't stand to lose your job, Sean."

"Nor you neither, Michael," Pokey sneered.

"It went fairly well for a first rehearsal," Annie reported to her employer. "They're nervous, they are, and afraid of losing their jobs. I'm not sure they'll all stay with it."

All the next week the women wondered if the men would return for rehearsal. Betsy asked Patty if she'd heard anything.

"I think Sean will shame 'em into it, if he hasn't already. Don't let on you know, but he's had a soft spot for you, mum, ever since the day they brought you into the pub all passed out."

Betsy felt herself redden. She didn't want to remember, yet she knew it was that event and her search for the Rileys that had paved the way for her present venture.

"Will Michael do it?"

"If the others do, he will. I'm sure 'o that!"

Betsy thought of ways she could change the story, tone it down. Better that than lose the cast.

When Sunday came, all but Pokey were there.

"He's afraid of losin' his job, and he's a wife and three to feed, with another on the way."

"It's been revised somewhat," Annie told them. "Perhaps you'll like the new ending better."

She described the changes she had in mind.

"Do you mind if I have a word with the men, Annie?" Sean asked.

They talked in low voices among themselves. Then Sean said, "It's your creation, but the men say, if we're goin' to do it, let's go all the way with it. Just like you had it 'afore."

Annie felt her heart leap. She had tried to convince herself that she'd be content with the new ending, but she was very moved that they were willing to do the original version. During the practice, she was impressed with how hard they worked, and at the end even offered to practice among themselves during the week.

Pat approached her. "There's one thing, though. What would you think, mum, if we was to have some of the scenes in the pub? It'd be more realistic like."

"I'm afraid you will not gain the sympathy of this audience by appearing to fritter away your time and money in a public saloon."

"Frittering away, is it!" Pat was upset and for a moment Annie was afraid she'd alienated him.

But Johnny said, "She's right. They wouldn't understand. The pub's what holds us together. But they wouldn't know about that."

At the third rehearsal Michael said, "I was wonderin' Mum, if we could put a little humor in it. The boys, well, we're accustomed to havin' a bit of fun with it, you know."

"He means bawdy humor," Patty, who had come along, whispered to Annie.

"Right you are, Michael," agreed Pat. "It's a mite stiff, don't you think, mum? Perhaps the folks will be expectin' to get a bit o' a laugh."

They certainly were, thought Annie. Even the men, for whose cause she was working, thought it too sober. Annie didn't know what to say. How could she make them understand that this was not a piece for vaudeville, and that jokes would ruin the whole purpose.

"That would be another kind of show."

"Well, couldn't we fit 'Let the Ole Cow Die' in there somewheres? It's not a foul song, and the folks might enjoy it."

"No, the lady's right. She knows what's she's doin, she does. Leave it to her, boys."

Sean had rescued her. She gave him a smile, and the rehearsal continued. When the others had left, Annie approached Sean.

"I don't see any place for humor in this program. But you've a fine voice, Mr. Sullivan, and perhaps you could start us off by singing *The Rose of Tralee*. As a solo. Everyone likes that, and it would put the audience in a receptive mood."

Sean's expressive face showed a mix of pleasure and embarrassment. "I'm touched mum, that you would want me to sing that song. It's one of my favorites."

During the week before the ball Annie and Betsy thought of every possible thing that could go wrong.

"Where will the actors stay before their performance?" Annie asked Betsy.

"I'll work it out," Betsy promised.

"How are they going to get the scenery they're makin' up the stairs?" Annie wondered.

Patty came to Betsy chewing her lip. "I can't do it, mum. I just can't."

"What's the trouble?"

"I'll forget me lines, I know I will."

"Let's go over them now, Patty."

Betsy practiced with the woman, but Patty was not comforted. "In front of all those people. I'm not like Michael— he enjoys it."

"You'll be fine, Patty."

"Did you find a second woman?" Betsy asked Annie.

"I'm afraid I'll have to take that part."

"Well, that will be wonderful! You'll be right there to guide them."

Betsy had so many last minute details to work out she could not afford to think about how the presentation would be received. She ran into the chairman of the Benefit Ball at the produce market.

"How's the entertainment coming? All prepared for Saturday night?"

Betsy nodded. "There will be a piano, won't there?"

"Yes, of course. Who's in your cast?"

"Oh, no one you know, I'm sure."

"Is it a variety show?"

Betsy smiled. "Afraid not."

"Well, I'm sure, whatever you've put together, we'll be pleasantly surprised."

"Yes, you'll be surprised."

Betsy got away from her as fast as she could.

The first time Annie met Cal was during a storm. All the special effects of heaven were putting on an impressive show. Thunder followed so closely behind lightning, that it was clear the brilliant daggers from above were not far off. Annie was waiting for it to let up, before she dared leave the Willis's.

Cal shook the rain off his coat, and removed his galoshes. "And who do we have here?" he smiled at Annie.

Betsy introduced her son to Annie, told him what a brave thing she was doing for the miners and trammers. Annie was embarrassed as Betsy sang her praises, but it didn't stop Betsy from going on.

"Don't tell your father, but she's working with me on a skit to perform for the Miners' Benefit."

Cal raised an eyebrow.

"I really should go," Annie remarked. "My husband will be concerned."

"I'll walk you home," Cal offered.

"Oh, you needn't" Annie protested.

His mother spoke up. "That would be splendid, Cal."

On the porch Cal sprung open his large umbrella and escorted her down the steps.

"How did you meet my mother?" He had to shout over the rain and wind.

"We're organizing a skit together for the Miners' Fund."

"What's Ma doing for this project?"

"She's doing the writing. I'm sure she can tell you about it herself."

Cal couldn't believe his ears.

"Pa won't like that."

Bolts of lightning followed by thunder ignited the dialogue.

"And how do you feel about it, Mr. Calvin?"

Cal took a deep breath. "I don't know if Ma told you, but I'm a shift captain, and as such am— assigned to management."

"And so you side with the Company? You're anti-union?"

Cal knew he'd reddened. He was glad it was dark, and the woman couldn't see his face. "Until recently I hadn't given it much thought."

The rain came at an angle, mostly toward Cal. Then it changed directions suddenly and was coming at Annie. Cal tilted the umbrella to protect her.

"And now?" Annie said.

"I'm not sure. It's all so complicated. There are two sides to everything."

"Not for those of us who don't have enough to eat, or never know when we say good-bye to our husbands if we'll ever see them again."

Cal muttered, "I suppose not."

"So give it some thought, will you?"

"Yes, ma'am."

They were at her door. She thanked him, got inside as quickly as she could, and closed the door against the storm.

CHAPTER FIVE

The day of the ball a slow fear began to creep over Betsy.
At last she put on the gown she'd made for the occasion. A
vibrant rust-colored taffeta trimmed in black velvet, it brought out
the dark shades in her own hair. Even Jeremy commented on how
smart she looked. Still, as she secured some last minute props, and
reassured Patty once more that she'd be just fine, Betsy wondered if
what she was doing was insane. Well, he is in a cheerful mood for
once. That's a good omen. He had not asked what the skit was about,
and for that Betsy was grateful.

The hall was beginning to fill when they arrived. Red Jacket's
finest, as Mrs. Wisely called them, had indeed turned out for this
occasion. It was the most important social event of the season.
Aromas of sweet- smelling goose greeted them on the stairway. The
hall had been decorated with fresh branches of maple, displaying all
the brilliant colors of fall. The tables held boughs of pine and gold-
flecked cones. Place cards, carefully made by some artistic individual,
donned each table setting.

Betsy saw the women all decked out in beautiful gowns, but no
more stunning than her own, she concluded.

An orchestra sat on the stage now, playing classical music. After
the meal and the skit, they would play popular music for the dancing.
She wondered if they'd play *Peg 'O My Heart* and *You Made Me Love
You*. Betsy looked up at the stage, the black velvet curtains that
framed each side. In less than two hours her little troupe would be up
there!

She wanted to check on them in the small back room, where they
were assembling to wait for their cue. The pieces of scenery, hinged
and easily set in place, should be there by now also. Sean had seen to
all that, bless his heart.

But just then, champagne was served, and it was difficult to escape
as Jeremy kept engaging them in conversation with other couples.
Betsy had two glasses before she'd had anything to eat. She felt the
effects, and though she would have liked more, when Jeremy said,
"I've think you've had enough," she refrained. She must keep her
head, and besides, it was important to keep Jeremy in good humor.

Pleased that she'd deferred when the tray was passed, he took her
arm and guided her toward the Parkers and someone she didn't know.

"Mr. Tyson, I'd like you to meet my wife, Betsy. This is Mr. Tyson, Dear, one of the stockholders of the Keweenaw. Mr. Tyson is visiting us from Boston."

Betsy blanched.

The new surface captain joined them. Betsy tried to focus on conversation that would be expected of her. "And what are the duties of a surface captain, Mr. Fielding?" she asked.

She barely took in a word as he regaled her with the responsibilities afforded him. Was Annie here yet? She must get to the back room and see if everyone had arrived. Why did Jeremy pick now to hover so?

"Well, in summary, ma'am, I'm responsible for just about everything that happens above board."

There was amused laughter.

"Maintenance of all the buildings, tracks, employment—"

Just then a bell sounded, that summoned them to their dinner places. Betsy suddenly realized she was famished, as she hadn't eaten all day. Eyeing a plate of pickled turnips and beets she wished she could start nibbling on these at least, but no, it seemed there were to be speeches first. A growing clamor of spoons against glasses rose. The assembled hushed.

Mrs. Wisely rose and received a warm round of applause. Betsy could feel her heart trying to escape, and wished she could slit the corset so tightly imprisoning her.

"At this our fifth annual ball for the benefit of the Miners' Fund," Mrs. Wisely was saying, "it is my great pleasure to see so many faces. Faces that belong to the responsible citizens of our community, who though in sufficiency themselves, are not unaware that there are many who are less fortunate. While we are the backbone of society, we are not immune to the suffering of our miners, who are the muscle of this community. And so this benefit was begun to help these very people, who when adversity strikes, will know that we are here, behind them, to support them in their hour of need."

Betsy started coughing, and excused herself. Darting to the back room she found Annie, Sean, Pat, and Johnny, the piano player. Annie introduced her to the players

"Annie, thank God you're here." Looking around she noticed the absence of Patty and Michael.

"Where are the Rileys?" she fairly hissed.

"Rest yourself, Mrs. Willis. They'll be along shortly, I'm sure," Sean said. He rose and took her hand. "It's good to see you again, it is."

"They were supposed to be here half an hour ago." Betsy laid the yellow rose she'd brought for Patty on the table.

"It's his missus, is my guess," interjected Pat. "Probably havin' last minute stage fright again, that'd be my opinion."

"What'll we do if they don't come?" asked Johnny.

Sean cleared his throat. "Oh, that's premature, Johnny. In any case, Michael won't let us down. If he can't get his missus to come, he'll at least be here himself. Wouldn't miss it for anything."

Johnny piped up. "Perhaps you could play her part, mum, if you don't mind my suggesting it." He was addressing Betsy.

"Never!" She caught her breath. "If it comes to that, you, Sean, as narrator, can tell the audience what's supposed to be happening."

"Yes, mum."

She looked around. "You brought a wheelbarrow?"

"Michael's bringing it."

Betsy swallowed. "The scenery's here. Good."

"Aye. But the paint's still wet. Be careful not to get none on your dress."

The warning came too late. The hem of her new gown had already brushed the pale yellow board, and picked up the color.

Apologies came fast. "We should have told you sooner."

"It'll come out in the wash, mum. It's only water paint."

"Never mind. Just go over your lines quietly, and I'll come back to check on the Rileys before dessert."

She was ready to scream. Patty again! And now her new gown! Tears she must hold back stung and threatened to overflow. She found the Ladies' room, and took a moment to compose herself.

When she returned to the table, Jeremy asked if she were all right.

She nodded, clutching her fists under the table.

Suddenly her appetite was gone, and she found it difficult to eat the delicacies she would have relished before. She picked at the peas and chestnuts, but the goose, roasted in apricots and brandy, was left untouched on her plate. She only wanted to drink more, but knew that could prove disastrous.

"You're not eating, Betsy." Jeremy observed.

"I'm just nervous," she admitted.

"I've never known you to have a case of nerves."

"Some of the cast isn't here."

The orchestra was playing some frenetic melody reflecting Betsy's mood.

"Jeremy, do excuse me again, while I see if they've arrived."

She fairly fled to the back room.

Still no Rileys. *Why are these people so unreliable?* she thought, remembering her search for Patty when no one had sent her any word.

The chairwoman's husband approached her as she headed for her seat.

"Mrs. Wisely would like to know where you'd like the piano for the skit."

Betsy hurried back to the dressing room to confer with Annie, then back to the man.

"Perhaps two or three feet more to the side, thank you."

"Very good, ma'am. And I'm to tell you to be ready to go on as soon as dessert's been cleared. Before the dancing."

"Yes." Betsy dabbed at the tiny drops of perspiration erupting on her upper lip before resuming her seat.

A woman leaned from across the table. "I understand you're providing the entertainment. I'm sure it's very amusing, and I'm looking forward to it. I expect we all are."

Her companion chimed in. "Yes, your reputation precedes you, Mrs. Willis." To her friend she said, "She's very good at this sort of thing."

Betsy fairly leapt backstage. This time she was met by a full cast, albeit a crying Patty.

Michael looked up. "Sorry to be so late, mum. Didn't mean to give you a fright. Had an awful time getting' Patty to come, I did."

Betsy breathed a sigh of relief. "Well, it's a good job you did. Just try to pull yourself together." She looked at the woman's pleading face, all red-eyed from crying so long. Well, that would work just fine for the part.

Michael tried to comfort her. "Yes, Love. Just think of all those dandies lookin' up at you. You don't want to be a fright for them, now do you?" His miserable attempt brought on a new wave of sobs.

"Hush now," Annie said. "They'll hear you out there."

Betsy turned to Sean. "I'll come and tell you when it's time to set up the scenery."

She returned to the table, unaware of what was being chatted about around her.

As people were finishing their coffee, Mrs. Wisely rose to make an announcement. "We will have a short break now, to allow the tables to be cleared, and the ladies to visit the powder room. The men, of course, may choose to indulge in their favorite pastime— smoking of the cigar. Then we will all meet back here and be treated to what, I am sure, will be a delightful piece of entertainment."

Again, Betsy felt the blood leave her face. She wanted to run, and this was her chance. But if poor Patty could stick it out, so must she. She made her way back to the actors. Annie was comforting Patty.

"Is everyone ready?"

Patty had stopped sobbing, but her face was still all red.

"It's time to take the scenery on."

While the orchestra removed their chairs and music stands, Annie and the actors placed a hinged partition on the stage, meant to represent shabby living quarters.

"Patty, where's your apron?"

"Oh!" She let out another wail. "I forgot it, so upset I was."

"Never mind, now."

The guests were returning to the dining room.

"Everyone speak up good and loud," Annie was saying. "It's not the pub you're playing to. It's a big hall, and there are about three hundred people out there, each paying dearly for this evening's. . ." She swallowed— "entertainment."

"Who's going to tell 'em the title of our skit?" asked Pat.

"Sean will. But first I'll introduce him and his song."

When Betsy left, Annie turned to her little company of actors, "If there was ever a place to put your cause before those who can effect change, this is it. They mean well, they really do. Tonight is your chance. Make the most of it."

She looked at each of them. "You're all very brave, and I'm proud of you."

Sean was turning his cap in his hand. "It's you that's brave, mum. And we all salute you."

"Aye, aye."

"We got somethin' for you. It isn't much, but it's from our heart, and we wanted you to have it in remembrance of us."

Sean handed her a little box. "Open it, mum, if you have time."

Annie hadn't expected this. Tears threatened to overflow, in gratitude and genuine surprise.

She removed the paper, and found inside a little pin in the shape of a bee.

"It's to go on one of your frocks, mum. Not pricey, it wasn't. Just a token of our thanks for all you've done for us."

Annie tried to conceal her feelings. "I don't know if I've done a thing— perhaps more harm than good. But I thank you, deeply." She couldn't let them see her cry.

There was much scuffling as everyone found their seats. Once again a cacophony of clanging spoons brought a hush to the assembly.

"And now we have reached that point in our program where we will be treated to the fruits of one of Red Jacket's artistic talents. Her gifts will be bestowed upon us this evening, as this clever lady has agreed to provide us with an original skit penned by her own hand. I know we can all expect to be highly entertained by our first lady of the arts and her troupe of actors. And now I am delighted to give you the beautiful and talented Mrs. Jeremy Willis. Please help me welcome her."

Betsy saw Jeremy's hands come together first. He rose quickly, and as he did, he set off the cue for all others to follow. She couldn't look at him as he beamed at her with pride. Why now, why now was he finally paying attention to her? Oh, Jeremy, it is too late. I know it is too late!

She rose and wedged her way between chairs of clapping guests to the front, where a small set of stairs brought her up to the stage. She looked out at the gathering of well-heeled men and women, all of whom were standing in recognition of her.

Oh, God, help me! Have I created a monstrous thing, or can I really move these people?

Somehow she found her voice.

"Before the promised skit, I should like to introduce to you one of the finest Irish tenors I have had the pleasure to hear. He will sing for us *The Rose of Tralee*. I give you Sean Sullivan." Betsy joined the others in the wings.

Polite, scattered clapping accompanied Sean's entrance to the stage. Johnny took his seat at the piano and Sean signaled he was ready. He filled the hall with the timbre of his voice, surprising more than a few that this hitherto unknown talent was among them. When he finished a great burst of applause followed him off stage.

Betsy tried to take a deep breath. At least that part had gone well.

At this point Sean was supposed to announce the title of their melodrama, The *Trammer's Tribulation*, but he only said, "And now our little troupe will present a skit for you." He did not introduce them by name as they said they wanted to remain anonymous.

"In the first scene, we find Harry at home with his missus, Betty."

Annie motioned Michael and Patty to go on stage.

"You'll be fine, Patty," Betsy whispered to the frightened woman.

Michael took his wife by the hand and brought her center stage. Patty forgot to pick up the broom, so Michael handed it to her.

"How was it in the mine today, Harry?"

"Hard, hard work as usual."

"And you get so little pay." Patty managed to squeak out.

Betsy wanted to kiss Patty.

As she continued to sweep the floor, Johnny struck up a chord, and Michael began singing *We're Poor but We're Happy* to the tune of *The Old Grey Mare.*

"We're poor, but we're happy, and we're starting a family. Now we are two, but soon we'll be three."

In the middle of the song Sean and Annie, playing friends of the couple, came to visit, joining in the chorus. There arose a murmur, as many recognized the tall woman as Big Annie, the rabble-rouser.

There followed some dialogue about how hard their life was.

"I've not a cent to buy Tim and little Alice shoes. And winter's almost upon us," Annie complained.

Michael's voice rang through the hall. "We thought it would be better in this country, but we break our backs, and what do we get for it? Not even enough to eat."

Betsy was able to peek through an opening where the curtain didn't quite meet the proscenium. The audience was attentive, waiting for something funny to laugh at, she surmised.

Sean added his woes and the scene ended with a short reprise of their song. Betsy could tell the guests weren't enthusiastic, but at least they weren't throwing fruit at the actors such as she'd seen at some performances. The applause was minimal and Sean came on quickly to introduce the next scene.

"Now a terrible thing has happened. There's been an explosion at the mine. One man's been killed and our Harry seriously injured— he has lost his arm. And so distraught is his wife, she has lost the baby. And got sick to boot. This scene takes place a month after the accident."

Michael returned to the stage, this time with one arm inside the jacket to suggest the lost limb. He sat down next to the cot where Patty was lying. His friends arrived.

"I've brought you a bit o' soup. There's no meat in it, though." Pat said.

"Here, try to eat something, Betty. Pat's brought you some soup."

"I can't eat," she wailed. "My baby! I've lost my baby!"

"Hasn't the doctor come to see her?" Sean asked.

"We can't afford a doctor."

"Poor Harry! Whatever will you do?" Pat shook his head.

Michael said, "I don't know. I can't work in the mine any more. Not with my arm gone."

"It's beasts of burden we are. Picking up after the miners. Heaving and hauling all the rock they bring down." Sean said.

"And not getting half the pay," Pat added.

There was an audible change in the attitude of the audience. Murmurs, and even shouting were heard. At first puzzled by the sudden change, it dawned on Betsy that with the omission of the title, it was only now understood this play was not about the miners, but trammers! They had no doubt anticipated how the Miners' Fund would come to the rescue of this family, making them all feel very good, for having contributed to the charity. Betsy felt weak.

They sang, *I'm a Low-Down Trammer Deep in the Hole*.

"Got no cash, a trammer am I,
Pushin'' the barrow up hill 'til I die."

The men mimed the movements, bending to pick up the heavy rocks.

They strained with their loads, placed them in the wheel barrow, and pushed it up the grade. When they had finished, there was no applause.

Betsy winced in horror. She didn't know they were going to sing this song. What must her husband be thinking?

"Harry," Sean spoke up. "Go to the employment office, and see what they can do for you. After all, you lost your arm in service to the Company."

"That's right," said Pat. "If they have any heart at all, they'll come to your aid."

"From cradle to grave, they take care of us. Isn't that what they say?" Johnny struck a chord.

They sang a song by the same name, recalling the paternalism of the Company, and ended the scene on a hopeful note.

A few in the spectators, anticipating the outcome, got up and left the room.

Sean faced the audience. "The next part is at the employment office. For this scene, I will play the part of the employer."

Betsy had been careful not to let them use titles like agent, or captain. Nor did they use anyone's real name.

The men removed the cot and pushed on a desk and chair. Sean hung a sign that said "Employment", and sat behind the desk.

"The Company cannot support you the rest of your life, lad. No, I'm afraid there's nothing we can do for you." He spoke in a blustery, boisterous manner.

"But I've heard of cases where miners were given a pension."

"Ah, well, miners, yes, in some cases. But you're a trammer, eh?"

"You mean there's nothing to be done for trammers a'tall?"

"No, lad, afraid not."

"Well, I'm willin' to work. Is there some sort of job I could do on the surface?"

Sean shook his head.

"The Wash House— I could clean up there, take care of the towels and such."

"No opening. And if there was, it would go to an old or injured miner."

"Then you do nothing for the trammers?" Michael shouted.

Betsy grimaced. Michael was putting more into this than he ever had before, and she could feel it having an adverse effect. She could hear murmurs from the audience.

Sean shrugged. "I don't make the rules."

"Then what can I do? We can't pay the rent. We've been given our notice."

"The by-laws clearly state—"

"That we should starve!" Michael shouted.

Betsy jolted. She wondered if Michael had lost control. She looked back at the audience. Everyone appeared uncomfortable, and the murmurs were growing louder. Suddenly a loud boo rang through the hall.

"In the last scene," Sean was trying to project his voice over the noise of the crowd, "Betty and Harry are homeless, out on the street in a storm, with no food and no place to go. My friend and I will play the gentlemen."

A general moaning and a few hisses rose from the audience.

While Michael practically dragged the now-terrified Patty across the stage, Johnny played a dirge on the piano, that he followed by rattling a large piece of sheet metal, signifying thunder.

As the passersby entered, Michael held an empty cup to them, and Patty raised her arm to shield against the rain.

"Please, sir, help a cripple, who can no longer work." The gentleman pulled his coat up against the wind and walked on by. The second man came on from the other direction and did the same.

The skit ended as Harry and Betty stumbled off stage, with the music of the dirge swelling in volume, Johnny hitting several more chords for added emphasis.

There was no applause, only a growing crescendo of boos and hisses. Betsy caught some remarks:

"In very poor taste."

"Damn disgusting."

"She was supposed to amuse us."

A great shuffling of chairs and commotion followed as some left altogether, while others awaited the hall to be cleared for dancing.

The piano player for the orchestra practically pushed Johnny off the stool. He immediately began pounding out light and peppy tunes.

While Annie's team hastened to remove the set, they collided with members of the orchestra carrying on chairs and music stands.

Before she dared allow her own feelings to surface, Betsy went to her actors, finding Patty once again in tears. None of them looked happy, and Pat was angry. He threw his cap on the floor.

"They don't give a fig about the likes of us. They'd as soon the whole lot of us was swept out to sea, and back to where we came from."

Annie was strong and unflappable, but Sean was concerned about Betsy. "How are you takin' it, ma'am?"

She shook her head. "I don't know yet." She took a deep breath. "I suppose I'll sort it all out when I get home."

She looked them over, Patty was giving off muffled sobs under Michael's wing.

"We tried." Betsy put on a brave smile. "If we touched even one heart, perhaps it will help. We knew we were taking a risk."

It was hard to look at this lamentable group of players. They reminded her of scenes from the works of Charles Dickens.

"I thank you from the bottom of my heart," she finished.

"I think we best pack up and get out of here before they give us the boot," Sean said.

She watched them struggle down the steep and narrow back stairs with the awkward pieces of scenery.

"Don't forget your bits and pieces," Annie called as she followed them down.

When they were gone Betsy went back to the tiny room where they'd waited to do their little show. It seemed strangely empty and forlorn. The only sign they'd ever been there was Patty's yellow rose, lying wilted and forgotten on the table. Just an hour ago, there'd been a hushed kind of excitement— a dream that just perhaps they could somehow make a difference.

She could still hear Sean. "We're either damn fools, or some kind of heroes."

Betsy had found it hard enough to face the earnest, hardworking troupe after the debacle. Now she had to deal with Jeremy.

Greeted with averted faces or worse yet— glares, she inched her way back through the crowd. The tables had been removed and she could find him nowhere. Making her way downstairs to the smoking room, she glanced in, was met with hostile looks, and retreated. A few men were outside, taking a breath of air. Jeremy was not among them.

She hired a cab, and gave her address. But just as the driver turned the first corner, Betsy called, "Wait! I'd like to get out here, please."

"Are you sure, mum?"

"Quite sure."

She paid the man, and took her leave of the car. It was a long way home, but it would give her some respite from the denunciation she was sure to face at home. Faltering along the path between the road and the pond, she found a log to sit on.

She needed to clarify her own thoughts before she faced Jeremy. Clearly he was humiliated and furious, or he wouldn't have abandoned her at the hall.

The moon was full, and reflected dizzily in the moving patterns of the water. Betsy walked to the edge and saw her own reflection swaying in tandem with the moon. Transfixed, she stared at it until she felt woozy, and found her way back to the log.

How could I have fooled myself into thinking those people would appreciate having the hardships of the trammers rubbed in their faces — especially, at such an occasion? They don't want to know.

She berated herself again for thinking she could get away with anything of a serious nature, when they were there to have a good time.

Finally, she rose and stumbled along the path. Her gown snagged on a thorn bush. She yanked it loose and heard a rip like a hissing snake. She didn't care. She would never wear it again. Her shoes, too, were doubtlessly ruined by the stones.

Finally she reached home.

Opening the front door, the only light she could see was from the red coal in Jeremy's pipe glowing from the parlor. She tried to make her escape upstairs, but he waylaid her.

"Come in here, Betsy."

Dutifully she returned, collapsed in a seat in the drawing room.

She waited.

"What in God's name made you think you could get away with it?"

She felt numb. "I don't know, Jeremy."

"You will never live it down. Do you realize that?"

She said nothing.

"Cast any aspirations to society aside." He raised his voice. "You are done for, Betsy!"

At this moment all she wanted was to get his tirade over with. The less she said, the sooner he would finish.

"And if you don't care about your own reputation, have you any regard for mine? Do you have any idea of the disgrace you have thrown in my face?" He waited. "Well, do you?" he thundered.

"If there's disgrace, it is mine."

Jeremy rose and banged the ashes of his pipe against the cold fireplace.

"Do you think you can disassociate yourself from me? Society will not. You are Mrs. Jeremy Willis, an extension of me! In your selfish willfulness you have brought me down with you."

"I don't give a fig about Society."

"You have put my career in jeopardy, woman!" he bellowed at her. "I work for the Company. They could discharge me!"

By now his face was crimson. He was pacing the room like a lion on the hunt, coming in closer to his prey with each cross.

"Did you fail to notice that Henry Parker, and the entire management of the mine were there? And did you not meet Mr. Tyson, the visiting stockholder from Boston? Why do you think the stockholders back east sent him? To see how we do things here, Betsy!"

"How in God's name could you have been so stupid!"

Betsy bristled. The hair on the back of her neck began to stand on end, and she knew she couldn't hold her temper much longer.

"What you have done tonight is despicable. Conceived in deception and disloyalty to all whom you should hold sacred."

"I did not deceive you!"

"When did you give me the slightest inkling of what you were planning?"

"You never asked!"

"I trusted you were arranging something amusing for the guests, as you were charged to do."

"I was given no instructions."

"You knew what was expected of you. When I wouldn't act on your behalf for those people, you took matters into your own hands!"

"Yes!"

"And turned what should have been a light piece of entertainment into a disgusting political ploy, entirely out of place."

"I was trying to—"

"What were you thinking, Betsy?"

"I had hoped Red Jacket's finest, who believe themselves to be so charitable, would be moved to compassion when they realized nothing was being done for the indigent trammer."

"They know, Betsy. Are you so naive you don't recognize that their goodness glands will only swell so far? Do you actually believe they enjoyed being told they're not doing enough? Did you really think that would make them reach deeper into their pockets? Did you?"

He was standing over her now. She could feel the sweat spring off his face onto her own.

"I had hoped—"

"You had hoped to use this occasion for your own self-aggrandizement. I think you enjoy a scandal."

"That's not true."

"You think you can live outside the rules of Society, Betsy. You will rue the day. Mark my words— you will rue this day!"

CHAPTER SIX

Walter Radcliff strode down Front Street in the little town of Ripley, adjoining Hancock. He glanced up the hill toward the house in which he'd spent his most miserable years— with his stepmother, Catherine, and his sissy of a little brother, Jorie.

Catherine had been dead these many years, and Jorie had gone off to work in the west.

On a whim he decided to go look at the house. It was late fall, and he slipped on the wet leaves as he climbed the hill. Once the pride of the town, this magnificent house was now abandoned, dilapidated. The roof sagged on the western side, and moss covered a good deal of it. Paint had peeled off the siding. A broken rain gutter hung at a precarious angle from the roof, swaying in the wind like a finger telling you to stay away.

There'd been a time when he thought he'd have a good stake in the sale of the property. He'd fought for it for years. But some discrepancy in the title history had made it impossible to sell. It had been held up in probate indefinitely. It was not even insured.

Walter slinked around to the back. Mudslides had caused the steep hill abutting the house to push against the house itself. Strange mushrooms grew on this new topography.

He reached above the shed door, and his fingers found it— the duplicate key he'd had made years ago. Always handy if he wanted access. Inside, dust covered everything.

"Shit," he said as he walked into a large cobweb covering his face.

A picture of his stepmother lay on the table in the parlor. He stared at it for several minutes, remembering her disdain for him, before throwing it to the ground and stamping on it.

Walter knew he was considered the black sheep of the family. Even his father had agreed with her to have him sent away, all because of a few tricks he'd played on his little brother— Jorie, who got all the attention, all the love. Well, what did it matter now? He'd moved on, could make choices of his own.

Climbing the stairs he heard a cacophony of creaks. He saw two mice scamper away, and wheezed at the odor of their droppings.

He couldn't resist entering her room. Her all-white furnishings looked grey and shabby now. A few ornaments remained on the dresser— her ivory comb and brush set. Yes! And that blue jar that held the cream she'd so lovingly applied to Jorie.

Always Jorie, never him. He remembered the day he'd come back after Catherine was dead and found Jorie in her room. How he'd picked up the globe, tossed it from hand to hand, over his shoulder, knowing all the while Jorie was holding his breath, for fear he'd break it.

The rest of the house held little interest for him. He made a cursory tour, looking to see if anything of value remained.

Long ago he'd hired a dray to transport the player piano and better furniture to his lodgings. He'd sold them at auction. Everything else seemed to be about the same. He didn't fancy anything he saw.

About twelve years ago Jorie had come back to claim his bride, Kaarina Pakkala, and Walter'd had to play one more trick on him. He had seen the wedding announcement in the paper. He'd left a note at the desk of Jorie's hotel, signed "Kaarina", saying that she'd changed her mind and just couldn't go through with the wedding. Not to be fooled, Jorie had strode over to Kaarina's house and cleared the matter up. After all, he'd been corresponding with her for over a year, and knew her handwriting. Walter thought the joke had been fun anyway.

A little later that day Walter ran into his old friend Flem. His real name was Fleming Crocker, but everyone called him Flem.

Walter saw the limp. "What happened to your leg, Flem?" Walter asked.

"Got hurt in the mine."

"Will it heal?"

"Don't know. It's been awhile."

"Let me buy you a drink."

"I won't argue."

They were in Houghton and went to the Ball and Chain to raise a few.

Walter told him about going up to the old house.

"Anybody living there?"

Walter shook his head. "The place ought to be torn down."

"How come?"

"It's a fire hazard."

"Fire hazard." Flem laughed. "Now wouldn't that be a sight? It would be fun to see it go up in flames."

"Yeah?" Walter's eyes lit up.

Frenchie came by. A town eccentric, he said politely, "You boys joined ze union yet?"

"Yup," they answered simultaneously.

"C'est bon."

Although a miner, whenever he was out soliciting membership, Frenchie was impeccably dressed in a black suit, bowler hat and red carnation.

"Hey, Frenchie, when's the strike gonna be?" Flem asked.

"When we get ze beaucoup members."

"I'm talkin' it up," Walter added.

Frenchie did a little soft shoe and tipped his hat. He was known for his little antics and mime shows.

They snickered when he left. But they were both itching for a strike.

Flem was eager to get back to the conversation they'd been having. "Hey! You hated her enough. Could you do it?"

"Burn it down?" Walter passed his hand across his face. "I don't know. It would take some planning."

"'Course. You wouldn't want to get caught."

"I don't know."

"I dare you, Walter! I dare you to do it."

"And what will you give me if I do?"

Flem dropped his head. "I don't know. Ain't got much."

"Didn't think so."

Still the idea of burning down the house on the hill percolated in Walter's head. If he couldn't get his share out of it, what good was it, anyway? It kept gnawing at him until he knew he had to do it. He spent hours deliberating on various ways. Which would be the least likely to get him caught?

Finally it hit him— dynamite. What a show that would make! The lethal material could be used for more than busting up rock. As a miner, he knew how to set the plug, how to light the fuse, and how much time each foot of fuse would give him to get away.

Getting the dynamite was no problem. He'd get some at work— a little bit at a time. But he couldn't carry off a bundle of fuse for the job. He'd need enough to give ample time to get back down the hill and across the bridge to Houghton, where he could witness the explosion. He'd go to the Ball and Chain. There he'd have plenty of witnesses, if need be, who could testify he was nowhere near the house.

He sketched out on paper the layout of the fuse he'd plant in the house. He'd loop it back and forth, being sure it didn't jump across to another section. He figured carefully how much he'd need.

Fuse line could be bought locally, but that would surely throw suspicion on him. So he took the train to L'Anse, bought it there, and returned to Hancock.

He was so excited and nervous when he got home that as he cut the fuse, he accidentally stabbed his hand. At first startled, he held his arm up and sat motionless watching the blood run down his hand and arm. It dripped off his elbow, ran crookedly down the wooden table leg and pooled on the ground. It was several minutes before he felt any pain, or did anything to bandage the wound. The dripping vermillion, forming patterns on his arm as it crossed his veins, held him for a few moments in a trance.

Walter knew he'd have to wait until the time was right. He figured a Saturday night would be good. In the pubs, where men were relaxed and most were deep into their cups, watchdogs would be few. And they'd be sleeping in late on Sunday morning.

So it was that in early November Walter made his way to the old house about two in the morning.

He encountered no one on the street except a drunk, singing happily as he staggered home.

Walter let himself into the house in the usual way. He placed the dynamite charge in the center of the lower floor. Jumping the stairs two at a time he began laying the fuse in his step-mother's room. From there, he unwound the fuse, snaking it in and out of rooms and down the stairway.

Walter's heart beat harder every moment; he couldn't remember being so excited.

He continued zigzagging the fuse around rooms in the lower floor, until he was back to the charge. Letting the charge and the fuse kiss each other, he hurried back upstairs.

His hands were shaking, but he managed to light the fuse. Stumbling down the stairs, he fled from the house as quickly as possible. He tore down the hill, raced along Frontage Road, and crossed the bridge to Houghton.

By the time the sparks hit the dynamite, he would be long gone. There would be a helluva blast. Flames would rise, making a wonderful sight, with sound effects, too. Better than fireworks.

There he allowed himself a moment to look back. What he saw amazed him. There was smoke rising from house. No blast. What had gone wrong? Why this wimpy smoke and no explosion?

He hurried along to the saloon. Whatever had happened, the house was on fire, and he needed to be with those who could furnish an alibi if necessary. He ordered a double whiskey and tried to remain calm until somebody noticed the fire.

That didn't take long. In a few minutes somebody was running along the street shouting, "Fire across the lake!"

Almost everyone vacated the saloon and scrambled out to see what the call was about. Men rushed across the bridge to see what was on fire, and to help put it out. Walter ran along with them. They sped along Frontage Road and up the hill. Flames were rising from the structure now, all from the upper floor.

Walter heard the bells of the fire trucks as they approached, both from Hancock and Houghton. He was too confused to figure out why the fire had started upstairs. He couldn't think about that now. All he knew was that if it reached the dynamite there would be a tremendous blast that would take a lot of blokes with it.

Suddenly, when the men climbing the hill were no more than a hundred yards from the house, the explosion did go off. It was a sight, all right, sending flaming timbers in every direction. Large shards of glass pierced the night air illumined by the fire. Those nearest the house ducked, ran down hill, covering their heads. Screams of fright, injury and awe echoed down the valley.

Walter saw two men catapult into the air, then roll down the hill on fire. Standing near the back of the crowd, some distance from the house he threw up. He was shaking and faint. His knees buckled, and he sat down, as if he meant to. Someone came along and asked how he was. It was Earl Foster.

"You all right?"

Fearing the man had recognized him, he nodded and said, "Yes, it's just so sad to see the old place go up like that."

Foster smirked. Who had a better motive? This was the Radcliff son, who had loathed his step-mother, hated living here.

But this would have to wait. Earl had to help the firemen keep the crowd back. With his suspicions ignited, it wasn't likely to leave his mind soon.

Fire trucks coming from as far as Red Jacket brought their water supplies. But there was little the firemen could do to douse this fire. They formed a line to keep folks back from the explosion. Some saw to the injured.

As he lay wide awake that night, Walter finally figured out why the fire had started upstairs. It was the rug, of course. Why hadn't he thought of that? It was one thing to let a burning fuse run along a surface of rock, quite another to lay it on inflammable material. How foolish he felt! But what did it really matter? He'd accomplished his purpose.

There was a news article in the paper the next day. The fire chief of Hancock was quoted as saying, "The explosion was set deliberately with dynamite. Several, who at first thought it was an ordinary fire, rushed up the hill to help firemen put it out, but upon approaching the site, were stopped by a mighty detonation. So far, the architect of this heinous crime has not yet been apprehended."

'Architect'. Walter liked that word— it made him feel grand.

Earl Foster had Walter Radcliff brought in for questioning.

"Sheriff, all you have to do is ask anybody at the Ball and Chain. They saw me there. We all ran across the bridge and up the hill together. Ask 'em"

Walter's story was well backed up, which didn't convince Earl. He held him for three days in the jailhouse, renewing the questioning each day. His suspicions gnawed at his mind and wouldn't let go.

The delay of the explosion, after smoke had been observed, made Earl believe there must have been a hell of a lot of fuse running through the house.

"Where did you get the fuse, Radcliff?"

"What fuse!" Walter fumed.

"Fuse and dynamite. You have access to both."

"Where would I get all that fuse?"

Earl had called local and nearby out-of-town stores. No one recalled anyone buying fuse lately.

"You had a motive, too. You hated your step-mother."

Walter threw his arms up in the air. "That was a long time ago. Jesus."

Earl investigated Walter's living quarters and found nothing. The only unusual thing he saw was a trail of dried blood running down a table leg. But that proved nothing. Cupboards, closets held no telltale evidence. Earl was certain this was Walter's venture. But after three days he had to let him go.

CHAPTER SEVEN

To some extent, Jeremy's prediction came true. Women who'd been Betsy's friends for years either snubbed or pitied her. Jeremy was cold and distant. He didn't suggest they attend a single social event, or even go for an evening walk.

Rose remained her faithful companion. And of course she had her lovely AnnaBeth and two wonderful sons. Deeply humiliated, Betsy cocooned herself from the public. She stayed at home and gave her attention to the younger members of her family.

Barroom brawls were not unusual in the plethora of saloons that dotted the Copper Country. But the Willis boys had never been involved in them. This past year, Roy had been much too happy to bother himself about the petty quarrels that erupted on the barstools. In fact, when he could see one coming on, his response was to buy a round of drinks for every man who could hold his temper.

But now Roy was spoiling for a fight. He knew it when he left the doctor's office that blustery November. He knew it when he stomped down Walker Street, and he knew it when he pulled on the heavy iron handle of The Red Nugget. It didn't matter who it was with or what it was about. And he didn't much care about the unlucky guy who'd get in his way.

Two hours later the saloon keeper called Jeremy Willis to tell him that his son had tried to take on every man in the bar, that he was in bad shape, and somebody'd better come and get what was left of him.

When Jeremy and Calvin got there, the bartender had sent everyone home. He was sweeping up the broken glass that lay about everywhere.

"Where's my boy?"

The barman motioned to the corner. There, on the floor lay a man, battered and bruised almost beyond recognition. Jeremy and Calvin hoisted Roy's unconscious body, laid him in the cart, and took him home.

Betsy assembled her first aid supplies as best she could, and braced herself for an ugly sight. She thought she was ready for the worst, but nothing prepared her for the ghastly spectacle spread out on the kitchen table.

"Get another lamp," Jeremy barked at Calvin.

Betsy pulled herself together, and started the water boiling.

She fought back faintness and nausea as she tended to his wounds. His eyes were both bloody and swollen, his nose broken, and his face punctured with the imprint of a lumberman's cleated boot. When she turned his head, she saw his right ear was torn. His body was badly bruised, and it seemed each time she cleaned an area, more cuts were revealed.

"We'd best call Dr. Follett," Jeremy said.

"No!" Betsy's response was perhaps too strong. "I'll take care of him myself."

"His ear's half torn off for God's sake! You're going to sew him up?"

"If necessary."

"Why? We'll get the Company doctor. That's what he's paid for."

"Let me take care of it!"

Doctor Blake had died shortly after retiring and Betsy wanted nothing to do with Red Jacket's new doctor. Peter Follett. Doctor Peter Follett. Too many memories.

She examined the ear, picked a glass shard from it.

"Calvin, get my sewing box."

"You're not serious," Jeremy said.

"He's unconscious. He won't feel a thing. I've put needle to thread a thousand times or more—"

"But not to flesh."

"—And not a few times to hide. How do you think I made the children's slippers, when they were little?"

Calvin came back with the box. Betsy sterilized a needle, slipped strong flaxen thread into it and began her work.

"For God's sake, Betsy."

"If he doesn't like it, he can go to the physician himself when he's able."

She finished the sewing, painted the puncture wounds from the cleats once more with tincture of iodine and applied bandages.

"Now it's your turn." She faced her husband.

"To do what?"

"He has a broken arm. You'd better set and splint it."

"Jesus," Jeremy said under his breath.

Again Calvin was the errand boy. Jeremy sent him to fetch a board which could be used as a splint.

Betsy winced as she heard Jeremy struggle with bone against bone; and once Roy awoke, gasped in pain, and passed out again. She fashioned a sling for him, and when Jeremy had finished setting the arm, she slipped Roy's arm gently into it.

The men carried him upstairs to the room he'd shared with his brother since they were small boys.

"Go to my bed tonight," she told Calvin. "I want to stay with Roy."

Betsy lay awake in Calvin's narrow bed a long time waiting to hear some sign of life from her son. Finally it came in the form of low groans, deep wounded animal sounds. He tried to turn, cried out in pain.

Betsy crept into his room, and when he came to enough to ask what happened, she explained as much as she could. He seemed to remember nothing past going to The Red Nugget in Red Jacket.

She continued to lie awake hours after Roy had gone back to sleep, wondering what could have occasioned such violence. She wrestled with these questions all night. At five she left Roy's room and crawled in beside her husband.

"Jeremy, tell me. Why did he do it? What happened?"

Jeremy lay on his back, looking up at the ceiling. Having slept fitfully himself, he was now fully awake.

"What's wrong with him? Has he told you anything? Please tell me, Jeremy."

She saw Jeremy swallow hard.

"He's sick, Betsy."

"What kind of sick?"

He almost choked on the word. "Syphilis."

She gasped.

They were lying several inches apart. He heard her uneven breathing, then the quiet sobs. Past differences melted, at least for now. They were both Roy's parents; they'd face this together.

He touched her shoulder. She turned tentatively to her side. Then with one sweeping move he pulled her gently to him.

"Roy?" She was incredulous.

He nodded.

"How do you know?"

"Doctor Follett called me just as I was leaving work yesterday."

"He told you?"

He said Roy was in such a temper when he left his office he thought I'd better stay alert."

"Syphilis? It's certain?"

"Tests were sent to a lab."

"How can they be sure?"

"Betsy, they *know*."

"And the cure?" She was afraid to hear the answer.

"There isn't any. Mercury helps sometimes, but it only postpones. . ." his voice trailed off. "He can't marry, of course."

Betsy shuddered. "Oh, my God!" She tried to absorb this. "What are his symptoms?"

"For now, sores, lesions."

"And then what?"

"Well, they'll heal and he might appear to be well for quite a long time— years perhaps. But then....well, who knows? Each case is different."

"Tell me, Jeremy, I want to know."

"Betsy, there's no point—"

"Will he be like Uncle Albert? Go blind, then crazy? Tell me, Jeremy!"

"I don't know. But there are different stages, Follett said. The serious symptoms— the ones you mentioned— they can take a long time to come on."

He pulled her to him, "He will probably live for years."

She started crying softly in his arms. She shuttered, thinking of Uncle Albert, the laughing stock of the town, finally ending his days at Newberry's Lunacy Sanatorium. Was this to be the fate of their first born son? Even as he held her, she felt a tear of her husband's fall onto her forehead. And her heart went out to him in a way it had not for years, for it was this son into whom Jeremy had poured all his hopes, just as it was Calvin into whom she poured hers.

She didn't know how it had turned out that way, but Jeremy had cherished his first son, and mostly ignored his second. Betsy had taken up the slack.

In the morning she left her husband's bed and crawled back to Roy's room. It was noon before he was fully awake, and with it came the pain. Betsy tried to soothe his wounds with comfrey, but Roy pushed her away.

"Leave me alone," he kept saying.

"Can I get you anything? Are you hungry?"

"Go away."

After waiting hours for him to awaken she was now exiled. How could she tell this son who was a virtual stranger that she didn't blame him for what he'd done to get himself in this mess? How could she let him know that she had succumbed to the same urgency in her youth? Others would judge him, she knew, accuse him of throwing away his future, his life. He would judge himself more harshly than anyone.

At noon Jeremy managed to get a draft of brandy down his son's throat. It seemed to ease him back to sleep.

By mid-November Roy's barroom injuries had healed sufficiently for him to go back to work. Remote and sober, he no longer sought nor endured the company of others. Robust laughter and slaps on the back were no more. Even Calvin was shut out. Roy put all his energy into his work. He tried to be fair with the men, but beyond that brooked no conversation.

December of 1912 had more snowfall than most folks had ever seen. All over town, from door to street, people were erecting high wooden sidewalks three feet above the ground. When it snowed, they could be swept off with a broom. Children liked to play under them, making hide-outs and forts.

On city streets, huge wooden rollers drawn by teams of horses compressed the snow, so sleighs could navigate the road. On city streets more snowplows were being employed than ever before. Snowshoes and sleds came out of cellars and sheds sooner than usual, to the annoyance of adults and delight of children. The smell of wet wool mittens and scarves came home with the children.

The Keweenaw Peninsula was just the dog's ear of the larger Upper Peninsula— the most northerly point. With the wind sweeping across it, assaulted on all sides by Lake Superior, it wasn't unusual for snow banks to get as high as thirty feet. Some families were snowed in. If exit were necessary, their only escape was through an upstairs window.

Calvin sat in his room, finishing an elaborate design to fit around a mirror for AnnaBeth. It was made of thin, flexible bamboo sticks, and twisted into a pattern to encompass the six inch piece of glass. If only the pieces would stay in place once they were glued. It was very frustrating when they sprang back in defiance.

Calvin watched the blizzard continue to swirl around the fruit trees until everything was so white that, as close as they were, he could no longer make them out.

He wondered if they'd have a tree this year. Usually he and Roy trudged deep into the woods to select a fine fir. It would be kept outside until Christmas Eve, then brought into the cold back parlor. When he was small, his first vision of the tree was Christmas morning. He thought good ole' Saint Nick had put it there during the night. This year, with all the snow and Christmas only five days away, he didn't see how they could manage a tree.

Although his wounds were healing well, Roy's arm still gave him such trouble that finally his father got him to see Dr. Follett. The arm was reset.

That night as Betsy was preparing for bed, Jeremy knocked on the door. "May I come in?"

She was surprised, waited to discover his purpose.

He stood in the doorway watching her pull the pins out of her hair at her dressing table. "I have to eat my words. Doctor Follett told Roy he couldn't have sewn his ear up any better than you did."

"Humph." Inwardly she cherished the compliment. "And the scars on his face?"

"They're permanent." He looked at her tenderly, softened his words. "But they'll fade."

"Why did he do it— fight?"

But she knew it was a silly question. He fought because his whole life had gone over the cliff like a runaway horse and buggy. Having Jenny was out of the question. So was living out any kind of normal life, as the disease would take its toll year after year.

Finding these thoughts unbearable, Betsy turned her mind elsewhere. She finished taking the pins out of her hair, shaking it loose over her shoulders.

Her hair was still a beautiful flaxen shade. Jeremy seldom saw it down anymore, and realized he missed this. He missed brushing it gently, the way he used to when they were close. He had given her the ivory brush, comb and mirror set for her twentieth-fifth birthday. He picked her brush off the table, began stroking her long silken hair. She raised no objections, surprised him by closing her eyes and leaning her head back against him, giving in to the comfort of being cared for, the sensuality of the touch.

He continued in silence, and when he felt he could no longer prolong it, he set the brush down.

"Thank you, Jeremy."

"Good-night, Betsy."

He started to leave and she found herself wanting to keep him there.

"What did he tell Jenny?"

"I understand he told Tobias, who insisted that Roy tell Jenny to her face that he couldn't marry her. So Roy managed to blurt something out to Jenny. Her father had to fill her in on the rest."

She shook her head sadly. "They still love each other."

"It doesn't change anything, Betsy."

Remembering her own feeling of abandonment, Betsy felt for the girl who'd been forsaken by her beloved. And her tears spilled over again for Roy, who would have to pay his whole life for finding some relief for his need.

She looked so full of woe that Jeremy came back to her, took her in his arms and held her a long time. When he pulled away, she murmured, "You don't have to leave, Jeremy."

And so he lay beside her. There was no joining that night, but somehow out of their son's misfortune, and from the ashes of their own relationship, they had managed once again to create a tenuous bond.

There were many rumors as to why the engagement was off. The only thing for certain was that they were no longer seen together, and Tobias Foster admitted to a few that the wedding was off. Beyond that he was silent on the matter. He stopped attending his poker club.

Jenny was seldom seen and barely recognized when she was. Her dazzling signature smile was gone.

Rumors circulated as to who had broken it off. Had Jenny, because of that terrible brawl Roy got himself into? The postman said that to see her red eyes, it was obvious he jilted her. But the butcher allowed as it had to have been the lass that chucked him, just as in his case. Otherwise why had poor Roy brawled?

CHAPTER EIGHT

With the moon still casting a glow on the snow, Cal could hear his father outside shoveling. Well, certainly after yesterday's storm the shoveling was necessary, but he felt a little guilty. He had planned to do that job. He got dressed quickly and went downstairs.

There was a note on the kitchen table.

"Betsy, I have to leave early to finish taking inventory. Sorry, forgot to tell you last night."

As Cal started to build up the fire, he heard his Pa drive off in the sleigh.

Roy came downstairs. "In that case, "I'm not going in."

"To work? You sure?"

"They'll probably close most shafts today. Anyway, Pa took off without us. How are we supposed to get there in this weather on our own?"

"He's left us before, when we weren't ready, and we got there," Cal said.

"Not in two feet of snow that hasn't been plowed yet. Hell, the drifts are covering the front parlor windows. Anyway, he left early. Didn't give us a chance."

So they stayed at home. With nothing to do but eat, by lunchtime they were restless.

"Let's get the tree," Calvin suggested.

"Are you nuts? In this?"

"I can't stay in here any longer."

Calvin got his leggings, pulled them on. "You coming or not?"

"Well hell, if you're dumb enough to go out there in this crap, I guess I better go with you. What the hell. Somethin' to do."

So bundled up with snowshoes on their feet, they slid, crawled, fell, and laughed their way up the hill toward the woods beyond. Half way up, their foolery led to pushing each other down, and Roy managed to roll his brother most of the way back down the slope.

But Calvin didn't care. He was so glad to see his brother laugh again. He'd have climbed that hill a dozen times just to give Roy some fun.

Deep in the woods they were still laughing.

"Hell, you can't tell a fir from a rock. They all look the same!" Roy howled.

"Pyramids," Cal said.

"How about this one?" Calvin shook the tree Roy was standing close to so fiercely it sent clouds of snow in his brother's face. And so the rough-housing, wrestling and laughter continued.

It was four o'clock, starting to get dark, as it did this time of year. Betsy was worried.

"Jeremy, they've been gone too long. Out in that snow, away from any help, if they need it."

"They're grown men, for God's sake. They can take care of themselves."

Suddenly laughter broke the silence, then the stomping of feet. Betsy rushed to the back door, and saw the boys shaking the tree. They leaned it against the house.

"Oh thank God! Come in and shut the door. I thought something must have happened to you. You've been gone so long, and it was getting—"

"Hey, Ma, it wasn't easy climbing the hill in this snow."

"Sometimes it was up to our armpits."

"And picking out a tree when they all looked like pyramids was a real job too."

They said this seriously. Then, just looking at each other was enough to send them into further explosions of laughter.

Well, they were safe, and they were happy. What more could she ask of them?

"Thanks for getting the tree, boys."

"It wouldn't be much of a Christmas without one, would it?" Calvin remarked, unraveling his lengthy muffler and showering the entire kitchen with snow.

Betsy decided to forgo the lecture about taking their outer wraps off in the shed. It had been so long since she'd heard her oldest son laugh.

Betsy and AnnaBeth provided a fine dinner on Christmas Eve, with roast beef and the root vegetables kept in the cellar. Homemade bread, plum pudding and black currant wine added to the feast.

Christmas day was a time for the whole family to be gathered together in the back parlor.

Betsy made hot chocolate in the morning to go with the breakfast cake she had gotten up early to bake. As soon as everyone had gulped theirs down, the family headed for the parlor. Roy already had a fire going in there.

Betsy lit the candles on the tree with AnnaBeth's help and everyone clapped. Then there was laughter.

Try as they had, the boys had not been able to find a "good" side to the tree. But Betsy allowed that it looked "natural" and AnnaBeth said she loved it more for being so misshapen.

Calvin had wrapped his gift for AnnaBeth in tissue and put it under the tree the night before. Partly hidden as it was behind some larger packages, she didn't see it right off. She sat shyly back, and waited for the others to open their gifts.

He was glad that Ma was pleased with the mauve slippers he'd bought her, but he was most excited just waiting for his sister to find the little masterpiece he'd made for her.

Suddenly Roy, sitting on the floor, reached over a pile of presents to get one with his name. Calvin heard something crack and crunch. With his heart in his throat, he knew what it was. She hadn't even seen it.

"What was that?" Ma asked. "Did something break?"

"Sounded like it." Calvin reached down to uncover the gift. The glass wasn't broken, but the trim was now a pathetic pile of sticks.

"What was it?" AnnaBeth asked.

"Nothing." Calvin mumbled. He didn't want to tell her what the gift was he'd been working on all week for her.

Roy spoke. "Looks to me like it was some kind of fancy mirror. Probably for you, AnnaBeth. I'm awful sorry."

Calvin looked at Roy's stricken face and added, "He didn't mean to. Just an accident."

"Cal, is it true? Is that what you made for me?"

His cheeks reddened. What had been his delicate little masterpiece now lay like a pile of pick-up-sticks. Why had he thought it was so wonderful? He was ashamed of it now.

"You can fix it, can't you, Cal? The glass isn't broken."

She was pleading, picking up the pieces of her treasure. But all he could think of was all the work he'd put into it, how disappointed his sister was and how sick his brother was. His head was aching. He had to get out of here.

"No, I can't," he called over his shoulder, and started up to his room.

AnnaBeth ran after him, chasing him up the stairs and into his room. She held the fragments of her gift in her hands.

"Don't feel bad, Calvin. If you don't want to fix it, it's all right. I know you worked hard on it. Didn't you?"

"Not that hard. It was dumb. Flimsy."

"I'm sure it was beautiful— I can tell, here on this side, where it isn't broken. Anyway, what matters is that you did it, that's what counts. I'll always remember that."

She was making him feel worse. Poor AnnaBeth, who had never had much of anything, who everyone sort of forgot— AnnaBeth was trying to make him feel better.

"Thanks."

"Ma said you wrote me a poem."

"When did she tell you that?"

"Last week. She said that's why you wouldn't let me in your room—that you were working on it."

"I was working on— the other thing."

"Oh, Calvin, where is it?"

"Where's what?"

"The poem! I want to see it. Give it to me, Calvin."

"Naw. Not now."

"Oh. Well, I have something for you," she spoke in her bashful way. She reached into her apron pocket and extracted a small book, bound in soft leather.

"The Sonnets of William Shakespeare. Lordy, AnnaBeth, where did you get this?"

"At Boynton's Bookstore. I thought you would like it."

"Indeed I do!"

Opening the front cover, there on the blank page, in her finest handwriting AnnaBeth had inscribed, "For my brother Calvin, who is the light of my life. Love, AnnaBeth Willis, Christmas, 1912."

He was embarrassed and again the tears threatened to flow. This time he let them fall freely down his cheeks, one landing on the word `love'. He looked up at her then, afraid she might misinterpret them, but they were matched in her own eyes. For once, she had hit a winner, and she knew it.

"Now can I see my poem?"

She was more clever than he'd given her credit for. "It's under the lamp."

She retrieved it, and Calvin watched her read it slowly. Suddenly, she shot up and gave him a big hug. "It's wonderful!"

He sat up to disengage himself. "You'd say that if I wrote `figety-figety-figety fog.'"

"Will you read it Calvin— aloud?"

He'd felt overly sentimental writing it; reading it out loud was too much.

"No," he protested.

"Please." She pushed it under his nose.

How could he refuse her? He took the paper.

"'To AnnaBeth.'" He darted a quick look at her. She was settling down on the bed, ready to relish hearing the verse written just for her, read to her in the poet's own voice. She closed her eyes.

"'*Oft like a shadow, she stands apart*
Following me with eyes alone.
Ashamed, I send her back my heart;
I'm not a god upon a throne.
But little does she know 'tis not I
But her in whom the deities lie.'
It's not very good," he finished lamely.

"It's beautiful! Is it a sonnet?"

"No. It's not long enough for one thing. I don't think it's long enough to even call a poem."

"Yes, it is. It's long enough for me, anyway."

Then she started rocking in that jerky way of hers, that he'd come to know meant she wanted to say something, but was not quite sure of herself.

"I didn't know you— noticed, so much. I mean, that I watch you."

He was flustered. Why hadn't he written something about flowers or squirrels? Before he had to respond to that she was on to something else.

"What's a deity?"

He groaned. Now he'd have to explain that part. It was all too embarrassing.

"It means dragon— you think I'm it, but it's really you."

He was trying to keep it light, but she looked confused, the way she did when she couldn't comprehend a conversation or article; he couldn't leave it that way.

"No, I'm just kidding. It means, well, that you look up to me, but it's really you I should be looking up to." He was standing by the window, so as not to have to look at her.

"Why?"

"AnnaBeth, come on. Can't you be satisfied?" What good was poetry if you had to explain it?

"No, not 'til you tell me."

"It's just you're well, so, so . . . pure. You don't have evil thoughts like me. That's what it means."

"Calvin, you don't have evil thoughts!"

"How would you know?" Had he shocked her?

"I'm the one with evil thoughts."

"You?"

"Yes. Things you can't even imagine."

"Tell me, then."

"No. It would truly horrify you." But she was enjoying the hold she had on him.

"I bet."

"It's true."

"Then tell me," he implored.

"Promise you won't tell?"

"Promise."

"Well . . . about things disappearing."

"What things?"

"Just well . . . mostly people."

"People! What people?" He was the one being shocked.

"Well, one in particular."

Before he could get it out of her, Ma called them to join the family, and with a sly smile, AnnaBeth darted out of the room and down the stairs.

Calvin decided those few moments with his sister were the best part of this disastrous holiday for him. At least he knew where he stood with her. And they were more alike than he had ever imagined.

CHAPTER NINE

It was early February, 1913. The knock on the Clemenc door was unexpected. So early in the morning, the only light was the moon shining on the frost-covered ground. Joseph rose from his bed, drawing a blanket around him, as he felt his way through the cold house to the door.

"Who is it?" he called.

"Frenchie."

"Whatcha want?"

"Open ze damn door, will you? Mon dieu!"

Reluctantly, Joseph opened the door, ushering in a blast of frigid air.

"Well, come in then, 'fore you turn this place into an ice house."

Frenchie entered quickly, rubbing his hands together, slamming the door behind him. There he stood with a red carnation in his buttonhole.

"We need ze beaucoup men for ze union. You will join us, oui, Joseph?"

"The WFM? What for?"

"Membership in ze Western Federation of Miners— it ez low. N'est pas? We have to make big ze membership now, so we be ready to fight in ze summer."

He mimed a great battle, but Joseph was not amused.

"What are you talkin'? You know there ain't enough funds to carry on a strike yet."

"Joseph, we can't wait longer. If we don't get it off ze ground now, it will be too late for zis year. We don't want to be making ze strike come next winter, n'est pas?"

Frenchie shivered— perhaps for effect, perhaps because he was genuinely cold.

"We got to start early to be sure zis zing is over 'for hard wezer sets in again . . . Will you make your name here, Joseph?" He offered a pencil and a pad with a list of names.

Joseph twisted the end of his mustache, coughed. "I don't think so, Frenchie. Not now."

Frenchie looked disappointed. "Oh, Joseph. We must be togezer on zis. Mon dieu!"

Joseph shook his head.

"I gotta be on my way zen— talk to ze ozer men."

Frenchie was gone as quickly as he'd come.

The cold draft traveled all the way into the bedroom. Awakened by the noise, Annie stirred under the covers.

"What was Frenchie here about?" she asked

"Sneakin' around in pre-dawn hours getting' signatures to join the union."

"What did you tell him?"

"I ain't getting involved in that. Company won't give in."

"Nothing will change until you make a united front."

"Lay off, Annie. This is men's business."

Annie could barely conceal her anger. "It everybody's business, Joseph. Families suffer when there isn't enough food on the table—"

"And how do you think payless days is gonna feed a family?"

"We can't just keep caving in—"

"Enough, woman."

Annie bit her words and turned over. No use talking to Joseph. She wondered if he'd ever vote for a strike. But there might be something *she* could do.

Calvin missed the brother he'd known— missed his hearty laughter, his sense of humor. He had thought they were as close as two brothers could be, not that they talked a lot— they just understood each other. But now Roy had created an impenetrable wall that even Calvin couldn't chip. Conversation between them became stilted, superficial.

The laughter they'd shared the day they got the Christmas tree couldn't be sustained; it had dissipated as quickly as the wine they'd shared that evening.

Cal could see the pain in Jenny's eyes too. Running into her as she was coming out of the cobbler's in February, he offered to accompany her home. She agreed, but he couldn't think of anything much to say to her as they negotiated the slippery walkway on the way to her house. When they came to her gate he looked at his feet and mumbled, "I'm sorry the way things turned out— with Roy."

"Thank you."

He looked up. "For what?"

She shrugged. "For saying that. Nobody else has."

Calvin was silent. If they were aware of the wind and cold, they ignored it.

"I feel like I'm wearing a scarlet letter."

He wasn't sure what that was, but he got the gist.

"You didn't do anything."

"Still feels that way. Everybody knows why he broke it off. Everybody knows he's got— " She stopped in horror at what she was about to say.

Calvin felt an urge to save her. Something soft and vulnerable about her made him loose his tongue.

"Do you still love him?" he blurted out.

She didn't answer right away, and he regretted having asked.

Then, "Yes. But not in the same way. There isn't any. . ."

She searched for a word.

". . .Innocence. It's all gone. And the despair of it all."

"For you?"

She seemed surprised. "For him." She lowered her eyes. "Well, yes, for me too, but mostly for him."

"Do you ever see him?"

"I've sent him letters. I've told him I want to be his friend, but he doesn't answer."

"It's his shame, that's why he can't face you."

She nodded.

"What will you do?"

Jenny shook her head.

"You'll find someone else."

"I haven't been able to think about that."

But that night she did think about it. She began to have thoughts she hadn't had since she'd first met Roy. Desire mingled with shame, as a dialogue ran in her mind.

How could you do this to Roy?

He brought it on himself.

But he's already paying such a price, how could you twist the final knife, rub his nose in it?

He's hurt my life a lot. Do I have to let him ruin it?

This would kill him.

He's killing himself.

And then—

Am I attracted to Calvin just because he's Roy's brother? Am I trying to punish Roy?

Her mind ran wild, and finally she put her feet on the ground, remembered that nothing at all had happened with Calvin. Nothing. She combed back through their conversation and couldn't find a single word he'd said that could give her cause to believe he had an interest in her, other than a natural compassion for his brother's forsaken sweetheart. She was sure he was genuinely concerned. Perhaps she'd imagined the rest.

For weeks Calvin watched her face flash in his mind, her words play their mournful melody in his ear, and longed to help her create a happier song. He yearned to see more of her. But how could he ever expect Roy to understand, to forgive him? How could he deliver such a blow to his brother, his best friend? He wished Roy would open up, come back to his old self. Maybe he would be all for it, would see it as a way of making things right with Jenny, sort of balancing the scale.

But Roy didn't open up, and Calvin kept his desires to himself.

He tried to concern himself with the unrest of the miners, and the growing membership in the Western Federation of Miners. That could only mean trouble for the mining companies. And Calvin had conflicting loyalties.

The compassionate looks from family members bothered Roy. He felt a kaleidoscope of other sentiments coming from them too: pity, contempt and resentment that he'd brought disgrace on the family. Real or imagined, this is how he felt. There were no more guiltless times. He was always conscious of his shameful state and the awareness that everyone else was too.

Even at work, he didn't command the respect he once had as shaft supervisor. It was subtle at first, and then not so restrained. A shift captain began to argue with him. Slurs were made behind his back. If they didn't know about his disease, they knew he'd broken off with the girl he was engaged to, and that invited scores of speculations and was a juicy topic for saloon banter. And no one could ignore his mutilated face.

Wretched with his prognosis, and miserable at having lost Jenny, Roy wanted only to be alone.

Finally, he decided he couldn't stand the prying eyes of friend, family or foe. And all this talk at the mine about a strike. All around him—discontent. He quit his job and took a room in a boarding house down in Hancock, just north of the Portage Lake Bridge, directly across from Houghton. It was far enough away, he figured that the gossip would be minimal. Sooner or later he'd get a job, in the Hancock mine.

Surprising all, Henry Parker appointed Cal to replace Roy. Lester Rhodes was in line to become a shaft supervisor. He'd been a shift captain for several years, and was considered to be responsible. When Roy Willis left, Rhodes had every right to expect that he'd be the replacement. But that was not what the superintendent of the mine had in mind. Lester Rhodes remained one of the shift captains.

On a blustery March weekend Cal decided to visit Roy in Hancock. He was shocked at the shabby boarding house he found his brother in.

Roy didn't seem all that happy to see him, but at least invited him to his room. It held only a narrow bed with sinking mattress and a single chair. Roy flopped on the bed, and Cal took the chair. "What brings you here, brother mine?"

"Just wanted to see how you were doing."

"I'm doing just fine," Roy said with false enthusiasm.

Cal didn't know quite how to deal with this. He said, "Glad to hear it," but he knew it wasn't true. In the corner he saw a pile of dirty laundry.

"Shall we go get a bite to eat somewhere? You must have discovered a couple of spots by now."

"I eat my meals downstairs, and I'm not hungry now."

Roy wasn't making it easy for him. They sat in silence. Cal tipped his chair back, only to feel the back legs about to give out from under him.

Finally he said, "Want to go for a walk?"

"Not now. I'm resting."

"Do you— feel sick, Roy?" Cal ventured.

"Hey, none of that. I don't want to talk about it."

What could they talk about? Cal wondered if it had been a mistake to come.

"Well, is there anything I can do for you? Anything you want me to go out and get for you?"

"Nope."

Finally Cal said, "Maybe I should leave, eh?"

"Naw. Not now that you're here."

Well, Cal supposed, that was encouraging, but it was sure awkward.

"If you're going to stay overnight, there's another mattress in the closet."

Cal nodded. He'd have to feel his way through this fog.

"So how's our glorious family?"

Cal ignored the sarcasm. "AnnaBeth's getting over a cold." Pa seemed to have lost his sense of humor, and Ma had withdrawn into herself, but he decided to say nothing of this.

As sundown approached Cal was finally able to rouse his brother. They would go to a saloon, but Roy wouldn't go to any in Hancock. He insisted on going across the lake to Houghton, even though with every other door a saloon, there were plenty to choose from here. The paper said there were a hundred sixty seven in the county, forty-six of them in Hancock, twenty-three in Houghton, and another seventy-four in Red Jacket! And men came from neighboring towns to add to the drinking population.

The ice was already showing signs of breaking up in March. Not being thick enough to trust, they proceeded the long way— going down to the bridge and crossing there. They chose a saloon on the west end of town. The brothers looked around— nobody they recognized. They perched themselves on barstools, and each ordered a double shot and a pint. When they were on their next round, a fellow they'd known from school slithered up on the stool next to them.

Calvin saw him coming, muttered "Weasel" under his breath. Roy caught it, tensed in anticipation.

"Hear you got the pox, Willis." For emphasis, Weasel spat his wad of chewing tobacco several feet across the room directly into the spittoon. Having won several spitting contests, it was his single talent.

Roy said nothing, took a long swig of whiskey.

"She gave you the clap, and you're givin' her a bastard. I call that a fair trade!" He popped another plug of tobacco in his mouth.

Roy froze, but refused to change his expression. Calvin wheeled around at the stranger, prepared to take him on. There would have been nothing unusual about yet another brawl in a saloon, but Roy put out a restraining hand.

"Don't. Leave him. He doesn't know what he's talking about."

The man wiped his nose on his sleeve. "That's what I hear. Everybody knows it's yurs."

Roy slapped some money on the bar and rose to leave. Calvin followed. Roy headed out the door and directly down the embankment for the lake.

"Roy, the ice is thin! Come on back— we'll take the bridge."

"You take it. I'm going this way."

"Don't be stupid— you could fall in!"

But Roy wouldn't stop. Calvin couldn't leave him, so he too, tumbled down the bank. He stumbled where he couldn't see. He cried out to dissuade Roy from this foolishness.

The first part of the ice seemed solid enough. When they were about a third of the way across they heard the ice crack. The sound echoed eerily through the valley. If they'd needed a warning, they'd surely gotten it. Calvin stepped back, but Roy streaked fearlessly ahead, maintaining his pace.

There was no moon. Calvin was losing the shape of his brother.

"Roy, are you crazy?"

"Guess I am. Isn't that part of the game?" And he continued across the ice.

Calvin stayed alert to the direction of the cracking. He managed to skirt the thin area, finding more stable ice. In the process he lost all sense of Roy's presence.

Finally, he reached the other side. Clawing his way up the muddy bank to the road, he took in his surroundings. There was no sign of Roy.

Calvin trudged slowly back to Roy's place. There was a light in the window. He took that as a good sign.

His brother was already in his room, stripped to his long underwear.

Tossing the spare mattress and a blanket on the floor for Cal, Roy murmured, "It would have been all right you know, if the ice had given way. Don't try to save me, little brother."

And with a quick puff he blew out his candle and climbed into bed.

Calvin tried to make discreet inquiries to find out if it was true that Carlene Tallfeather was with child. Finally, he rode out to her cabin, half way between Red Jacket and Hancock, in an area heavily wooded with pine and oak.

He did not want to go there. He was braced against her charms, and certain he would not fall to the same fate as Roy. But he found the task extremely distasteful. He had no idea what he'd say to her. He almost hoped she wouldn't be home, but he could see the chimney smoke from the road.

He had taken the small sleigh, and the old stallion. Although April, it was so cold ice crackled beneath the runners of the cutter. As he made his way to her door, the snow squeaked beneath his boots.

When she opened the door, Calvin could see that she thought it was Roy, so much alike in appearance were they. Her eyes opened wide, then narrowed.

"You're his brother."

"Yes."

"Come in, then."

Carlene Tallfeather came of an Ojibwa woman and an Irish miner. She was one of the few native Americans still living in these parts; most of her people had been removed from the Keweenaw decades before. She had little to do with her mother's people, who lived further south, and nothing at all with her father's. She kept to herself in a small abandoned woodsman's cabin she had fixed up the best she could.

One glance at her told him the rumor was true. He didn't know how far along – maybe six, seven months, though he knew he was no judge of such things. He closed the door behind him. For a few moments he put his attention on getting every bit of snow off his boots. It seemed to Calvin the noises that swept through the cabin were laughing at him. The wind howled in the cracks, and the windows rattled in their frames. Finally, he had to look up.

"Sit down," she said, never doubting he would.

There was little furniture in the cabin— a mattress on the floor, with a bear rug for covering, an old rocking chair into which Carlene eased herself, and a large table. He sat on the only remaining piece of furniture— a small stool.

"Take your coat off, if you want."

He didn't want. He wasn't taking anything off. He was very sure about that.

They sat in noisy silence, with the rush of the wind whistling down the chimney, the rocker that squeaked and moaned, and the crazy dancing forms in the fire.

As his eyes adjusted to the dim light, he took more in. Looking upward, his eyes fastened on the many bunches of weeds hung from the rough wooden rafters. The sudden sound of wolves howling nearby put him back on alert, but Carlene seemed unconcerned, kept a steady, inquiring gaze on him, waiting for him to speak.

Finally he blurted it out. "Whose child are you carrying?"

"I think you know. Else you wouldn't have come."

"How can you be sure?"

She considered him a long time. Then, holding her gaze steady she said, "If you were a woman and you'd only slept with one man, you'd know."

Calvin was embarrassed and dropped his eyes. He was annoyed too, for he couldn't believe her.

"Are you telling me you were a virgin 'fore Roy came along?"

"No. But I hadn't been with a man for three months before, and none since."

He was silent for a time, pulling in the sounds from outdoors, of the wind and the wolves.

Then he brought himself back. "How far— are you?"

A rude burst of sap spit from the fire, making him jump.

"Seven months."

He knew she was watching him, and he couldn't bear her gaze, so he stared at the fire. The room was smoky. Perhaps her flue needed attention, he reflected, and watched thin wisps of smoke escape the burning birch and enter the room.

Somehow she wasn't what he'd expected. He didn't know what that was, but surely not this simple expectant mother with the solemn face and large dark eyes.

He wasn't sure if anything she said was true, but he reckoned he'd gotten all the pertinent information he could— at least her version of it.

His eyes were burning from the smoke; he had to get away from here.

But it was she who rose.

"Did he send you?" Calvin stood up too.

"No."

She nodded, and he thought he read the slightest hint of disappointment.

"How do you . . . keep yourself here, make a living?"

"You're thinking I'm a whore," she muttered

He colored, but he didn't think it showed in the firelight. "I didn't say that."

"In the summer I grow herbs— for medicines, some for cooking too. The women come for them."

He glanced again at the things hanging down from the rafters. Was this where his mother got the stuff she made into medicinal tea?

"You support yourself selling weeds?"

She was silent, just watching him in that peaceful way of hers with eyes that seemed to read his soul.

"Herbs," he corrected himself. "I didn't know you could make a living at it." He wondered if they did any good, or if they were as useless as snake oil. He couldn't remember if any of those peculiar brews his mother had made had helped.

"I also hunt and fish. I don't have many wants."

She was still looking at him in that strange way that he couldn't figure. Was she amused by him?

"They come— mostly women. And they come to be healed."

So she was a medicine-woman, one of those Indian healers he'd heard about. He wondered if she danced around and cast spells he'd heard about.

"How did you meet Roy?"

"Your mother sent him, to get some herbs for your housemaid."

He blanched. He wondered if their mother knew the fatal net she'd thrown him in.

"Don't you have some potion for that?" He was looking at her belly.

"I wanted to keep the child."

"Wanted it?" He could hardly take this in. She wasn't married, and furthermore—

"I didn't know when I decided to keep the child. And now it's too late."

Calvin tried to grasp what she was saying.

"And I didn't know I was sick when your brother. . . was here. I'm sorry."

"I'll tell him."

"Thank you."

His last remark was meant to be sarcastic but he was glad she took it straight.

"I guess that's all I need to know." He turned to go, then looked back at her. "You're absolutely positive it's his."

"Yes."

"Good-night, then."

He opened the door, would have been gone, but she touched his sleeve.

"How is he?"

"Sick."

She couldn't say 'sorry' again, it wasn't enough. It had been woefully inadequate the first time, leaving her embarrassed, confused. So now she said nothing, closed the door after him, and pulled her chair closer to the fire. She sat there staring into the glowing embers, rocking harder, harder, rocking herself into a trance, where she might see their futures in the flames.

Cal went again to visit his brother. They were playing cards. Things had gone so poorly the last time, it was hard to go back. What made it worse was the message he had to deliver.

Finally he blurted it out. "I went to see Carlene."

Roy looked at his brother with suspicion.

"What the hell for?"

"I thought you should know if it was true — what Weasel said."

"Damn it, I didn't ask you to do that! Just stay out of it!"

Cal took a deep breath. "She's only got two months to go, and she swears it's yours. Says nobody poked her for three months before you and nobody since, and she didn't know she had the pox when you were there, or she wouldn't have done it, and she didn't know she had it when she decided to have the kid, and now it's too late to do anything about that."

He took a huge gulp of air and exhaled with satisfaction. He'd gotten the whole story out before Roy could shut him up.

"There, I've said it." He waited for more verbal blows from his brother.

Roy was slow responding. "You believe that?" he asked in a low voice.

"I didn't at first, of course, but, well, she seemed so. . ."

"Sincere?" Roy sneered.

"Well, I got the feeling she was telling the truth."

Roy turned on him. "So you think her bastard is mine?"

Calvin shrugged, shuffled the cards for a long time, and finally placed them before his brother.

A week later Cal returned. Two other boarders were in Roy's room playing cards. Cal was glad to see his brother had some company. Roy was a good poker player, but he wasn't doing well tonight, and called it an early evening.

When the others left, Roy threw his cards on the table. "What do you think I should do about her?"

"Maybe give her some money."

Cal thought he saw his brother nod, ever so slowly.

CHAPTER TEN

The miners and trammers were angry. Their jobs had always been risky, but now the men felt real fear. For years there had been a system with the two-man drill. One man drilled, the other helped support the heavy tool and kept a lookout for danger.

Now the mining companies were putting in the lighter one-man drill. There was no back-up, no protection for the miner. There were so many fatal accidents, it was called the 'widow maker.'

The men were strained to the limit by long shifts and short wages. Complaints had gone unanswered. The one-man drill was the last straw. Many were ready to strike.

Frenchie was buying drinks at the saloon for anyone who'd sign up to be a member of the miners' union.

"You meaning to bring on a strike, Frenchie?"

"Oui. Me and ozers. If we can get enough members. Have to have more money before we can make ze strike."

"How many members you think we need?"

"Zousands."

A man called Fergus said, "You know union headquarters don't want trouble yet. We ain't organized and we don't have enough membership and money. Denver ain't going to like this."

"What do you zink I'm doing? Getting' membersheep and money."

The piano player, accustomed to Frenchie's antics, began to play some chords. They thumped out louder and louder as Frenchie mimed out collecting money, his load getting heavier and heavier until he almost collapsed.

The drinkers clapped and whistled.

"We don't have any local leadership. Hell, who we got here knows how to run a successful strike?" Fergus said.

"I know a man. He's a good leader," Flem said. "He's holdin' a meeting Friday night at the community hall."

"Be sure your be zhere." Frenchie added. He said it like he meant it. He turned around in a circle and gave each man the evil eye. Then he laughed.

"What's his name?"

"Zey call him ze 'Redeemer.'"

"He'll liberate you from your paycheck," Fergus scoffed.

"All we need iz naysayers like you, Fergus. Have a leetle faith."

Still, Frenchie signed on twenty new members that night. He was an affable man, with his humor and inimitable personality. Everyone in town recognized him.

By mid-summer there were nine thousand members of the WFM in the Keweenaw Peninsula.

Betsy wrote to the editors:

As if dangers in the mine weren't already intolerable, management has now seen fit to cut their costs further by replacing the two-man drill with the one-man drill. It is truly a widow-maker, and accidents have doubled since its use. Something must be done to make our mining companies more cognizant of the preciousness of human life!

B.T. Wilkins

Carlene rose from her rocker. Visitors rarely came at night, and never so late. It was almost eleven.

"Who's out there?" But she thought she knew.

"Roy."—

The dry oak leaves had clung to their branches all winter. At last, surrendering to new life, they swirled about in the blustery March weather.

"Come in, then."

The gust of wind whipping the leaves into a tarantella created a macabre effect around Roy's scarred face. Carlene sucked in her breath, as Roy closed the door. The wounds had healed, but his face was still covered with bright red scars and pits where the cleats had been planted.

Well, at least she hadn't turned away in revulsion, like he'd expected her to. He offered no explanation, just stood turning his cap in his hands.

She'd thought he might come after his brother's visit. But then again, maybe not.

"Sit," she said, taking her seat on the stool.

"I can't stay," he mumbled.

"I don't want you towering over me, Roy Willis. Sit down."

Reluctantly he settled in the rocker, still twisting the cap in his hands, while she waited for him to speak. Twice he opened his mouth but nothing came.

Finally, "I don't know if your kid is mine or not, but I guess it is. So I want to give you something for it. I figured I could leave some money with you now and more later from time to time," he spilled it all to get it over with.

Whether he'd come here to make peace with a god he couldn't understand, but nevertheless feared— or some other reason, he didn't know.

"I don't want your money, Roy."

He didn't think he'd heard right.

"I didn't come asking you for it, did I?" she said softly.

"Why don't you want it?"

"I did something terrible to you. I didn't know then, but still I did. You don't owe me anything."

Roy didn't know what to say, so he said nothing. Carlene lit a cigar, taking a few puffs and passing it to Roy as she had before their troubles. He took it, and they sat in silence, passing it back and forth between them. He listened to the familiar crackling of the fire, and rocked in tandem to some unknown feeling.

Finally, "How will you live— without money, I mean?"

"I'll be all right."

"Are you sick?" he asked softly.

"Not now. I was."

"Will the kid be okay?"

"I don't know."

They sat a few minutes more, and then he rose to go, leaving the envelope of money on the rocker.

By the door he looked at her a long time and felt a tenderness he'd never known when they'd been together, and certainly not since she'd given him the pox. Maybe it was that they shared the same horrible fate. The thought crossed his mind of embracing her, just holding her quietly for a minute while they shared this common bond of despair. But the moment passed. She had opened the door.

"She wouldn't take it," he told his brother.

"How come?"

"I left it anyway."

"Why didn't she want it?"

"'Cuz of what she gave me."

"Oh."

"I got it off my conscience, anyway."

Every time she thought about it, Annie's heart thumped in her chest. She could hardly wait for the next day. Val Tory and two other women were going to join her in starting their own union! The women's auxiliary No. 15. The ladies of Hancock had an auxiliary, and so could they. If Joseph would do nothing to fight for justice, she would have to. While she worked, her mind raced through the plan she'd hatched.

Annie threw the gray scummy water from her scrub bucket on the ground outside, and pumped fresh water into it. She had one more floor to scrub for Mrs. Peters. Then she would be finished here for the day.

The next afternoon she trudged a mile and a half through muddy spring roads to Val Tory's house. Val couldn't leave her five children, and Annie had none. She brought her mending basket with her. There was no time for idle hands.

Annie was surprised to see Nellie Hamstead there. Nellie was a widow. She said more than once, "My husband was killed in that copper mine, and I don't even know what the stuff looks like." Well, of course, she still had her boys to fight for. They were following their father's steps.

When they were all there Annie said, "Our mission is to persuade the men that they have to fight against the one-man drill."

"And better pay!"

"Shorter hours," added Nellie.

"Yes, of course, but it's the new drill that's brought us together. That's what will incense other wives enough to join us," Annie emphasized. "It's a single cause which we can all unite behind."

"What about all the different languages?" Val asked. How can we communicate with them?" Val asked.

"We'll enlist leaders from all countries to talk their own into becoming members."

"I don't think I could work with a trammer's wife."

"We have to."

They were divided on this important matter. Being miners' wives, they h
ad never mixed with trammers' families.

"We don't want those women in our auxiliary."

"Yes, we do," said Annie. We need everyone we can get. Trammers have to compete with miners now, who lost out to the one-man drill. We need their membership too."

The argument continued, but in the end Annie won. She would start with some of the wives of the men she'd met during the skit.

It was exciting to be taking some action about the state of affairs.

When next she was at Betsy Willis's, Annie told her about the women's auxiliary.

"How can I help?" Betsy asked.

"If you'd be willing, we'd be mighty obliged if you would ask your Patty to join. And then if she could speak to the Irish wives."

"Yes, of course," Betsy promised.

Annie left with joy in her heart. The organization was growing. They would be ready when the strike came. And she was sure it was in the air.

Most adults knew a second language, as they or their parents had come from various countries in Europe. The women would approach those of their ethnic group.

With every breath she drew Annie was more exhilarated. She had galvanized the women of this town. By the end of two weeks they'd enlisted two hundred fifty women in their auxiliary.

"Whatcha bothering about that for?" Joseph asked. "Waste of time. Women can't do nothin' to change things."

"More than you're doing, Joseph Clemenc. You won't even join the union."

"Ain't yer affair. It's men's business."

"You're wrong about that. Whatever conditions the men work in affect us too," she countered.

It occurred to Joseph about once a month that he had a wife and that he could have sex from her. With little ado, he'd tap her on the shoulder, she'd turn over, he'd do his business, and then go back to sleep. Needless to say, Annie didn't get any pleasure from this. But she didn't refuse him either. She had one request— that he interrupt the act before his climax. Neither of them wanted a child now.

When Annie became involved in the strike, he was so ashamed he stopped approaching her at all.

"What were those women doing here?" Jeremy bellowed. He had come home early, and watched the auxiliary members depart like cockroaches, scurrying to safety.

"I will not lie, Jeremy. I feel very strongly, as you know, that something should be done for the miners' and trammers' families."

"Not in my house!"

"It's my house, too," Betsy said.

"What's gotten into you?" He slammed his fist on the table. "Don't you know by now that I stand on the side of the Company? That's what our family represents!"

"It's not what I represent!" she countered. "You should know that by now."

He raised his fist. She looked him straight in the eye. Finally, he lowered his arm, but between his teeth he said, "Listen to me, woman! You're not to have that rabble here again. Do you understand me?"

Betsy left the room. A few minutes later Cal entered. "I heard what you said to Ma."

"Stay out of it."

"I don't like it that you talk to her that way."

"Well, isn't that too bad? I suppose you're on her side."

"I don't know yet, Pa. But I think you should allow her to make up her own mind, and follow her own inclinations."

"Do you now?"

The argument went on. Day after day there was either fighting or silence. The serenity of the household had been destroyed.

Yet Jeremy still expected his due in the bedroom. Several nights Betsy refused him. Irritated with the refusals and her position about the miners, one night he pushed her out of bed. Her ankle hit against the heavy brass knob on the chest of drawers. Betsy howled. Jeremy procured some ice for her. Her ankle swelled up, bruised and caused such pain that she was limping.

"Go to the doctor, for God's sake! Go see Dr. Follett."

"No!"

"Why not?"

"Leave me alone."

Cal fashioned a crutch for her.

Two days later Betsy took a cab to the auxiliary meeting at Val's. When she returned home, the house seemed strangely empty.

Finally, she found AnnaBeth in her room. Her hand jumped to her mouth.

"What happened to you?"

Her daughter's face was swollen and her eyes were red.

"What's wrong? What happened, AnnaBeth?"

AnnaBeth swallowed and was reluctant to talk, but Betsy insisted. Finally she said, "Father got mad at me."

"What did he do?"

"He hit me."

Betsy was astonished. "Hit you! Whatever for?" Betsy turned the light on.

AnnaBeth shook her head, and closed her eyes.

"AnnaBeth, you must tell me."

"I can't!"

"You must."

Betsy waited. "If you don't, surely your father will."

Her daughter gasped. "No!"

"Then *you* must."

AnnaBeth coughed, stuttered, and finally spit it out. "I didn't know he was home. I didn't hear him come in. I was in my room . . ."

"Yes?"

"He opened my door, and saw me—" she cringed, "touching myself."

AnnaBeth buried her head in her hands and cried.

Betsy wanted to be sure she understood. "You mean— down there?"

AnnaBeth sobbed and nodded.

At first stunned into silence, Betsy quickly recovered. "Oh, my darling." She rushed to her daughter's side, and enclosed her in her arms. "It's all right. Go ahead and cry. I'm so sorry."

Betsy was aware that AnnaBeth was twenty-five years old. It seemed more and more likely that she'd be a spinster. She'd never had a beau. Once, when she was twenty, she was love-struck by a young man who showed an interest in her. But Jeremy would have none of it.

"Are you out of your mind, girl? He's a delivery man! You fancy a delivery man? I'll see that he never comes here again."

And he didn't.

Five more years had gone by. The poor girl had no doubt longed for someone, and had found the only release she could— reading romantic novels and acting out her fantasies.

Betsy was furious. Of course Jeremy would think it wrong, deplorable. But to strike her—

She looked at her daughter's face, more swollen than before. "How many times did he strike you?"

"About five, I think."

"Oh, my God. AnnaBeth, I am so sorry."

She retrieved some ice for the young woman's face, and waited for her husband to come home.

When he finally did, she confronted him. Jeremy did not apologize. "What she was doing was odious."

"Did you just burst into her room without knocking?"

"I heard moaning. I thought she was ill."

Betsy bristled with indignation. "Why did you strike her?"

"Have you no sense of propriety?" he said.

Although ten years her senior, sometimes she thought he was at least a generation older than she.

"Oh, God." Betsy shook her head. "I suppose you've never done that."

"I'm a man! And you will not question me. Unless you want some slaps yourself!"

CHAPTER ELEVEN

A ll of Red Jacket seemed to be outside on this unseasonably warm May morning. The many gullies that ran down hill bubbled over with spring run-off. Where no walkways were in place, folks navigated the molasses-like mud, most with good spirits. The oozing earth signaled winter's demise at last.

Calvin was standing on the bank of a pond baiting his fish hook when he spotted Jenny. He jumped, because in truth he had just been thinking about her. More than thinking, he'd been imagining all sorts of interesting things to do with her. Surprised and delighted, he grinned at her. She looked so delicious, with her hair up and only a few wayward strands falling around her face. He wanted to nibble her neck.

"Any bites?" she said.

"What! Oh. No, not yet."

"Maybe they're still asleep, eh?"

"I guess." He felt woefully inadequate in the fine art of speaking to young ladies.

"I was just going for a stroll," she explained. "It's too heavenly to stay indoors."

"Can you stay a while? I've got some lunch— nothin' special, but some leftover chicken and sweet cider."

"I wouldn't want you to go short."

"Oh, don't worry about that. I had a big breakfast. Anyway, there's plenty."

"All right, then." She smiled at him and looked for a place to sit.

Calvin parked his fishing pole. He spied a fallen maple. Quickly he removed his jacket, and draped it over the damp bark for her.

"Are you sure you won't be cold?" she asked, pulling her heavy sweater tighter around her. "It's still chilly."

"I'll be fine."

They sat together munching chicken, apples and biscuits. Calvin felt wonderful, just to be near her. The fallen tree lay at a steep angle, and Cal kept sliding down a bit toward Jenny. At first it embarrassed them both, and he'd retrieve the few inches he felt would be proper to have between them.

The fact that they couldn't always think of something to say was camouflaged by their apparent focus on food. When they did speak, it was in fits and starts. The words bounced around in his head, but didn't come out.

Jenny said, "I reckon spring is early this year, eh?"

"I'd have to agree with you, Jenny."

He took a long swig of cider, trying desperately to corral his thoughts.

She rescued him. "Have you noticed the trees blossoming all over town?"

"Oh, yes. Our cherry blossoms are all coming out."

"They must be beautiful."

"You ought to come over and see them," he said.

Jenny made no reply, and he covered the gap by offering her cider from a mason jar.

"Hope you don't mind sharing the same bottle. I didn't know I'd be having company, or I'd have brought some glasses." He wiped the jar with his clean handkerchief and handed it to her.

"It's fine. I didn't know I'd be your luncheon guest, or I'd have brought some cookies."

"I'm sorry I don't have anything for dessert."

"No, don't be. I just meant. . . Oh, dear."

"What have you been doing with yourself?" This was a dangerous stab in the dark, but for the moment it was all he could think of.

"I have a new job at the ladies' clothing store."

"Do you fancy it?"

"Oh, yes, I do. It's a lively place, with women of every age coming in all day."

"Every size, too, I reckon."

She laughed. "Oh, yes, every size."

Then they both laughed so hard Calvin choked on his cider, and Jenny said her ribs would burst if she didn't stop. That seemed, finally, to put them at ease.

"And you, your work is going well?"

"I have more responsibility now."

"What do you do?"

"I'm a shaft supervisor." He didn't like to brag. But then why had he told her?

"That sounds important."

Calvin explained how there were several shafts, a supervisor for each. He added that the top dog was in charge of all underground operations, although of course, his office was on top.

"On top?"

"Of the ground. Not in the mine. And then, underneath him—

"Underneath?" And they both laughed again, although they weren't sure why.

He bumped into her again. This time they were both amused. And he didn't try to recover the space between them.

Calvin went on to explain the hierarchy of the mine staff, from the owners in Boston, to the dregs.

"And who are the dregs?"

She had the sweetest little rose of a mouth he'd ever seen.

"Trammers. They're usually the Poles and the Slavs. It's the meanest job in the mine. They have to load all the rocks the miners blast out onto carts, and push the carts up the incline to the lift. It's very hard work."

He didn't think he'd ever seen such white, even teeth.

"Why are they Poles and Slavs?"

"Because they don't have any status. At least not yet. They were the last to get here. There's a real pecking order— Cornish, Irish, German, and so on. And the Finns don't want to work underground, so most cut the timbers for the mine."

"Do you need many timbers?"

He wished he dared brush the crumb of biscuit off her cheek.

"Oh, tons. That's what keeps the mines from collapsing. There's probably as much timber underground in these parts as there is above."

"Oh, my! I didn't know that."

"They're called stulls— the structures made of timber. Huge eight by eights." He glanced up. "I'm sure you're not really interested in all this mine talk. I'm boring you."

"Oh no! You're not. I am interested. Truly."

He looked at her, puzzled. "Why?"

She dropped her eyes and turned away. He realized he had embarrassed her, and that was the last thing he wanted to do. Again he was sorry for saying the wrong thing.

Unable to express what they were really thinking, they seized their inspiration from the squirrels chasing each other and chattering about things they both knew. Neither heard the words, only the ardor behind the telling. Cal picked up his fishing pole again. Before he had it in the water they saw the surface of the pond twitch as a fish jumped.

"At least they're coming to life now," he said.

Jenny watched him as his focus turned entirely to his task. She noticed how he licked his lips and took up a certain stance— almost as a runner would. Not relaxed, as she'd seen others fishing.

Finally, she felt it was time to go. The last thing she wanted to do was overstay her welcome, and she was sure Calvin was cold without his jacket.

As she rose, she finally asked what she'd put off all afternoon. "How is Roy?"

"He's-- all right.

Then, looking up she said, "I used to love him so much."

"*And now?*" he wondered.

Her gaze wandered away, and she caught a strand of hair blowing across her face. "I pity him. A great deal."

"He wouldn't want your pity."

"I 'spect not."

She reached for her bonnet, had trouble with the bow. With more assertion than he knew he had, Calvin reached up and tied it for her, fussing with the ribbons, taking longer than necessary.

She seemed amused by the seriousness with which he took this task, and a little shy. But she smiled at him, and he thought maybe she'd enjoyed it a little bit too.

When she left, his mind raced, scanning, dissecting everything she'd said. Had she deliberately let him know her feelings for Roy had changed, so that he would know the field was open? He couldn't tell. She had no guile, he thought, so probably she just spoke her mind, and that was all it was. Still, they'd had a good time together, and he knew, for his part, he'd favor seeing her again. In fact, he'd like to court her.

There was of course, the problem of Roy. Cal tried to think of some way to ease into the subject with him. He had been going down to spend part of the weekends with Roy in Hancock.

Two weeks later, he was playing poker in Roy's room with several other boarders. He lost heavily. When the game was over and the others had left the room, Calvin knew he couldn't put it off any longer. A pitcher of hard cider stood half full between them.

"Let's have another, Roy."

Calvin poured, watching his brother.

With his heart in his throat, he tried to sound off hand. "Think you'll ever see Jenny again?"

"Doubt it."

"You never run into her?"

"Did once. Turned the corner and went the other way before she saw me."

"Do you think she'll find another fellow?" Cal tried to sound casual.

"Hope so, for her sake. Why you askin' so many questions?"

"I saw her a couple weeks back."

Raising his glass, Roy's elbow stopped mid-air. "Where?"

"She was out for a stroll down by the pond where I was fishing."

"Oh." He set his glass down. "Did she say anything?"

"She asked about you."

"What'd you tell her?"

"I told her you were melancholy."

"Jesus. What did you say that for?"

"She was very concerned, interested."

Roy shifted in his seat and took a gulp of cider.

"What is she doing with herself these days?"

"She's hired on with Mrs. Ruelle at the women's store."

"Does she have a beau?"

"I don't think so."

Roy was quiet for a bit, chewed on the stub of his cold cigar.

"Seems like you spent quite a spell of time with her."

It was Calvin's turn to be quiet, but he was sure Roy could hear his heart beating.

His brother's eyes narrowed. "Are you trying to say you fancy her?"

"She's a nice lady," Calvin stalled.

"Seems like maybe you want to be her beau, eh?"

"I don't know. I only just saw her the once." Which wasn't quite true, but almost.

"Maybe you'd like to see a lot more of her?"

Calvin colored, dropped his eyes.

Roy leaned forward. "Are you asking me for her hand, little brother?"

"No, I just wondered how you'd feel if I started seeing her."

"Don't that beat all!" Roy guffawed. "My sister-in-law!"

"Roy, hang on— nothing's happened—"

"Part of the family— cozy picture, that!" And he burst into bitter laughter, tipping his chair and glass back alike as he poured its contents down his throat.

He had jumped to the last chapter before Cal had finished telling him the first.

"I'll be the laughing stock of the whole county!"

Roy sat up abruptly. "My God, brother, I can't even face the woman!"

And Cal regretted ever having brought it up.

Several weeks passed and the brothers didn't speak of Jenny. But Cal and Jenny kept seeing each other, furtively.

Finally, Cal said to Jenny, "I'm tired of sneaking around like we're doing something wrong. I think we should get married."

"Now?" Jenny uttered in amazement.

"Very soon. He's never going to like it, but he might as well start getting used to it."

"But you haven't even proposed to me," Jenny blurted out.

"Oversight." He smiled sheepishly. "Will you, my dearest Jenny, marry me?"

She burst out laughing.

"What's so funny?"

"Just the way you said it."

"Well, will you?"

"Yes, of course, dear Calvin."

And so it happened, on the fifteenth of June1913. Not a large affair. Only the immediate family was invited. On Jenny's side, her father, as well as her Uncle Earl and Aunt Cora attended. On his side Cal's parents and sister AnnaBeth were there. Roy had been invited but did not attend. Disappointing to the wedding couple, but a relief, too.

"Better this, than if he'd come and made a scene," Cal commented.

Cal's parents had offered the young couple the guest house on their property. Small, but sunny and inviting, it was already furnished, and a delicious retreat for the newlyweds.

Roy lay on his bed next to an empty bottle of whiskey. For weeks all he'd been able to think about was his brother's wedding to his former sweetheart. He didn't want to imagine them together. He'd tried to relieve his misery by pretending it was he who was removing each bit of feminine clothing his bride was wearing. He'd take her in his arms and carry her to their four-poster bed, adorned all in white. Exploring every bit of her perfect body, he'd respond to the touch of all her curves and crevices. Her body would rise in anticipation, and he, finally possessing her, would consummate the throbbing desire that had been burning in him for over a year.

And then, by himself, he'd explode on his worn mattress, in a shabby room, far from Jenny. This scene was often followed by slow, then escalating sobs, for he would never have Jenny, or any other woman. The third act of this sad saga was his getting drunk, finally passing out. Only oblivion could offer relief. For a time.

He would not, could not go to the wedding. She was his, dammit! What kind of brother would turn the knife as Cal had, taking advantage of the state of affairs that had led Roy to break off with his fiancée?

There was a short honeymoon, with the promise of a longer one when the fate of Cal's shaft was stable.

On their wedding night, the inevitable was put off by both of them with a barrage of small talk that kept going into the wee hours.

Cal had never been with a woman, and wasn't sure he could perform under demand, as it were, as much as he wanted to. Jenny's face was like a mirror of his own state, a false gaiety sparkling between the frown lines on her face. Finally, Cal suggested they go to sleep, and Jenny readily agreed.

In the morning, as he sensed the first stirrings of wakefulness, Cal felt her thigh against his. Immediately aroused, he turned gently to his bride. Her breathing came fast, but he could feel the stiffening of her body. Well, not too surprising, he decided— a young woman with no experience. She was scared. He would be patient. The short honeymoon ended, and still the marriage had not been consummated.

Finally, in the third week of their marriage, Jenny gave herself to her husband. He had the feeling she didn't really enjoy it, and of course, it was painful, being the first time. He promised her it would get better.

And it did. At least it didn't hurt anymore. In fact, in a limited sort of way, his young wife seemed to enjoy the pleasures of the night.

CHAPTER TWELVE

Cal waited impatiently for reports of the rock that came from the new shaft. The results were mixed; some days the percentage of copper was high.

"How high?" Jenny wanted to know.

"As much as six percent."

She looked doubtful. "Is that good?"

"Very good. We're happy with anything over two percent."

But other weeks there was mostly poor-rock, not yielding much copper at all, and Cal would come home discouraged.

"Conglomerate. That's all we see, day after day."

Jenny tried to soothe him. "You have to be patient, my dear. You've told me that over and over."

"It's not just the copper," he confessed to Jenny. "It's Rhodes. He's jealous that I got Roy's job, He's bitter, talking behind my back, trying to undermine my authority."

"He was passed over," Jenny offered.

"Yeah, well he's a bad sport. I may ask Henry to send him to another shaft."

When doubts about the shaft filled his mind, Cal withdrew into himself and spoke little. Then just as quickly his temper would improve and he'd be his old self again— lively and teasing Jenny.

For some time now she had noticed his extraordinary cheerfulness, and guessed the reason, but waited for him to speak of it.

Then one day he could hold his joy in no longer. He found his wife working at the wood stove, picked her up and swung her around the room. Startled, Jenny asked what it was all about.

"Here's to the No.9. The rock is loaded with copper, Jenny, very rich indeed!"

"You were right! Oh, Cal!"

"Too soon to be absolutely sure. But I tell you, Jenny, there's more to be made in Michigan copper than ever there was in California gold!"

"Truly?"

"Yes!" He laughed. "I don't think Henry thought I'd find enough copper to make a pot to piss in. Says those promising veins can fool you— just run out."

"Do they?"

"Sometimes. Although, he allows I have a good nose for copper, but it's costly to sink a shaft. And this one's especially expensive, being removed from the others. If I've made a mistake, it will cost the stockholders dearly."

"Oh, yes. Those poor aristocrats in Boston, who don't even know where Michigan is," Jenny said.

Cal shrugged. "We need them. It takes capital to operate a mine. Not like gold, can't pan for it. At one time there was copper found on the ground. But that's long gone."

"Well, if the copper's there, I know you'll find it. What does your nose say to this?" Jenny quipped, as she held a spoonful of venison stew up for him.

"Delicious. As long as you believe in me, I'll not give a fig what anyone else thinks."

Cal put his arms around her from the back as she tended to the stew. He was pensive for a moment. "Rhodes, of course, played the naysayer."

"Cal, what if you discover an enormous deposit like the Calumet Lode? Wouldn't that be something, eh?"

"Five hundred tons? Copper seldom comes in such neat packages, my dear. We're just hoping the strong vein doesn't run out."

Work continued at No.9. Months more were spent expanding the shaft once they had reached the desired depth. On Cal's recommendation, they had plotted out a plan to open toward the west, for his borings had indicated this was the most promising direction. But as the search went on, it became obvious that their efforts weren't paying off.

Cal would not give up. He sought out Henry Parker. "There's a promising vein leading north, Henry. I want to tunnel in that direction."

"You're the chief."

For a few weeks the vein they were pursuing was productive, but then it took a sudden dip downwards, making it inaccessible from the level they were on, and so proved no more rewarding than the western tunnel. Cal was still certain the site was rich. Having gone this far, another level should be opened up. Surely there was more copper here. The shaft was sunk another level deeper, and then another. More drifts were stoped out horizontally.

Finally, it looked as though they might have hit pay dirt.

"There's calcite, Jenny!"

"What does that mean?"

"It's a sure sign there's copper too. It's about time."

Cal got so excited he spent hours down in the shaft, looking after this new find like a mother hen.

"Perhaps you're watching it too closely," Henry suggested. "You know what they say about a watched pot."

Cal shrugged.

"Take a vacation. Take a real honeymoon."

Rhodes encouraged him to go. "The mine will still be here."

Two weeks later Rhodes brought it up again. "I think you should get away. You're getting on the men's nerves."

That evening he said to Jenny, "How would you like to go to Chicago?"

"Oh, Cal, can we really? Who will take over the shaft?"

"Well, that's a sticky wicket. I was thinking of asking Roy."

"Roy? Why?"

"Well, he knows the shaft for one thing. And I think it would help his self-esteem."

"Do you think he'll do it?"

"I don't know. All I can do is ask."

"And if he refuses?"

Cal shook his head.

Jenny asked, "What about Rhodes?"

"Rhodes will be sore, of course. But I don't trust the man."

Cal approached his brother with his heart in his throat. He hadn't seen him since a month before the wedding. When there was no response from knocking on his door, Cal tried the handle, and found the door unlocked. Before him lay his brother, apparently awake, but surrounded by the sights and smell of whiskey.

"Checking in on me, eh?"

"No, I've come to ask you a favor."

"Well, let's have some pleasantries, first. Where's your manners, little brother?"

"All right."

"How's my sister-in-law? The sweet Jenny Foster. Oh, pardon me, Mrs. Calvin Willis."

"She's fine. Concerned about you, of course. We all are."

"Aw," Roy said.

"I'm going to be away for a while. Going to Chicago."

"Business trip?"

Cal coughed. "Not exactly."

"Oh, what's the matter with me? Must be the honeymoon." Roy's sarcasm filled the room.

Roy turned sober and serious. "What's this favor you've come to ask?"

"I need someone to take over No.9 while I'm gone. I'm hoping you will."

"Gesture of pity, is it? I don't need your pity."

"No. I need you."

"You've got Rhodes. You don't need me."

"I do need you. You know the shaft. I can't trust Rhodes."

"Trust, is it? You trust me? And I should trust you?"

Cal was silent. Finally he said, "I thought it might do you some good."

"Do you, now? Do you know I hate that town and everybody in it? Have you thought about that?"

In the end, after several days, Cal persuaded Roy to take the job.

"I ain't doing this for you, Cal. You gotta understand that."

On the twenty-second of July, Cal and Jenny boarded *The SS North American* for Chicago.

Jenny had never dreamed of such luxury. The lavish appointments, the extra effort to make the passengers comfortable, all took her breath away. The rich walnut paneling of the dining room offered an elegant backdrop to the best cuisine available. The meals were choice, always with a variety of selections to choose from; local whitefish, caught in Lake Superior was the specialty.

"And Cal, the band will play every evening!"

Jenny hadn't had such a good time dancing since her wedding. They swayed to the music and played cards at night with another couple.

And it was there on the ship that Jenny at last gave herself freely to Cal. In the tiny cabin, they squeezed into one of the two narrow beds, clinging to each other, lest one fall out. It was amusing to them, and perhaps it was this that loosened the laces of Jenny's inhibitions.

A few days later they docked in Chicago. Cal had booked a suite at the Washington, Chicago's finest hotel, right on Michigan Avenue facing the lake. From their rooms they could see the waves lapping the shore.

Looking at a newspaper Jenny squealed. "Enrico Caruso is here, in Pagliacci. We must see him! Oh, please, Cal."

"It's probably sold out, but I'll see what I can do."

When Cal came back he was smiling.

"You got them!" she cried.

"Well, not yet. But the concierge assured me he could obtain some of the best seats in the house.

After the performance Jenny wrote to her father:

August 14, 1912

Dear Papa,

Tonight Cal hailed a hansom, and the driver took us to the theatre, where the great Caruso was singing. It was dreadfully hot, with hundreds of people packed tightly together, but I was enthralled.

People were dressed in all manner of the latest fashions from Paris and New York. If the curtain had remained closed, I'd have been satisfied just to see the parade of gorgeous confections I'd been treated to.

But the curtain did go up, and when the Italian star's voice filled the hall, it so permeated the hearts and minds of all present, it was as though he was singing to one single entity, and we were all part of it.

Near the end, you could hear the sound of ladies' pocketbooks opening and closing as our handkerchiefs were removed to wipe away the profusion of tears. All felt for the unfortunate clown, Pagliacci.

I didn't want the lights to come up when it was over, for I was quite comfortable in the excruciating sorrow at the story's unhappy ending.

Your loving daughter,
Jenny

Jenny fell in love with Chicago. But after two days it seemed to her that Cal was not in quite so joyous a mood.

"Cal, are you having a good time?"

"Splendid."

"You seem a little far away. Your head's still in the mine, isn't it?"

"I guess it is."

"Roy is a competent shaft supervisor. I wish you'd put all that aside while we're on holiday."

Cal nodded, but two days later he received a telegram from Henry Parker. It turned him ashen.

"EXPLOSION IN No 9 STOP SHAFT CLOSED STOP HENRY"

"What is it, Cal?"

He handed her the paper.

Jenny gasped as she read the cryptic message. "What are you going to do?"

"I have to go back."

"Henry didn't ask you to. If they've closed it, there's nothing you can do."

"You don't understand. It's my project. I started it, if it's in trouble I have to be there."

"Of course. When do you want to leave?"

Cal broke out in a sweat. Was Roy hurt? Had he, Cal, delivered the final blow to his brother, putting him in this position? He couldn't wait to get back.

The following day they boarded the *Copper Country Limited*. As the train traveled north through Wisconsin woods of pine and hemlock, occasionally Jenny caught glimpses of birch and aspen, already turning yellow. And in the Upper Peninsula, where the forests were still intact, the glorious maples had already turned out in their autumn splendor of crimson, orange and gold.

In her present mood, she didn't appreciate this beauty; it was the herald of another winter.

Cal barely spoke all the way home, and Jenny understood why: His dream had literally blown up. Roy's condition was unknown.

The screech of the train's brakes woke them from their separate reveries, as they pulled into the Hancock station. Cal hired a cab to take Jenny home and then to take him on to the mine.

That evening she didn't hear him come in, but his voice commanded her attention.

"A man was killed, and his partner injured in the new level."

"And Roy?"

"He wasn't hurt."

"Have you spoken to him?"

"Not yet."

She turned to see his drawn face. "How did it happen?"

Cal shook his head, listed possibilities. "Too much dynamite, too short a fuse for the men to get away. I should never have left." He sat at the table with his head in his hands.

"You can't blame yourself. Henry told you to take a vacation. Besides, what could you have done if you'd been here? It's not your job to be on that level all the time."

"I know. But Dixon, the shift boss, was out sick."

"Who took his place?"

"Rhodes."

"Where was Roy?"

"I don't know yet. I have to talk to him. He might have been on grass hiring a new man, or in another level. I'll find him tomorrow. With the shaft closed for the time, he didn't show up today."

On this warm evening, Jenny had fixed a cold supper with salad and ham, but Cal wasn't hungry.

"I'm going up to the hospital tomorrow and see what I can find out from the injured man."

The next night Cal knew no more than before.

"I couldn't talk to the survivor. He lost one side of his face, and appears to have lost his wits as well," he told Jenny.

"Is that temporary?"

"I don't know." He paused and starting pacing the floor. "The strange thing is the explosion didn't happen at the usual time charges go off. All day long they drill and fill the holes with plugs of dynamite. But they don't set them off 'til the end of their shift. That's what's supposed to happen."

"Yes?"

"The charges went off a full hour before quitting time."

"Why would they set them off early?"

"I don't think it was set off deliberately."

"Then what?"

"Maybe striking a match if they were standing too close to the fuse."

"Is that likely?"

"Shouldn't be. Flame shouldn't be anywhere near fuses."

"I don't understand."

"Men get careless when they're tired. They'd already worked a long day. Or it could have been a faulty fuse."

"And Roy? What did he have to say?"

"I haven't found him yet."

The next day Cal strode into Henry Parker's office. Cal preempted the agent before Henry could speak.

"I want to go down and see for myself what happened."

Henry Parker shook his head. "That's not possible. It's been capped."

"I thought it was temporary."

"We didn't know the extent of the damage then. It's too dangerous. The wall was blown out and nothing's stable." Henry Parker studied his cigar. "Besides, it's a sign of respect to the widow."

"Closing the shaft never put food on the table." Cal stopped to take a breath and keep his thoughts straight. "Why close the whole shaft because of an explosion on Level Eight? The other levels weren't affected, were they?"

"Cal—" Henry stopped himself, reached for his pipe. "So far we've put more into the Nine than we've taken out. This explosion really puts that shaft in the red, and we're not prepared to pour more money into it to get it up and running again. Not when there's no evidence that such action would prove profitable."

Henry looked up. "For the folks back east, this explosion was the death knell for the Nine."

"That wasn't my fault."

"I know that. But it all adds up to a rainy day for the Keweenaw."

"I want to look at it, Henry."

"I've already refused Earl Foster."

"Refused the sheriff?"

"Advised against it. There are other avenues of investigation to explore. People to talk to."

"Let me go down there."

"I can't let you do that."

Cal tried to absorb the finality of this statement. He swallowed hard. "What will you have me doing then, Henry?"

"For now you can manage the No. 6. And get a hold of your brother, will you? I have to talk to him."

"You haven't heard from him?"

"Nope. Talked to most the workers around here that day. A couple said they saw him leave the grounds. But nobody seemed too sure."

Cal felt the sweat run down his face.

All night he was restless, sleepless. In the morning he said, "Something's not right, I still can't make out why those fuses went off prematurely."

"You said it was an accident," Jenny replied.

"Maybe. But that doesn't explain why the wall caved in— something's fishy."

"Has Henry seen it?"

"No. Only Rhodes."

"And Rhodes never believed in the Nine in the first place."

"I think, given a chance, Rhodes would close it on any pretext. And I'd say he probably exaggerated the damage. Except it was heard a mile away."

"Have you talked to him?"

"He admits his vote was for closing it. But he emphasizes it was Henry's call."

"It should have been yours," Jenny said quietly. "You're in charge of that shaft."

"Henry got around that," Cal quipped bitterly.

In the evening, Cal said, "It's too coincidental. Rhodes encourages me to get out of town, and while I'm gone and he's running the shift, there's an explosion big enough to close the shaft, kill a man, and seriously injure another."

They were silent for a time.

Then Jenny asked, "If you suspect Rhodes of doing it deliberately, why don't you talk to Henry again?"

Cal shook his head. "It wouldn't do any good. I have no proof."

"Well, you could start him thinking."

"Henry wanted it closed too. I'd have to have something solid. He won't let me go down there, and nobody's talking."

"What about the other miners?"

"They were on different levels. They heard it, of course. And the reverberations caused some rock to fall there, too. Fortunately, no one else got hurt."

He stopped pacing and faced her. "There's something else fishy. I still can't find Roy."

"You think he had something to do with it?"

"No. I don't want to believe that. But where is he? I've been to his lodgings in Hancock. He hasn't been there since he took on the job here."

"Maybe he's ashamed that this awful thing happened on his watch."

"That's what I think. But it's a helluva way to handle it."

Earl Foster was at the mine for a second time to investigate the explosion.

"Don't know what you can do, Sheriff, I've closed the shaft," Henry Parker said.

"I have to talk to the people involved. Who was working the shift when it happened?"

"Roy Willis was in charge. Cal Willis was out of town."

"And who else was down there?"

"The man who was killed, and his brother who survived. The Trewella brothers"

"Yes, I know about them. Who else?"

"Rhodes, of course. He was shift captain. That seems to be all, at the time of the explosion."

"What was the coroner's report on cause of death?"

"Failure to survive."

Earl coughed back his reaction.

He had been at the hospital and found the survivor in a coma. It wasn't clear he'd ever emerge from it. Earl remembered the time about eight months ago when he'd arrested this Twister Trewella on the charge of setting a fire in the hole. He'd been given a light sentence— six months. And much to Earl's surprise, the Company had taken him on again, with the endorsement of Cal, who knew him as a hard worker. Cal Willis had even elevated his status to a miner trainee, under his older brother's tutelage.

Now there was an explosion while Trewella was down there. It didn't set right with Earl. Was Trewella at the root of this? Had he planned the explosion expecting to get himself and his brother to grass before the charges went off? Earl would have to do some more digging. Perhaps he hadn't acknowledged the significance of the first crime at the lad's trial.

Or maybe it was someone else, trying to foment a strike by demonstrating how unsafe underground conditions were.

And then there was the mysterious disappearance of Roy Willis. Could Roy have been involved with the explosion in any way? Why had he vanished?

"Have you seen Roy since the explosion?" he asked Parker.

"No."

Earl knew Roy was messed up, but he couldn't make it add up right. If Roy had no part of it, why had he absconded like that? He had to find him.

"What do you know about your brother's state of mind, Cal?" the sheriff asked.

"You're not saying—"

"Hold on there, boy. I haven't accused him of anything."

"But you're thinking he might have . . ."

"Sounds like you've been thinking."

Cal let out a deep breath and shook his head. "If I could just find him, and talk to him."

"You have no idea where he is?"

"No. And that's the truth. I've searched everywhere."

"Why do you think he ran off?"

"I don't know. I just don't know. He's been laughed at and taunted—and, well, he probably couldn't take one more thing."

Earl pursed his lips. "Could be. Sure need to talk to him, though. If you hear from him—"

CHAPTER THIRTEEN

Frenchie had used a lot of his own money in the beginning to get the miners to join the WMF. He was determined to build the membership enough to have a strike. He had no family, so his dollar stretched a little farther than it did with most others. He had an affable personality, and knew some words in several of the languages spoken in the Copper Country.

He'd seek out the ringleaders in each ethnic group, convince them, and get them in turn to persuade their fellows. The membership grew from three hundred to one thousand that spring. And when the companies made it clear that the one-man drill was here to stay, the membership grew into the thousands. Now they were adding the terrible explosion at No.9 to their list of grievances. It was another example of poor maintenance of the mines. A man a week was being killed in one mine or another in the Upper Peninsula, and two a day maimed for life.

Annie got her husband off to work, did her own housework as quickly as possible, and headed for the Willis home.

She cleaned the upstairs, and then approached Betsy.

"The men keep talking about a strike, but there's no action," she said.

"There will be. You get the women, and I'll get you the biggest flag you ever saw to lead your parade."

"Oh, Mrs. Willis," Annie's' eyes burned with excitement. This was a sure sign of support.

"I wish I could join you, Annie. I'm not as brave as you. I dare not."

"I understand," Annie said. "Just knowing you're behind us will give me courage."

In the days that followed Annie walked door to door in her neighborhood, enlisting the women in Auxiliary 15. She had to let everyone know how important it was to support the strike.

A knock on the door, and Cal found himself gazing at the most deformed face he'd ever seen.

"It's brave of you to come, Mr. . . ."

"Twister. Twister Trewella."

"That's right."

Cal could hardly believe the apparition before him. Surprised and elated that the man had recovered enough to come to him, he was nevertheless hard put to hide his amazement. Half of the man's face had been burned and mutilated, and was now warped into a ghoulish frozen smile. His scalp, too, had been burned. His previously full head of red hair now erupted in lonely tufts on one side only. They brought to mind a defrocked bird. Whiskers grew only on one side of his chin.

Twister sat with his head down, curling his cap. He had a habit of clapping one hand against the twisted side of his face, then forcing it down with his other hand. But soon he'd repeat the movement. Cal looked at him with compassion. It couldn't be easy for this poor wreck of a man to come to the home of the superintendent. He'd waited a long time to hear what he would have to say, he could wait a few moments longer.

Cal poured tea. "Sugar? Milk?"

"Thank you, Cap'n."

Twister put several lumps of sugar in his cup and a draft of milk. When he finished stirring it, he raised the cup to his lips with both hands. Due to the condition of his face, he couldn't drink it without making slurping sounds. He looked up, embarrassed. Cal returned a smile of encouragement.

When the tea was finished and he could no longer put off his mission, Twister said, "I've come ta talk to you 'bout what 'appened the day of the h'explosion."

"Thank you." Although straining his patience, Cal decided to let the man tell the story his own way before asking questions.

"It wasn't like what they said h'in the papers. You see, Mr. Rhodes was down there h'every day h'after you left. The shift boss, 'e'd been h'ailin' for a couple of months, coughing terrible, even blood, but ne'er missed a day o' work, as I'm sure you know. Now Mr. Rhodes says to 'im, 'Go 'ome, ya h'ought be in bed with that cough.' "

"I see."

"Me and Fred was following the direction you set h'out before you left, and the vein was beginning to look stronger. We hadn't brought the good stuff down yet, but we could see h'it ahead, a good vein."

Twister stopped, as if to make sure his tale was welcome. He slapped at his face.

"Go on."

"Mr. Rhodes, 'e changed the direction we were stopin'."

"Changed it?"

"Yes, sir. 'E said it was h'only by a few degrees, and would be better that a way. Said 'e'd been readin' rock h'all his life and knew what 'e was doin'."

Twister stopped to lick his lips. He looked at the empty tea cup.

"I'll get you more in a minute. Please continue."

"Me and Fred, we could 'ardly h'argue with 'im."

"Of course not."

"But we was wonderin' what you'd say when you got back, knowin' h'it was not h'according to your plan. So we drill and blast h'accordin' to Rhodes's h'instructions, leavin' kind of a corner where we changed direction.

"Then one day 'e says, 'Boys, we're gonna tidy this h'up. We're gonna take h'out this bulge and straighten h'out the drift. Now we suspicioned 'e was tryin' to 'ide somethin', straightenin' h'it out, that way. But we follow instructions. 'E's got other levels and shafts to check on, you know, but 'e stays down there with me and Fred, and keeps tellin' h'us to drill more holes. And 'e 'ad h'us puttin' 'em real close together.

"'E don't want us takin' any breaks, h'either. We got so tired Fred, 'e h'ask if 'e could bring down a couple h'of blokes workin' h'on the level h'above to spell h'us, but 'e says 'No, boys. You can get the job done. A couple of strong Cousin Jacks like you, and there'll be h'a nice bonus h'in h'it for you, too.' Me, I couldn't s'ay nothin'. I'm still a trammer, 'fficially. But Fred's been teachin' me h'everythin 'bout being a miner. I'm his h'assistant." He sat up a little straighter. "Trainee, they call h'it.

"Then Mr. Rhodes, 'e makes h'us drill bigger holes, so's to 'old more charge. The walls h'in this new part, they h'aren't timbered yet, and Mr. Rhodes, 'e won't give h'us time to do h'it. With nothin to 'old the wall back, and h'all that dynamite, we're getting' scared. But the captain, he jus' says, 'No point in takin' a long time to do this, I wanna git h'it done.'"

Twister stopped, looked at his empty cup and saucer. Though Cal could hardly wait to hear the end of this tale, he got up to get the man more tea. And thinking he was probably hungry, he found some cold bacon and a heel of bread on the stove and gave him that too.

Cal watched him as he consumed the food, impatient for him to continue his story. While he waited he noticed for the first time how specks of powder from the blast were imprisoned under the man's skin, giving it a bluish, dirty appearance.

When he'd devoured every morsel on his plate, Twister continued. "H'after we finish drillin' we start fillin' the 'oles with the charges—'im too. 'Uge amounts. Next we set the fuses. 'E sets a few 'isself, and then leaves h'us to finish, while 'e goes up to grass. Then we fire 'em like 'e told hus. We knew there was going to be one 'ell of a 'splosion, but those charges should'na gone h'off for a long time. Still, we weren't takin' h'any chances— you never saw two moles run so fast. But we've only gone a few yards and h'all 'ell breaks loose. The last thing I remember is flyin' through the h'air like a cannon ball."

Twister stopped, seemed unable to go on. Finally, he took a deep breath and said, "Reckon my voice got trapped h'in my throat just now. Fred, 'e never got h'out." He swallowed with difficulty. "'E was my brother."

"I didn't know."

"Yes, Cap'n."

Cal waited, finally asked, "What do you think happened?"

"Well, the way I figure it, one h'of them fuses 'ad to be real short, or looped h'over itself, so the spark jumped. H'it must have been connected to one of the big charges."

"You didn't notice any particularly short fuse?"

"No, sir. The fuses are different lengths h'anyway, so they won't 'all go off h'at the same time. Once we started firin' 'em, we were workin' real fast, so's to get out a' there. Guess we didn't notice."

Cal eyed the man carefully. "And how do you account for the premature explosion?"

Twister wet his lips, darted a couple of quick looks at Cal. "Well, lemme put h'it this way. Me h'and Fred didn't h'use short fuses."

Cal nodded. He looked out the window at the long shadows the afternoon sun was casting on the front lawn. He wondered if he'd done the right thing, taking this man on again, after the near disaster he'd caused before.

"Did Mr. Rhodes ever come to see you in the hospital?"

"No, sir."

"Did you ever get the 'bonus' he promised?"

"No."

"One more thing— in this new direction you were blasting, did you see the vein?"

"No, sir, only poor rock."

"Thank you."

When he'd left, Cal raced upstairs to find his wife. "Jenny, the man talked! He knows everything!"

Jenny stared at her husband. "Do you believe him?"

"I'm not sure. If what goes around, comes around, he sure got his comeuppance. But he had so much detail, so much about Rhodes. It all makes sense."

Jenny joined in Cal's excitement as she listened to his report of the miner's visit. It was the first piece of hopeful news they'd had in months.

"What will you do now?"

"Go to Henry."

"Will he believe the man's story?"

"He'll believe evidence. I'm hoping with Twister's story I can talk Henry into letting me open the shaft to examine it."

"Will Twister testify to Henry?"

"He says he will."

"I know Rhodes resents you, but what did he hope to accomplish?"

"To discredit me. Pretend he'd followed my plan and prove there was no copper there. With no real wins so far, it wouldn't take much to convince Henry. The explosion was to cover his tracks. And if Henry closed the mine, so much the better."

"But why did he involve others, who could talk?"

"One answer is that there weren't supposed to be any survivors. I don't know if we'll ever know if the fatal accident was deliberate."

Cal waited impatiently for Monday morning to go to Henry Parker's office.

During the whole telling of the story, Henry gave no indication whether he believed it or not. Cal felt uncomfortable waiting for a reply. His throat was dry. He was struck with the thought that Twister must have felt the same way two days earlier telling him. He sat quietly while Henry cleaned his pipe, giving great attention to it. Cal watched him fill it, tamp it down with his little finger, and finally, light it.

After drawing on it deeply he said, "You're making a terrible accusation."

"I'm just reporting what the survivor said."

"Passing on rumors."

"I don't see it that way, sir."

"This is the same damned bloke who set that fire last year! You expect me to believe his story? A helluva witness he'll make."

"I believe him."

"If there's any falsehood here, he'll be back in the slammer."

Cal waited again while Henry let the news percolate some more.

"I know there's been bad blood between you and Rhodes, but I can't believe he'd go that far. You're saying he destroyed company property, and put men's lives at terrible risk— maybe tried to kill 'em both."

"If you'll let me go down there—"

"Open the Nine? Not on your life."

"It's the only way we'll ever know.

"Henry was quiet. "Some things are better left alone, Cal."

"If you never know what really happened, could you ever trust Rhodes again?"

Henry reddened, and looked annoyed. "You're going down the wrong hole now, Cal."

They sat in silence for a while. Finally, Henry said, "I'll send for Twister whatever-his-name-is, and hear his tale."

Henry rose and Cal took his cue to leave. "Stop by tomorrow. I'm not promising anything."

Cal left feeling he'd gotten as far as he could expect on the first overture.

The rest of the day he puzzled over and over the information he'd gotten from Twister, and the response from Henry. Practically sleepless that night, he returned the next day with bags under his eyes.

"I talked to your man," Henry began.

Cal nodded, waited for more.

"I tried, but I can't think of any reason not to believe him. Cal, the Nine's a mess. How's going down there gonna tell you anything?"

Cal's hopes rose. "You still have my plans?"

Henry nodded.

"I can tell if he changed the direction, even a little."

"Not if it's as blown up down there as . . . Rhodes says it is," he finished lamely.

Cal's confidence was growing. "We'll see."

"Christ, it's dangerous to even ride the car down. At the bottom—"

"Let me worry about that."

Henry's pipe had gone out. Cal waited again as Henry fussed with it, got it going. Finally Henry said, "I'll get some men to uncap it. Come back Thursday morning."

"Thank you, Henry."

"I'm not promising anything," he said again. "And for now, I want to keep this under wraps. Don't hang around here."

On Thursday Henry handed Cal his plans for the No.9. Cal flipped the pages until he came to the one for the level where the explosion had taken place. They were the last plans he'd drawn, and he'd made it plain to Rhodes before he'd left for Chicago how he wanted them carried out.

The man who operated the car was waiting for him at No.9. They strode the short distance to the opening.

"'Mornin', Cap'n, sir."

"Good morning, Tucker."

"Good to have you back, sir."

He was hardly "back" but he didn't want to argue the point with the operator.

"Mr. Parker tells me you want to look over the damage on Level Eight."

"That's right."

"That was some explosion, that was. Me, I've been listenin' to explosions all my life, but that was some doozey."

Cal nodded.

"S'pose they told you how Mr. Rhodes he took off ahead of the others, couldn't wait to get to grass. He sure looked some relieved when he stepped off at the top."

"You brought him up?"

"Yes, sir. And I brought up the Trewella boys too. One dead and the other looked ready to join him."

"Who loaded them on the car?"

"Pete Lesser from level six went down there and got 'em both. First the live one, a' course— that would be Twister. Pete held on to him all the way up. He was still unconscious, Twister was. Then Pete went down there again and got his brother."

Cal approached the man-car. "It's running all right?"

"Oh, yes, sir. Took her down this morning to make sure."

"Thank you."

Cal turned on his headlamp, stepped into the car, and signaled Tucker that he was ready to descend. The car jerked in to motion, complaining loudly at being pressed into service after being retired for so long. Wheels squeaked in need of oil as they clattered against the rails. Without the weight of a load of men, the car jumped and bumped against the rails.

Always before there'd been the sound of hammering, drilling, men's voices, or charges going off. Today Cal was conscious of the rush of wind in his face, the creaking of timbers supporting the shaft, and the increase in temperature as he descended into darkness. For a frightening moment the car baulked, like a rebellious mule, and Cal held his breath. Then in the distance there was an air blast that reverberated and echoed through the many chambers of this mine. Finally, the car lurched on.

When it came to a stop, Cal got off. He took a few deep breaths and surveyed his surroundings.

Tucker said, "I'm going back up top, if you don't mind, sir. Pull on this chain when you want me to come and get you."

Cal could not show his fear to the man, and nodded. He listened while the car skipped and jumped its way back to safety.

He had never been down on any level alone. In the absence of the usual clamor, he noticed sounds he'd never heard before— the dripping of water, scurrying of rats. He stood still for a moment as one, too big for a cat to attack, came toward him. He heard small pieces of rock fall to the ground from various directions. And the wind— such an uncanny sound in this otherwise silent tomb.

Finally, he realized the only way to quell his fear was to get to work. He secured one end of a ball of twine to a rock. He walked cautiously along the empty drift with the twine until he came near the rock pile caused by the explosion. Here he fixed the string to the floor with another rock and took a compass from his pocket. His plans called for the drift to be cut at two degrees west by northwest. He held the compass against string in the section that had been stoped out before he'd left.

"Right on the mark."

He jerked the string loose and wound it up. Ahead he could see where the wall had been blown away, but not as much as he'd been led to believe. The broken rock had not been trammed out, and he had to climb over the rubble to get to the other side. The drift extended beyond the explosion. Cal moved enough rock to clear a path. On this new stretch he laid his string. Carefully, he placed his compass down, and let out a loud whistle.

Back on grass, he said, "Henry, go down there with me. I want you to see it."

"You'd better have something extraordinary to show me."

Reluctantly, the agent for the Keweenaw Mine Company agreed. Henry Parker didn't like to descend into the bowels of the earth.

At the shaft Tucker was waiting for them.

Parker was more nervous than Cal had been. White knuckled, he clung to the bench all the way down, and sat as far back on it as he could.

When they were on flat ground they traversed the quarter mile of the old stretch, and Cal showed Henry with the compass and twine that the first section was as planned. Then he helped the portly Henry over the pile of rock caused by the explosion.

"I thought the damage was worse than this," Henry commented.

Cal could see the sweat run in rivulets down the man's face, under Parker's helmet lamp.

They stepped cautiously along the new stretch, Cal often having to support Parker. Cal fastened the string with rocks again. Then he laid his compass on it.

"Have a look, Henry."

Henry knelt on the ground, holding his lantern near the compass. Drops of perspiration fell on the glass. Henry picked it up, cleaned it off and put it back.

"Did you say it was supposed to continue at two degrees?"

"Supposed to," Cal answered.

They could plainly read: twelve degrees.

Lester Rhodes stood opposite Henry Parker.

"I'm short a shift boss today, over in No. 4. Can this wait, Mr. Parker?"

"No, it can't. Sit down."

Lester sat down. "What's so important?"

"When Willis was in Chicago, and you were operating No.9, did you use Willis's plans?"

Lester looked puzzled. "Certainly."

"Did you have any problems following them, or reason to change the vectors?"

"No."

"You're sure?"

Lester hesitated. "The vein was running out sir, as I've told you before. But before we gave up on it altogether, I tried a slightly different angle."

"I was down there today. It's not only obvious you changed the vector, but that in doing so you deliberately abandoned the vein— that is plain to see straight ahead in the old course."

"You were down there?" Lester stammered.

"You didn't count on that, did you?"

Lester said nothing.

"You were punching above your weight, Rhodes."

"I thought—"

"And with your planned explosion—"

"Sir, I had nothin' to do with the explosion!"

"How can you say that? You worked the men like beasts, high-tailed it out of there before all your charges went off—"

"But I didn't do nothin' to cause an explosion!"

"You meant to cover up what you'd done and close the shaft. You are responsible for the death of one man and serious injury of another.

In addition, you caused grievous damage to company property resulting in great loss of revenue."

"That's not true—"

"Get your tools and get out."

"Mr. Parker, sir—"

"Get out—"

"It was somebody else."

"What are you talking about? Who else was down there?"

"Roy Willis. Roy went down just before I came up."

Parker took this in. "Did he say why?"

"He was in charge of the shaft while his brother was away, so it wasn't for me to question him. I was only the shift captain."

"Roy!" Jenny cried. "How could it be Roy?"

"I don't know."

"Do you believe that, Cal?"

"I don't know what to believe. I've got to find him. Talk to him."

First he had to locate Tucker. He was working another shaft car now. When he found the man, Cal was almost afraid to ask the question.

"Did my brother go to Level Eight the day of the explosion?"

The man looked blank.

"Roy Willis."

"He was down there a few times. On that day? Not real sure, sir, with all that was happening— the explosion, then tryin' to get the men up to grass—"

"You're not sure!" Cal bellowed.

"Is it important?" the man ventured sheepishly.

Cal started to speak, then strode quickly away.

Further questioning of Twister led to his concurring that Roy had been on that level, but he hadn't seen him for a few hours the day of the explosion.

"If 'e came down late, with the noise h'of the drills h'and our scramblin' to finish the job, might not have noticed." He wet his lips. "Besides, sir, since the h'accident, my brain gets a bit h'addled sometimes."

"Why would Roy do such a thing?" Jenny couldn't believe it.

"I don't think that he did. Could be Rhodes just passing the buck. He couldn't deny changing the vector. But he wouldn't want to admit to a deliberate explosion, would he?"

Cal paced the floor. "I've got to find Roy."

But two weeks of looking for his brother turned up nothing. Apparently no one had seen him— not in the pubs, nor the streets. Roy had no telephone, but Cal had been to his lodgings in Hancock four times; it seemed no one had seen Roy there since the explosion. Cal left messages for him, but never heard back.

Because of his willful sabotage of Cal's plan, Rhodes was dismissed. Sheriff Foster arrested him. Rhodes admitted to changing the vector "slightly".

"Why?" Foster asked him.

"Thought there might be more copper going that way."

"And my mother was a cottontail rabbit," Earl said dryly.

Rhodes looked up, startled. "Well, we weren't getting' anywhere with Cal's plan. I thought maybe if I was to discover somethin' better, I might get, well, some credit for that."

"The reports do not substantiate what you're telling me. All who have visited this scene say you turned away from a clear vein of copper."

The long and short of it was that Rhodes was ordered to pay a certain sum back to the mine for damages, and a six week stay at the county's best. But no charges were brought against him for the explosion and death of the miner. Without Roy, and Twister's fractured memory, there wasn't enough to go on. The question just hung there.

And the shaft remained closed.

After he served his time, Lester Rhodes vanished. The sheriff figured the man knew he couldn't get a job anywhere in any mine. He could no more cast off his reputation than his shadow. Even discounting the suspicion that he had caused the explosion, the fact that he had counter-ordered the cuts to be made was enough to make him a pariah in the industry.

Earl still wasn't convinced that Rhodes hadn't caused the explosion. The fact that he made a run for it out of town made him look the more culpable. But he'd gone as far as he could on that trail. At least for now.

Earl turned his attention to finding Roy. He deputized a man in Hancock and another in Red Jacket to search as well. Although it didn't seem to fit his character at all, Earl couldn't help thinking that maybe Roy, bitter with how his life was spiraling down, may have caused the explosion. He might have done this to ruin Cal, or at least to dash his brother's hopes that he was going to find the mother lode in the No.9. Could Roy Willis be so crazed as to deliberately set off an explosion resulting in someone's death?

CHAPTER FOURTEEN

Meanwhile other problems were taking Earl's attention. The one-man drill had caused accidents and deaths in various Keweenaw mines, and the miners were rebelling. And that alone was helping to raise membership in the Western Federation of Miners that spring. The long shifts, the poor pay, and now the new one-man drill had fomented a call for long overdue change.

Polite letters were sent from the union to management, asking for meetings to negotiate improvements. But the miners were ignored. Management wouldn't meet with the miners. Nor would they answer the letters.

"Negotiate with them? You must be joking." James McNeary knocked the ashes out of his pipe.

"Just wanted to make sure, sir," the newspaper man said.

"Never. The trouble-makers are an unlawful, murderous lot, and totally without our support. Most of our miners are loyal employees, and would never join a union."

"Unions are up-and-coming. Progress and all. Someday—"

"Progress! We'll not have that kind of progress in Michigan. The WFM is headquartered in Denver. They'll never get their claws in the Keweenaw."

"I know. I was just saying a lot of them have complaints—"

"Oh, yes, I know. Not enough stulls in place is one of their grievances. "Timbering costs us money. The men cost us nothing."

"And the one-man drill. That's the latest. Do you think the explosion in No.9 had anything to do with the men trying to bring on the strike? Trying to bring the Company down?" Able Vassar asked.

"Who knows? But we will not give in an inch," McNeary went on. "Who do they think built the schools, the churches for them? There's a church for every denomination you've heard of and some you haven't— synagogues, too. We've taken care of them, helped families when good men met with accidents. Built the library, the hospital."

Just thinking about it angered McNeary. He stood, knocking an ashtray off the desk.

"God, what more do they expect?"

"You don't have to convince me, sir." Able Vassar from the *Mining Chronicle* agreed. "The Company's done everything for them."

Then, as if he were alone, McNeary said, "I used to know a lot of them, personally— good men. And I took good care of them, like children."

He fingered the chunk of copper.

Then turning back to Vassar he said, "I'll never acknowledge the union. If they think they can swarm over me like a hive of bees they're sadly mistaken. And no raises now— not under threat! The Company does not belong to them. It belongs to the owners in Boston and their stockholders. I represent their interests. I've no fear of these rebels."

"What kind of funds do these trouble-makers have? I mean in the unlikely event that they do strike."

McNeary snorted. "Very little. Lloyd Tobin at the bank let me in on that little secret. They don't have enough to feed a tinker for a month. And they don't have enough membership in that silly union to call a strike vote. The WFM is more meddlesome than menacing. Most of the men know where their bread is buttered. I don't think we have anything to worry about."

"I'll keep writing it like it is— do what I can to dissipate the tension."

"Good man. Appreciate it, Able. You've a fine paper. And we appreciate your loyalty. Not like the muckrakers that come from out of town."

"Thank you, sir."

Still, James McNeary wrote to a certain detective firm in New York.

On July first Harry Berglund got off the train in Red Jacket, and decided the first thing he needed to do was find a room. He had no friends here. There was no on to help him get a job— he was on his own.

Signs were about town, directing new workers to lodgings. He needed a private room. There were reports to write at night, and send back to New York.

He figured he'd costumed himself well enough to blend in with other mine workers in town. His suitcase and clothes looked worn.

He found a room on the third floor of Widow Mason's house for a dollar a week. It was really the attic. Hot and stuffy; little breeze came through the single window. Besides a small cot, the only other piece of furniture was a scarred dresser with temperamental drawers. He found a small discarded board in the street. It was smooth— probably part of a cast-off piece of furniture. By placing it across his lap, he could use it as a desk for writing his reports.

He knew he'd have to start at the bottom. The No. 3 at Keweenaw had the worst reputation for safety. That's where new employees were sent. He was given the lowest level of work, as a trammer.

The detective firm he'd worked for these past three years had been hired by the Keweenaw Mining Company to send a man to spy on the workers and check on work conditions. Harry was their man.

On his first day of work he nearly escaped falling rock that should have been shored up long before. A nearby trammer yanked him out of the way.

"You gotta learn to jump fast around here. Helps to have eyes in the back of yer head."

Harry recognized him as a fellow Finn.

After work the man said, "*Sallikaa minun puoliajalla voit juoda, kamu.*"

Harry accepted. "And then I'll buy you one."

They went to a Finnish pub after work, and his new friend bought him a Finnish beer.

The man introduced himself. "Lubinnem's the name."

"And mine's Berglund. Harry."

"You don't want to work in the hole any longer than you have to. We hate it down below. Most Finns do the lumbering."

"But you—"

"No jobs open there, right now. I will get there as soon as I can."

But Harry had been hired to work in the mines. He wasn't allowed to reveal this to anyone.

Besides the hazardous conditions, the captain and foreman were abusive to the men, cursing and yelling at them continually. It was backbreaking work; Harry didn't know how long he could take it. When he got to grass, the hot water was gone and he'd had to clean up with cold, and no soap. He'd grown soft doing office and field work in New York. After two days below he was so sore he had to take a day off.

He wrote to the detective company that he agreed with the men— working conditions were loathsome and dangerous. There was faulty equipment and hazards at every turn.

Frequenting the Finnish saloons and pool hall, he met many alike who had quit the No. 3. Even if they had to wait a few weeks it was worth it to find work in another shaft.

There were always job openings in the No. 3, where a death or serious injury was reported every week. He said he'd seen enough, and could he come home now. The detective firm told him to stay on. The client wanted to know who the rabel-rousers were who were inciting a strike, who was stirring up the most trouble.

"Jesus, how does anybody stand it down here?" he asked Lubinnem.

"Got to put in time here, before they'll take you anywhere else."

"How long have you been working here?"

"A month. Figure in another month I'll try my luck again at the lumber site."

On his fifth day Harry had to leap fast to avoid a piece of falling rock. The next day, on his way down the shaft, the man car skipped his level. He had to climb up the old ladder one level to get to his level. In the darkness he could not see the two missing rungs, fell, and injured his knee.

He was out of work for eight days.

After witnessing two serious accidents the following week, Harry decided to quit the No. 3 and look for a job in a safer shaft. He'd heard the No. 6 wasn't too bad, and he hung around there several days asking for employment. He was told each time that nothing was available.

Finally, in the second week, he secured a position as a trammer.

At a Finnish saloon he raised a glass more than once with his friend Mike Lubinnem. On his third night there, a Finn was coming through with membership papers for the WFM. Lubinnem told Harry he'd better join the union if he wanted any help from them during the strike.

"Maybe," Harry said. "Short of funds now."

Membership drives were being carried out in every saloon and social hall in town.

"You're pretty sure there'll be a strike?"

"Gotta be. Safety conditions are getting worse and worse. We can't put up with this much longer."

"Do the Germans, Irish— everybody feel the same?"

The man assured Berglund they did, and told him details of incidents that raised his hair.

"A rock— part of the wall fell on a trammer without warning. The poor bloke was bleeding heavily, but they wouldn't start up the man-car and bring him up to grass until the shift was over. He bled to death before they got him to the hospital."

"Jesus! Is that typical, do you think, in all shafts?"

"Can't say. Depends on the shift boss, I guess."

"What responsibility, if any, does management take for these accidents?"

"Almost always blame it on the carelessness of the men. Or 'unavoidable.' Never accept responsibility themselves. Say the men know the dangers when they sign on. That's how they win any law suit."

Harry sucked on his pipe. "What about these air blasts?"

"Have you heard them?"

"One, just yesterday. Everybody 'bout jumped out of their skin."

"Spooky phenomenon. They shake the earth all around, and can be heard miles away."

"What causes them?" Harry asked.

"The Company says they don't know. But I'll tell you what they are—the sins of the forefathers."

"How's that?"

"For half a century the supervisors and captains didn't put proper supports into place. This underground community we're living in is practically hollow. They keep digging deeper and deeper—"

"How deep?"

"We're a mile down now, and very few rock pillars are left standing above to support the hanging walls. One hollow level on top of another. What you're hearing in those air blasts is the caving in of the mine. Old abandoned shafts."

Harry turned pale, and finished his ale in one gulp. Back in his room he wrote this up in another report to his company. His handwriting was getting jerky.

Cal continued to search for his brother. He visited Roy's old haunts and his friends. No one had seen or heard of him. Cal even rode out to Carlene's. No, she hadn't heard from him. She seemed as concerned as he that Roy had disappeared.

"Do you have any idea, miss, where he might have gone?"

"No. Just away from your people."

Jenny worried. "What do you think happened to him?"

"I don't know. Maybe he was so ashamed he took a train to Chicago, to lose himself in the big city— start a new life."

Cal still couldn't believe his brother could do such a thing. But since Roy had run off, and Cal couldn't get his side of the story, it was impossible to rule that possibility out.

He also knew a strike was imminent, and he wondered if the explosion was caused by someone to stir up discontent and bring the strike on.

Or, again, was his brother just ashamed?

"Ashamed— of what?" Jenny said."

"I mean if it was Roy who caused the. . ." his voice trailed off.

"No, no!" Jenny protested.

She began crying, ran upstairs to their bedroom and buried her head between their pillows. Cal followed her.

"What, what is the matter, Jenny?"

He held her close for a while, quieting her sobs, and trying to understand his young wife.

Later that evening, when they were in bed, just the sight of her swollen breasts made him yearn for her. How long had it been? Once again he attempted to arouse her. At first she seemed responsive, offering her lips to him. But as soon as his hands began to wander to other parts of her body, he could feel her tighten, freeze up. He let her go, and fell back on his side of the bed.

They lay in silence for a while. Finally she spoke.

"It's Roy. I feel so sorry for him. He's not a bad person, Cal."

"I know that."

"But his being held accountable for the explosion—"

"Not accountable. The sheriff wants to question him. He was, after all, in charge of the shaft."

She was silent.

"Are you blaming me, Jenny? For putting him in that position when we went away?"

"No, of course not. Never."

"Then what?"

"I blame myself," and she was sobbing again.

"You? Why?"

He couldn't grasp her meaning.

"If I hadn't, if we hadn't—"

"Hadn't what?"

She shook her head.

"Married? Is that what you're saying?"

"I don't know. I'm so confused."

"Are you saying your heart still belongs to Roy?"

"No, not that."

"Then what!"

"I don't know." She finally choked out, "I guess it's a feeling of disloyalty."

Cal felt all blood from his face to his groin leave him. A mixture of anger, confusion and sadness churned in him.

"He betrayed you, Jenny. He brought on his own troubles."

He could barely hear her. "Nobody deserves so much punishment," she whispered.

"Are you saying you should have married him anyway?"

"No!"

"Or become a spinster?"

"I don't know. But to marry you was to divide your family, set you two against each other." She raised herself up on her elbow. "And invite his hatred of me. He couldn't handle all that!"

"He doesn't hate you."

"He does. He truly does. Don't you see how our being together twisted the knife for him? He didn't even have family he could trust anymore." She took a deep breath. "First he lost me and then he lost you." She flopped back down on her pillow.

She had uncovered the very feelings he'd tried to bury. The guilt. Would Jenny ever be his? Or would the specter of his brother always hang between them?

CHAPTER FIFTEEN

Earl Foster had been the sheriff of Houghton County for a long time. About twenty years, he reckoned it was. For the most part he enjoyed it. Well, maybe that was the wrong word. He thought he was doing something worthwhile for the community. He thought justice was important.

But the sheriff could hardly believe it when his old colleague George McKinney, who had been the county judge for years and was finally retiring, urged him to run for the office.

Buck Boyce, the prosecuting attorney who had salivated over securing the bench for years, would be running for the position. But Boyce had tarnished his image in several recent court cases.

"Hadn't thought of it," he told the retiring judge.

"You're the best man for the job."

"I haven't even studied law, George."

"You know the law as well as anyone. And you've attended enough trials to know the procedure." George McKinney drew on his cigar. "Earl, you're a fair man— that's the most important thing."

"Not an easy time to be taking on that job," Earl pursed his lips. "With all the unrest and uprising among the miners."

"True. But if anyone can put out wildfires and make wise decisions, it would be you."

Earl swallowed hard. He had always admired George. They had been adversaries, friends, poker players and colleagues. But not on equal terms. It was always understood that George, being older and holding a higher rank, would have the advantage. And George had taken that advantage— sometimes teasing him, or treating him like a boy. Still they'd remained friends, if on somewhat different footing.

So the surprising proposal from the retiring judge caused his throat to swell up, and he found it hard to speak.

"I needn't add," said the judge, "that a recommendation from me won't hurt you a bit in the election."

"No, sir. I appreciate that. I do."

"And we wouldn't want ole Buck to take the bench, now would we?"

Earl looked hard at the older man. "Let me think about it, George."

"Don't take too long."

Earl discussed it with his wife, Cora.

"Breathtaking, it is— you being the judge! And you could stop running all over this county. You'd have a desk, and a courtroom. Oh, it sounds grand."

Earl wasn't at all sure he was up to the job, especially now, with riots starting even before the strike was underway. But finally he agreed to be put on the slate.

It was a closer contest than McKinney had forecast, but in the end Earl won. McKinney held a celebration for him at his antebellum house on the hill, and many friends toasted the new judge-to-be. Besides the joy and enthusiasm the evening brought, there was serious discussion about the political climate. A miners' strike seemed imminent.

"Who's going to lead them?" someone asked.

"In any situation where action is required," George McKinney replied, "Natural leaders emerge. One I'm thinking of is called the "Redeemer". Whether self-named or supplied by the rabble, I don't know. I heard he stands on barrels in the street and proclaims that he can lead the union to success. He offers private counseling to those who ask for it, and many do."

"How do you know all this?" Earl wanted to know.

"I have ways. Knot-holes all over the county." He ended with a sly smile.

The man called Redeemer was a local miner. Few knew him, and no one noticed anything special about him until there was talk of a strike. About five feet ten, thin, with brown hair, he had not stood out.

Then his knack for making speeches caught everyone's attention. He soon earned a reputation for being a strong union man and good leader. He gave rousing talks every night or two inside or outside the local social halls. Although he was a native, he was welcomed in most ethnic halls, too. He made the men feel better about the dangerous path they were about to embark on. He made their hearts swell with the power of the union.

"Men, unless we unite and join together to end our oppression, we are worse off than the black slaves of the south were— our work is harder, and we've barely enough to feed our families. Our condition is a pestilence! We must end this slavery! We must galvanize our strength. Together we can bring glory out of darkness. What can management do without us, I ask you?"

Such incendiary speeches were met with rousing cheers.

Redeemer had assistants in red hats milling through the crowd to capture their membership while the men were fired up.

The national headquarters of the WMF in Denver didn't think Michigan was ready for a strike. Even with the membership growing, it was plain they didn't have enough money to carry a strike for long.

"Not a good time. You don't have sufficient funds in your coffers," the president wrote.

But the union leaders from Denver couldn't prevail against the fury and upheaval in the Upper Peninsula. They were dragged into the fracas.

When it was clear that the locals meant to go ahead anyway, the national officers wrote letters to the Keweenaw politely explaining the complaints of their employees.

McNeary laughed. "So now the national's getting into it. Well, Denver's not coming here. I won't even answer their letters."

And he didn't.

The letters that the locals wrote weren't so polite. They demanded that the Company meet with representatives of the union. The companies ignored the letters, sometimes returning them marked 'refused'.

The man called Redeemer was taking pleasure in his work. He realized he had a talent for public speaking, maybe a calling. It gave him a real sense of power to stand on a barrel or pile of lumber and regale the boys with histrionic tales of doom and gloom that would plague those who resisted the forces of progress--and the power they'd feel as a united force.

He was grateful now for the elocution class he'd had to take in high school. The students were required to give a speech on some current events topic every two weeks. He'd hated it at first, but when he realized that he had a certain way about him that held his classmates' attention, he started enjoying it. He'd swagger up to the front of the room, run his hand across his face and offer a charming smile. He'd always try to find ideas that were amusing, and the class looked forward to his talks. Soon he did too.

It was paying off now.

"Unions are up-and-coming," he bellowed from the steps of the courthouse and in front of the livery alike. "It is time to recognize that only through unity will we ever have any power. One by one, we stand alone, with no voice, a straw in the wind. Together we can move the companies we work for— make them see what have long been our rights— a shorter work day, decent wages, and the end of the 'widow maker.' A union is a *brotherhood*, men."

He paused to wait for the emotional effect.

"Let us join together as brothers. Come sign up to be a member of WMF."

And they did. It was Redeemer's dramatic flair and charisma that pulled them in. He was a man who seemed to come out of nowhere, a purveyor of dreams, spawning hopes for a better life among the mine workers.

Judge Foster had heard about him. He decided to stand at the back of the crowd outside the courthouse as he left his office. About thirty men were gathered there, listening attentively to the speaker, and cheering him on. He recognized this man.

"Oh, my God! If that isn't—"

His thoughts were interrupted by someone bumping him, who in turn had been bumped by someone else. He was surprised when he looked up to see Big Annie. He'd seen her from a distance, and she certainly fit the description. He nodded to her and she smiled back.

"What do you think of him, Ma'am?"

"He has a very persuasive manner."

"Doesn't he, though. Kind of reminds me of a preacher at a revival meeting," Earl said.

Annie laughed. "You could say that. But he's getting the men to join the union."

"That he is."

A boy, no more than fourteen approached Redeemer after the meeting. "Can I talk to you, sir?"

"Certainly. What's your name, lad?"

"Percival, sir. Percival Wainwright."

"What's on your mind, young Percival?"

"Well, this is the situation." He wiped his nose on his sleeve. "I want to join the union. In a way I'm afraid not to, the way things are going. But I don't have any saved-up money to quit working if we was to strike. See, my father was injured in the mine three years ago—can't work no more, so I've my parents to support and six younger brothers and sisters. We have to squeak by as it is. There just isn't any money for union dues, and being out of work."

Redeemer put his hand on the boy's shoulder. "I understand. I really do. But you have to look at the big picture, son. You'll always be squeaking by unless we force the Company to make our lives easier. The union will be giving every miner an allowance while we're on strike. Now that should help, right?"

Flem had been taken on as assistant to Redeemer. His duties included finding tipplers in the saloons and persuading them to join up. He befriended every man he met. Then he'd get those who were obstinate about joining the union inebriated and relieve them of their funds.

He sincerely believed in the union, and felt that every miner should be a member regardless of what it took to get him there. He worked long and hard, often with little sleep. He would do anything to please Redeemer, even following him many nights to make sure he was safe.

Flem was feeling prosperous. He'd taken up smoking Cuban cigars and wearing better clothes, just like Redeemer. He bought a new plaid coat in blues and greens, which he decided made him look very distinguished. He came to be almost as well-known as Redeemer and Frenchie. He still had a strange gait due to his mine accident, but he didn't look like a bum anymore. Folks respected him. He was a living reminder of how important it was to unite and fight for basic safety precautions in the mine. Sometimes he used a crutch.

Redeemer collected union dues and franchised Frenchie, Flem and a few others to do the same. He spread it out in several banks to make it harder for the Company to get a good handle on how much they had. He appointed a 'board' to act as union whip on the rank and file. He made a point of seeking out the leaders in every ethnic group, encouraging them to bring their people into the union and support a strike. He often shared "secrets" with them, making them feel special. Redeemer was feeling more and more powerful.

Then one day he declared, "It's time."

On July 23rd, 1913 the strike officially began. Through showers and a strong wind blowing off Lake Superior, some five hundred striking miners marched down Calumet Avenue in perfect order to the Keweenaw mine that bordered Red Jacket. But when they got there, a volcano of long pent-up resentment and anger erupted. They were ready for a fight.

"Let's get'em!"

"It's about time!"

"The S.O.Bs."

"Bring 'em down!"

"Bloody bastards!"

"Fuck the Company!"

Ammunition was grabbed on the way— rocks, heavy sticks and iron bolts lying around were hurled at non-union workers. Officers were rousted in the Company offices. They were driven out of the building and clubbed. Company windows were broken. Tempers unleashed after long suppression created a horrendous tempest that went unabated.

"Fuckin' tyrants!"

"Slave drivers."

The adrenalin rose in them. A mob mentality took over. Miners approaching for the night shift were harassed and driven away.

Into the evening, the crashing sounds broke the silence of the darkness and woke sleeping babes in nearby homes.

That night McNeary had to close the mine.

"We'll see who wins this squabble," he said.

Still, he slept in a different bed every night.

On the second day of the strike, most of the mines in Houghton and Hancock were closed.

Dear Editor,

Finally the strike has begun! Mine workers whose tolerance has been strained to the breaking point have started marching and expressing their long-held resentments toward unfair labor practices. Let's cheer them on, as they pass our doors, and say a prayer for them!

B.T. Wilkins

The spy, Harry Berglund was clubbed on the head as he approached the mine for his shift. The next day he decided it was time to leave Red Jacket. With a swollen head, he gathered up his few belongings, and dashed for the train depot. He recognized the faces of a few fellow workmen doing the same.

Only when the train started moving, did he feel he could breathe. As it carried him south, he saw the faces of husbands, boys and sons in the rail cars bound north— it was like looking at himself in the mirror over and over. These chaps were ready to take the place of those leaving the Copper Country— scabs, eager for work. The Company wasn't looking for familiar faces; they were looking for men willing to work.

Annie had watched from the sidelines the first two days of the strike. She wouldn't be a bystander anymore. On the third day she awoke at four and couldn't get back to sleep. She was so excited about what she was about to do, it filled her with energy and courage.

"Where do you think you're going?" her husband demanded.

"To fight for justice!" she said.

By six o'clock she was marching down the main street, holding high the silk American flag that Betsy had given her. She was also wearing the little bumblebee pin the cast of the skit had given her. She was joined almost immediately by the women in the auxiliary and some who were not.

If the men could not bring about change, it was time for the women to show their bond of strength.

"We, the women of this town will make the Company bow to our demands!"

Annie was there at six o'clock every morning leading the parade. Even men fell into line and followed her. As many as two thousand Finns, Croats, Hungarians and Poles marched behind Big Annie for five to seven miles through the streets to the mines.

They marched every day and did not let up. On Sundays, she wore her pretty white Sunday dress trimmed with colorful ribbons.

Often, if she didn't see Jeremy's new motor car, she stopped by Betsy's on the way home. Betsy would give her a cup of tea, put Annie's feet up on the footstool, and eagerly listen to her stories of the day's happenings.

Betsy lived vicariously through Annie's drama— what she would love to be doing herself. Besides, she'd become very close to this woman during the preparation of the skit. She was always glad to see Annie.

Hurray for the women! It is not men alone who suffer from the unfair treatment of mine workers, but their whole families. Our women have formed an auxiliary, and they are marching too! Big Annie is leading the marches, and men as well as women are following her through the streets of Red Jacket and to the mine!

B.T. Wilkins

Betsy's eager attention and support filled Annie with confidence. It spurred her resolve to keep up the fight.

At first the women were peaceful, but many turned to behavior unknown to them before— committing atrocities men would not have thought of.

McNeary wrote the owner in Boston: "Today a tiny woman carried a bucket of human excrement down the street, and others followed her with brooms, ready to smear any non-union man they saw. And you would not believe the language of the politest women of these strikers."

Betsy was shocked to hear Annie tell of it. "They didn't!" She covered her mouth in horror. Then simultaneously both women burst out laughing.

McNeary was flummoxed by their involvement. Officers were not used to attacking women, and it seemed the gentler sex was getting away with far more than a man could.

"I think it is the women who are lighting the tinder to this rebellion," McNeary said.

One day Annie was cut on the wrist with an officer's saber.

"Can you stop this foolishness now?" her husband asked.

"No. I am only more invigorated by it."

It was true. Adrenalin poured through her body as she strode down the streets. She was fueled both by catcalls berating her, and shouts of "Go, Annie, go!" She barely noticed how tired she was until she reached home. Then, exhausted, she ignored Joseph's complaints, fixed simple meals, and retired to bed.

The riots continued. Strikers were smashing heads of those miners who wouldn't strike. Three days later Percival Wainwright was found dead on Keweenaw property.

As judge, Earl had been in office only a month when this unholy scene burst upon him.

The new sheriff cooperated with the Company but couldn't control the situation, even though he had deputized over two hundred Keweenaw employees to keep the peace.

When the rabble began setting fires to company property, McNeary asked Governor Ferris to send in the National Guard. The next day all of the state troops arrived in the Copper Country. They set up tents outside the armory and Keweenaw offices. They were there to squelch the riots and the strike, though they did not carry guns. Still, there were fights everywhere. Union men were beating up men who were still working in shafts that had not been closed.

After two weeks the governor called back half of the National Guard. McNeary was furious. He took stronger measures. He employed an organization of hit men from New York. If the WFM had developed a reputation for violence and head-bashing, the New York Barkers outdid them. They had been given free rein on how to handle the rowdy strikers. Carrying guns openly, the goons weren't shy about using them. House fires were started in the homes of known strikers. They put shame on the Keweenaw Mining Company. But no English-speaking newspaper in the Copper Country reported it.

The news of the strike had reached all corners of the country, and soon reporters from all over were coming to observe and report to their local papers.

"Betsy, your letters are being read!"

"Oh, it's a pittance, Annie."

"But it's working— the pen is very powerful."

"Many pens, my dear."

"Why are we still getting letters to a B. T. Wilkins?" Jeremy bellowed. He held a crumpled one in his hand.

"How can you expect me to answer that?" Betsy replied.

"It's the third one this week." He looked at her suspiciously. "Do you have something to do with this, eh?" He loomed over her.

"I refuse to converse with you when you treat me so." She left the room.

Frank Shavs joined other correspondents in the nucleus of the trouble. He followed the parades, tried to report the views of both sides to his Chicago paper. He was especially struck by the remarkable strength and endurance of the Croatian woman who carried an enormous flag down Red Jacket Avenue every day.

He approached her. "Isn't this flag too heavy for you?"

"I get used to it. Once I carried it ten miles."

"You didn't!"

"The men wouldn't let me carry it any further."

He asked, "Do you mind if I accompany you?"

She flashed her brilliant smile. "As long as you don't slow me down."

He wanted to talk to her, to find out why in the world she was involved in this mining fight, but she was moving so fast, it was hard to keep up with her.

"I understand you started the women's auxiliary. Is that true?"

"Yes, sir, it is."

"What do you hope to accomplish?"

She stared at him a moment, without missing a step. Her big blue eyes flashed.

"I should think it obvious," she retorted. "The mines can't run without the workers. If enough of them refuse to work, the mines will have to close."

"Please forgive me, ma'am. But can you tell me why you feel this is women's work?"

"I'll be happy to. A man's work and his wages deeply affect his whole family. We are striking for our families."

"I see. And you feel a woman can do as much as a man to convince the miners to stay on strike?"

"Perhaps more. It shames them into joining us." There seemed to be a twinkle in her eye.

"What about the danger? Don't you think about that?"

"If that were my focus, I should be cowering in bed under my covers. No, I don't think about that."

Frank Shavs admired her more and more. He wrote reports for his Chicago paper focusing on the bravery and long parades of the woman known as "Big Annie." It gave his stories a different point of view than other reporters' work. Soon he was marching with her every day.

On a cool evening in late August Annie came home to an empty house. The fireplace was cold, the house dark, and Joseph nowhere to be found. All his clothes and other belongings were gone. So Joseph had taken his leave. Maybe he'd left a note. She looked around in the bedroom and the kitchen. There was no note. Perhaps it was for the best. Whatever frayed bond they had once shared had long been torn apart.

She didn't expect him to have left her any money, but she looked anyway. Even the jar with her meager housekeeping money was empty. What was she going to live on? She had gotten so involved with the parades, she'd given up doing housekeeping for women of a higher class. Now it appeared she'd have to resume cleaning other peoples' houses. She decided she could do that in the afternoons, after the parades.

Why had she married him? It dismayed her to remember. She'd known she was too large to interest most men. Joseph was a bit taller than she. So she'd married him.

Why did she think she had to marry anyone? Well, what were her choices if she didn't? Lady of the night, maybe teacher, had she been educated enough. Wash and scrub woman— but she was that anyway. Marriage had not given her any financial advantage. Perhaps a bit with those in her level of society. Spinsters were pitied, not admired, usually burdening a brother and his wife or other such relative with their care.

As Annie's friends and followers realized she was a woman on her own, some began to give her money. She was their leader, after all. Someone would make a collection each week, put it in an envelope, and slip in her pocket. Not a lot, but enough to get by on, if she limited her diet to potatoes and beans. Sometimes, she shared them with her friends Val and Dennis Tory, and their large family.

All summer men were arrested by the dozens. In one day over one hundred were brought in. Earl Foster was put in a difficult position. He had long sided with the miners, who he felt were overworked and underpaid. Now, as judge, he was expected to take management's point of view, or at the very least maintain a neutrality that he didn't feel. He held hearings, dealt out sentences, and then in many cases, suspended them. But not all. The county jail was full, and the armory next to the Keweenaw was absorbing the overflow.

"I'm closing the social halls," James McNeary said. "Gathering places for discontent."

"But you can't close the saloons," Able Vassar pointed out.

"The social halls are a bigger problem. To some extent, men remain sober and serious there. They go to the saloons to drink and forget their troubles."

"How long do you figure this strike will last?"

"'Til the hooligans run out of money. And believe me, that won't be long. I have friends, Able, in the bank. I know their meager balance. It won't last two weeks, once they finally start passing it out. I will let grass grow under their feet before I'll ever acknowledge the WMF or any other union," he told the newspaper man.

The *Mining Chronicle* quoted McNeary verbatim.

Judge Foster believed him. The sheriff and his deputies continued to make arrests, Earl continued to pass sentences, but in many cases let the law-breakers off easy.

"The men on strike are law-abiding citizens who are expressing their right to free speech and protest," he stated.

McNeary called Judge Foster in for a confrontation.

"You may be the new judge of this county, Foster, but don't let it go to your head. You do not have the power to dispense with law and justice. You got that? Your duty is to mete out punishment where the law requires— not construct your own laws, based on your personal prejudice. There are honest miners out there wanting to go to work, and this anarchistic bunch is stopping them, attacking them. Is that your idea of a lawful society?"

Foster suspected that McNeary had enough clout in the county to get him ousted, if he alienated him too much. And Foster, brand new in his seat on the bench, had no clout at all.

Earl had a problem with psoriasis, and it served as a barometer of how distressed he was. The itch was getting worse.

His wife, Cora packed baking soda on it, and massaged his shoulders. "Breathe," she said, "breathe deeply, Earl. Try to forget it. At least for a while."

One day twenty arrests were made. Earl was shocked to see that fifteen who came before him were women.

"Good heavens, what's the world coming to?"

He held hearings, warned them about obeying the law, and suspended all sentences.

His brother, Tobias called in anger. Tobias was an officer at the mine.

"What the hell are you doing? Are you carrying a union card now?"

He got a terse letter of warning from McNeary. "I warn you, Foster, I can take you down."

"What are you going to do?" Cora asked him.

"Keep trying to be true to myself."

"You know where that's going to lead, don't you?"

"I suppose I do."

CHAPTER SIXTEEN

"**O**ne of two things will bring them to their knees. Cold weather or running out of funds," McNeary told the *Mining Chronicle*. "The strike will be over in a few days."

But for once in his life he was in for a surprise. Newsreels all over the nation had shown the plight of the miners in the Upper Peninsula, and other unions began to collect money to send to the Copper Country. From the AF of L to United Brewery Workers of America, money was collected and sent north.

The WFM assessed all members outside of Michigan two dollars a month.

Hurray for the strikers! They will not give up. Workers from all over the country sympathize with our men. They story is out! Management is unfair. Support the unions! Support the Labor Movement!

B.T. Wilkins

Again Jeremy was shaking a letter in his hand. "If one more of these comes I'm taking them to the post office to get to the bottom of this!" His face was flushed and he stamped out of the room.

Betsy realized something had to be done. For months she had retrieved the post before Jeremy returned home. But recently the postman had changed his schedule or his route. The mail came late afternoon, and often after Jeremy was home first.

She asked Annie if she could use her address.

"Of course, you can. I'll keep them safe for you."

Betsy gave her a hug. The problem was solved.

"Goddamn outsiders, poking their noses in our business," McNeary roared.

Cal knew exactly where his father stood in all this. Jeremy's store and most of the places the miners traded at were on Keweenaw property. They stood squarely on the side of management. At first sympathetic with the miners, the shopkeepers had long offered credit, but with the strike they started refusing to put bills on the 'tick.' The strike was hurting them, Jeremy included.

When Cal expressed concern for the miners, Jeremy took umbrage.

"Whose camp do you stand in, boy?" Jeremy asked his son.

"I can have sympathies."

"Sympathies are dangerous. Remember which side your bread is buttered on."

Jeremy had joined the Citizens' Alliance, a group of disgusted citizens who were tired of the endless parades, the shouts, the violence and the strike. He had been so vocal, he'd been made captain of the third district. It helped make up for the fact that business was slow. The scabs made purchases, but with so many shafts closed and miners out of work, it was not a good season economically.

He smiled. "Being made captain of our district, well, I consider it a large feather in my cap."

A peacock feather, Betsy thought to herself.

"You joined the Alliance yet, son?" Jeremy fingered the white button proudly.

"Nope."

Jeremy snorted. "You'll be tarred if you don't."

As a shaft captain, Cal was on the side of management. At least he was expected to be. With this rank came certain privileges and responsibilities. In the early days he hadn't thought about it much. He came into a situation by way of the status quo, and for a long time he hadn't questioned it. He and his brother had taken courses at the mining college in Houghton. Others had done the same. He had started as a miner, and with some education had worked his way up.

Many of the miners had enjoyed friendly relations with their bosses in the old days. Gradually, the companies had furnished churches, schools, and parks for their employees. Men felt cared for. If their tables weren't lavished with luxurious foods, they accepted that as their lot. But as the Keweenaw grew, and immigrants came from many non-English speaking countries, intimacy between employee and employer waned.

Cal's shaft and most of the others were closed. It gave him time to think about where he stood, what he really believed. Though he couldn't condone the violence that had started on the very first day of the strike, he felt sympathy for the men and their families. He knew he was straddling the fence, and that was a precarious place to sit.

It was true that this was not a partnership. The owners not only provided the setting for the work, but all the equipment for the workers to make a living. In addition, management had provided schools, parks—even supported the churches. They called it paternalism, and for a long time this had satisfied the workers.

But now accidents in the mines had doubled since the introduction of the one-man drill. Cal had attended the funerals of two from his own shaft. From the second, he was chased out of the cemetery by a distraught widow who blamed the Company for the accident. Left with seven children, she was in a desperate situation.

Cal was walking down Fifth Street when he could hear shouting from a block away. As he approached, he realized it was noise from the mob of mine workers who'd gathered to hear Redeemer speak. He joined the crowd.

"Miners in Minnesota are getting three dollars and fifty cent a day while we are only getting two dollars and fifty cents. And they only work an eight hour day. Did you know that? Are you satisfied to leave things as they are?"

Redeemer had their attention. Loud shouts of "No!" went up.

Again he was troubled by situation. He knew if he remained loyal to the company he'd become a shaft captain before too long. But he was feeling more and more uncomfortable.

Cal wished he had some knowledgeable and rational person to discuss this with. If only Roy were around.

The average weight of the strikers and their families dropped at least ten percent. Bellies hurt, children cried. The strike was hard on all who were out of work. But at least it was September— harvest season.

Annie had managed to keep up her vegetable garden. She didn't need all of those tomatoes and corn. Nor the lettuce or potatoes. She started giving the food to families who were truly hungry due to the strike. The Torys were among them— seven people there.

Other families were going hungry too. Betsy suggested a common area be set up down town, where anyone with excess vegetables could bring their food, and anyone in need of food could freely help themselves. Betsy and Patty made loaf after loaf of bread to donate to the cause. Annie and many others with gardens contributed to the tables set up on Fifth Street. Sean was enlisted to come with his wagon and take food to the poor trammers.

Although some families had too much pride to partake in the program, or distrusted food made from other ethnic groups, on the whole the program was very successful. No one need go hungry. In this season of abundance, with the good earth offering up everything from beets to barley, life didn't look quite so hard. And the program softened the hearts of many. Even families who had joined the Alliance sent their servants to the Rescue Row with donations of food.

"Who the hell's the leader of that rabble?" McNeary bellowed.

"They call him Redeemer, sir," Whipple told his boss.

"What's his real name?"

"I don't know. Don't know anyone who does."

"Hmm."

"I hear he's a lady's man," Whipple offered.

"That could be useful," McNeary replied.

"What would you like me to do?"

"I'll get Yellowbird on it." McNeary rose, dismissing his assistant.

Yellowbird was a prostitute, and an informer. She made good money from her first occupation and excellent from her second.

McNeary sent her to listen to the speeches, to notice whom he left with and where he lodged. Then he told her to be more forward, get him to notice her.

She did. In the crowd she asked questions, and he began to pay attention. Finally, one night they left together. He knew what she was, so no persuasion was required.

When the business he had engaged her for was over, they lay awake chatting. It seemed to Yellowbird that he was glad to have someone to talk to. Cautious, this man was no fool, and wasn't about to bare his soul to her or anyone else. But he did tell her what a charge it gave him to get up on the stump and command the attention of all those people.

"I suppose politicians feel that way. Actors, too," he laughed. He lit a cigarette and looked at her. "How'd you get into your line of work?"

She told him the truth. "My dad run off when I was twelve. I was the oldest kid, and two years later my ma told me it was time for me to make my own living. I knew what she meant. I knew how she was making hers."

"You've got a nice body." He dragged deeply on his cigarette. "Do you enjoy it— your work?"

She stared at him. No one had ever asked her that. "Not really. Sometimes it gets pretty scary."

"How so?"

She turned away. She didn't like talking about it.

"Tell me." He bit her nipple lightly. Then he laughed.

"Ouch! When they get out of control."

"Some of them rough you up?"

"It happens."

"Dangerous work."

"Doesn't seem to be a lot of choice. But then, if I was a man, I suppose I'd be a miner. That's dangerous too."

"Yup. You're very skilled at what you do."

She almost laughed. Usually, if they were satisfied, they said, "You're a good fuck."

She waited for him to say more about his work. She wanted to find out how really committed to the union he was.

"Do you see many accidents down below?"

"Lots." He put out his cigarette, and began to get dressed.

A week later she took a chance.

"You ever afraid one of the Citizens' Alliance men will take you down?"

"Naw. I've got eyes. Did you notice the man following us here?"

"No."

"He rides shotgun for me."

"He follows you everywhere?"

"Pretty near. I call him *Barnacle*," he smiled. "Him or one of the others are always around."

"No privacy," she quipped.

"That way I can't get into any trouble," he chuckled.

"And how did you get into *your line of work*?" She said it lightly.

"Opportunity. Challenge. It was there. I took it. Somebody had to lead the sheep."

"Does that make you the wolf?"

He gave her a wary look. Then he squeezed her lips hard with his thumb and forefinger. Finally, he laughed and kissed her.

She thought she had her answer.

A few days later she said to him, "Somebody wants to meet you."

Redeemer was escorted through the hall of the gods, as he later called it. He got a glimpse of fine art and furniture through every open doorway. He thought this would be a swell place to work.

"You've made quite a name for yourself," McNeary said.

"Thank you."

"Besides yourself, who would you say the rabble rousers are?"

"I'm not at liberty to say, sir. They pay my salary."

"And just how much do they pay you?"

"You're asking if I can be bought, sir?"

"I wouldn't have put it that way." The older man nodded, chewed on the end of his cigar, got out clippers and trimmed it properly.

"Come back if you're interested."

"In exactly what?"

"Doing the same thing you are now. But reporting to me. And telling the men it's time to hoist some rock. Union funds have run out."

The younger man gave a noncommittal nod.

"Keeping an ear out for the trouble-makers, hold-outs."

"I understand."

"I'm sure you do. I can make it worth your while."

"I'll think about it."

Redeemer left the office with a soft whistle on his lips.

Annie could tell that Frank admired her. She couldn't remember anyone showing such interest in her since she was a child. They talked as they marched along, at first mostly about the conditions in the mines and the strike, then about Citizens' Alliance which was causing the strikers so much trouble.

It wasn't long before their talk became more personal. She wanted to know if he'd always lived in Chicago, if there was any employment for women in the newspaper business. He told her he had studied journalism in a correspondence course, and no, he didn't know of any women in the business— not at his newspaper, anyway.

"But there should be. There really should. It would give a whole different point of view. Oh, I take that back. There is a Ladies' column once a week with recipes and such. But I didn't think that was what you meant."

"You're right. That's not what I meant."

Frank continued to accompany Annie in the parades. She thought he fancied himself her protector. Although she enjoyed his company, she didn't feel she needed a guard. Her conviction that what she was doing was right for her community was all the protection she needed. However, that didn't prevent her from being arrested.

The first time she was brought before Judge Foster, she was shocked to realize that this was the friendly man who'd spoken to her at a Redeemer gathering. How strange to see him now in a judge's gown.

She revealed no sign of recognition. Nor did he. She held her head high, convinced herself that she wasn't afraid.

Foster took off his glasses, and looked at her. "So you're the famous Big Annie, festering all the trouble around here."

Annie swallowed and unflinching, looked him straight in the eye. She thought she saw some kindness behind the harsh words.

"Yes sir, if you want to call it that. I call it my right to free speech, and my right to protest unfair labor practices." She stood proudly, still holding the American flag.

Judge Foster was silent. He seemed to be appraising her.

Although unnerved by him, she continued. "I believe the American constitution permits folks to gather, march and express themselves."

"In peaceful ways, yes."

Annie tried not to drop her eyes. "We mean to be peaceful, sir."

"But you aren't always, are you?"

"I cannot be responsible for everyone who follows me in the parade, but I have not advocated violence, sir."

Earl Foster nodded.

"I will let you off this time, Annie Clemenc, but I cannot abide violence, so let me be clear on this point. You will have to march peacefully. If you are brought in again for agitation and fomenting violence, I shall have to offer you a stay in the county's finest."

Annie blushed. She was dismissed.

Well, that wasn't so bad.

She was eager to tell Betsy.

"You were actually arrested?" Betsy asked in astonishment.

"Yes— dragged into court by two stout policemen."

"Oh, Annie, no!"

"It wasn't so bad. He let me off."

"This time. But you must be careful, my dear. He could put you in jail! Do curtail your emotions."

"Yes, ma'am."

Betsy gave her a hug.

Annie didn't always curtail her emotions. They ran so high, she had difficulty holding her tongue. Many of her followers did not curtail their tempers, either.

She was arrested three more times and hauled into court with a bevy of other women.

Judge Foster quickly passed sentences, then suspended them.

Many miners were ready to go back to work, but not enough of them to call off the strike. It dragged on into the cold weather.

"The pumps have been turned off in some of the shafts," Val told Annie. "And they're filling with water."

"Still, we will not give up. The company will pay attention to us."

"This is a message to the miners that they don't care how long we hold out!"

"I know. But we're not giving up, are we?" Her face broadened into a big smile.

Redeemer approached the management offices of the Keweenaw Mining Company. He was admitted by a secretary who took him back to McNeary's inner sanctum. He was beginning to feel at home here.

"You ready to talk?"

"I'm ready to listen."

The older man laid out the specifics of what he expected—persuasion, of a different kind, names of rabble rousers who wouldn't cave.

When he had finished, "Any questions?"

"Just the salary."

"What do you think you're worth?"

Redeemer threw out a figure.

McNeary whistled. "Can't go that high. I'll start you out same as a shift captain. Then we'll see how your efforts pay off, what kind of reports you send in."

Redeemer nodded.

"Sign here." A paper was pushed in front of Redeemer.

"I'll need your real name."

Redeemer hesitated. Then he picked up the pen and wrote it.

As he left the building his heart beat a little faster, just to think he might become part of management some day. Finally, he was getting some recognition. This was more exciting than a good fuck. And would last longer, too.

The man with the plaid coat stood outside watching his old friend enter the Company office. He waited until the other man came out, saw him fold a paper, and walk off whistling.

"Son of a whore!" The man with the plaid coat said. He broke a stick he was carrying against a tree, and strode off in the opposite direction.

CHAPTER SEVENTEEN

Anyone watching them for any length of time could tell they were in love. Frank was always by her side, and she favored him with many of her beautiful smiles. Still, she held him off.

"I've got a purpose, Frank. I can't afford to get distracted."

"I have one, too," he said, grabbing her around the waist when the day's parade was over.

He was patient, and finally managed to get a few stolen kisses from her one evening by her fence. Then longer ones. Annie felt sensations run through her body she didn't remember ever experiencing before. She lay in bed wondering about it. Mostly, she'd bleeen led to believe that sex was something men enjoyed and women endured. That had been her experience. But this was different. She wanted more than the scanty taste she'd had that evening. As she lay awake, it was the first time she'd let her thoughts stray from the course of the strike to anything else.

In the morning she slept later than usual. Embarrassed, knowing the women and some men would be waiting for her to lead the parade, she dressed hurriedly, skipped breakfast, and hurried out to join them.

Frank was not there. She realized as she marched along how much she missed him.

"I must get my mind back on focus. I can't afford to let him or anything distract me from my mission." She vowed to put him out of her mind, and for the most part, succeeded for the rest of the day.

But when she got home that evening his presence invaded her thoughts again.

"My God, I'm still a married woman," she moaned. "What can I be thinking?"

The next day Frank was at the corner when she left the house.

"I had to write reports yesterday," he said in way of apology.

"You don't have to come every day."

"I know. But I like to." He smiled in a way that made her stomach turn over.

They walked together toward the corner where the parade would begin. He took her hand, until she pulled away.

"People will talk," she protested. "I can't afford that kind of publicity."

People talked anyway. The sight of this out-of-town man attaching himself to Big Annie every day was fuel for gossip. Her reputation already was blown up, as the papers called her an agitator, lawbreaker and worse. To that was now added that she was a person of low moral character.

"I wouldn't care," she told Frank, "except as it may damage my standing as leader of the strikers. They don't deserve that."

She was with him during the day and thinking about him at night. No man had ever shown so much respect for her. They discussed all manner of issues, and he always listened respectfully to her opinions. He shared his thoughts, too, and told her how he'd become a news reporter.

"I grew up on a farm in rural Illinois. When I was eighteen I left home to go to the big city. Chicago held delights and fears I'd never encountered before. I began visiting local bars, picking up on the restlessness of its habitués."

"You knew even then you wanted to be a newsman?"

Their hips bumped, and again that sensation. "My God, what's happening to me?"

"Not exactly. I didn't know what I wanted. But I started listening. I heard a disgruntled man say 'Industries are growing in the east— mills and such. In Detroit, the automobile. And that revolution is moving west. You wait and see. An industrial revolution.'

"From there it was easy to write stories about them, and so I started free-lancing for the *Chicago Tribune,* always looking for the news-breaking story. I'd gotten in early, in 1910 when the newspaper changed from a broadsheet to a multiple page newspaper."

He let her read a couple of stories he'd written to send back to Chicago. Always, he'd slanted it toward her and all she'd done to lead the strikers.

"You make me sound like Joan of Arc."

"You are," he said. "I'll have to call you that in my next article."

Annie blushed, but she smiled too, to think she could have won this man's interest. And at first she tried to believe that was all it was—interest.

Her newly discovered rush of hormones couldn't refuse this young man altogether. Like her other passions, this one ran wild and untempered, keeping her awake nights when she should have fallen asleep as soon as her head touched the pillow. She imagined Frank beside her, kissing her, fondling her in places that had never been caressed. Fantasies filled her mind until at last sleep overpowered them.

"Let me at least come in for tea," he'd begged more than once. "It's cold out here."

He was right. It was November, and already there'd been several snowfalls. But she knew that wasn't the real reason. Finally she relented.

Frank stepped into Annie's home. It wasn't a bad house. It was exactly like all the others built in a row by the company, for the miners to rent. But despite its occupant's feminine efforts it had a forlorn feel, although very clean and tidy. There were no photographs except a small one which he supposed was of her parents.

"Shall I build up the fire?" he asked.

"Thank you, yes. I can't afford to keep it going all day when I'm not here."

The truth was that she didn't usually have a fire in the evening, either. After an exhausting day and a bite to eat, she took herself to bed. The house was very cold.

Conversations at her table turned to personal things. He wanted to know why she'd married Joseph. She wanted to know if he'd ever been married or had a sweetheart. No, to the first, yes to the second question.

"But she married someone else."

"I'm sorry."

"Don't be. I don't think it would have worked out."

He was touching her leg under the table. They talked on as though this wasn't happening. But when he rose and lifted her to her feet, she offered no resistance. He led her into the bedroom, and slowly unfastened her garments. She watched him as he did this, reveling in his desire for her. He smiled at her, almost shyly, and her hands reached up to unbutton his shirt.

She was amazed at the responses from her body as he touched her in different places. Her husband had never done that. With Joseph there was nothing to start with that might have excited her. But, oh my, it was so very different with Frank. She responded to him in every way. First her mouth, open and as ready as a hungry baby robin. She felt her back rise and fall as he encountered each facet of her body. And when he entered her, she could feel all parts of her swell, pulse and release. Her head swayed back and forth across the pillow. Swell, pulse and release.

When it was over, she rested on her back, but not for long. They were both impatient for more. He kissed her gently. He kissed her until her lips hurt. He forced her jaw to open so wide it hurt, but she didn't mind, and gave him more. She had never experienced such rapture.

Cal visited neighboring towns, inquiring in public places if anyone recognized the picture of his brother he was carrying. He got many false leads, but no real encouragement. He then turned to the newspapers, running classified ads in papers from Marquette to the town of Gay. When that didn't pay off, he sought assistance in cities as far away as Chicago and Detroit. He scoured all papers to see if he would get a response from someone who knew him, or better yet from his brother himself.

Cal had heard of a new drug that was supposed to cure or at least reduce symptoms of syphilis. It was called salvarsam, invented by a European scientist. Cal desperately wanted to find his brother and offer him this help. He could only hope that Roy had found out about it himself, and was using it.

Jenny gave herself to him, but not with any heart, Cal thought. If he could just find his brother and know that he was all right, then maybe he could win Jenny back.

When Cal offered a reward for the location of his brother, the responses poured in from West Virginia to California. He decided that was a bad idea.

There was one more avenue he hadn't explored. It gave him chills to think about it. Cal couldn't get it out of his head that maybe Roy had died in the explosion and no one knew. The poor rock that lay all about the scene had not been hauled out. Could his brother be lying beneath all that rubble? Although the thought of this had haunted Cal for many weeks, it was the last manner of investigation he wanted to pursue.

It would take a crew of trammers to go to Level Eight, load rock into cars, and at the other end dump the cars into skips. And there was a lot of rock to be hoisted up. If Cal could get Henry's permission to do it, he knew that he himself would have to supervise. His skin crawled at the thought of finding his brother there. And Henry wouldn't like the expense either, that probably would be for naught.

But once more he approached Henry Parker, asking that the shaft be opened. He explained his concern and the plan he had in mind. Henry was sympathetic to the mysterious disappearance of Roy Willis, but as Cal suspected, was not eager to embrace the expense of sending a crew of trammers to go down that shaft.

"I've looked everywhere for him. Run ads, made trips."

"Sorry, Can't do it, Cal. And that's final."

Annie's parents came by one Sunday afternoon in October. They seldom did; it was usually she who visited them.

"Is something wrong?" she asked.

"We're leaving for Detroit."

"Why?"

"There's work there. Good work in Mr. Ford's factory. Better pay, shorter hours," her father said.

"Your father's getting too old to work below. Surely, assembling of cars would be easier."

"I suppose so," Annie said.

"We'd like you to come with us, Annie."

"Oh, no, Mum, I couldn't do that!"

"Why on earth not? You've no man to hold you here," her mother said.

"I've my work. It's very important to me."

"You ought to get out of here before you get stoned," her father said. "What you're doing is no kind of work for a woman."

"I can't leave."

They were silent, as the autumn winds brought down a topping of leaves to cover the previous night's snowfall.

"When will you be going?" Annie finally asked.

"Day after tomorrow." Her mother sighed. "Well, I didn't really think you'd leave, so I brought something for you." She reached in a large blue cotton bag and pulled out a quilt. "It was your great-grandmother made it. I think you should have something from the old country. Will you take it, girl?"

"Of course. Oh, it's lovely."

"Well, now be careful with it. It's getting frayed here and there."

"I'll fix it. I'll put a new binding around it."

Her father was hesitant to leave, wiping his mouth, the way he always did, when he was fixing to speak.

"Your Joseph's down to the Ford place. Just thought you should know."

"How did you find out?"

"Friends, who went down before. Don't count on his coming back."

"I'm not."

There was a long silence. Annie was wondering if she'd ever see her parents again. Perhaps they were thinking the same about her.

"Write to us. Please," her mother finally said. "I'll send you the address."

"I will," said Annie.

Tezaurus brinuti o sebi," her mother said with watery eyes.

"You too— take care of yourself, *Majka*."

Annie kissed them good-bye. She went back in the house with the sadness of loss, feeling the absence of another part of her life.

Annie's friend Val Tory and other mothers took turns watching each other's children, so they could march in the parades.

They had been arrested several times. Usually, they were released within hours, but even Judge Foster was unrelenting when Annie attacked a non-union member without cause.

"That will be a ten-day sentence, Annie. You're not getting out of it."

The judge took off his glasses and looked at her.

"But you needn't serve it right now, if it doesn't suit you. You let the court know when you're ready. You have three months in which to do those ten days."

The time he gave her to delay the sentence was rather lenient, she thought.

Annie and Frank were marching down the street on a cold, blustery day in November, when a man approached her.

He tipped his hat and smiled. "You must be Big Annie."

She nodded politely. "That's what I'm called. "And you?"

He smiled modestly. "I'm known as the Redeemer."

"Ah. So we've finally met."

"Yes, ma'am."

Frank was trying to keep up with them, from behind, while taking notes.

"I have much thanks to offer you," she said, "since it seems to be largely to your efforts, that so many men have finally found their senses and joined the WFM."

"Yes, ma'am. As I am grateful to you for doing the same— with the marches and such."

"Do you know about our Women's Auxiliary? We have together made a mass of hundreds of women, who in turn speak to their husbands."

"Very commendable. You must be very tired by now, carrying this heavy flag every day, and marching for miles."

"Not as tired as you might think."

"But it's been four months now. Do you see any real progress?"

Something in his tone made Annie wary.

"Of course."

"You don't really think the Company will ever agree to a union, do you?"

Annie stopped in her tracks. She looked this man straight in the eye.

"Whose side did you say you were on?"

"Probably the biggest agitator isn't a man at all," Redeemer reported to his boss. "She leads all those marches, and gets women and men alike to follow her."

"I've heard about her."

"She's called Big Annie."

"Ah, yes."

"She needs to be stopped," Redeemer said.

"You take care of it."

Redeemer gave a lot of thought to how he'd take care of Big Annie. He turned different ideas over in his mind, relishing the taste of each. What would cause the biggest blow— to take her down, or take down those she loved?

But that wasn't all he had to think about.

Redeemer had to win the men over— convince them to do a turnabout. Did he have enough power over this assembly to reverse their course? He wasn't sure. But if he could do that, there was no telling how far he could go with this company.

He stood on the steps of the courthouse. He raised both hands to signal silence, and wiped his hand across his face.

When the crowd was still he said, "Men, you all know how hard we've tried, how we've tightened our belts. We have a good cause. We have fought hard. And we should be proud. But the time has come when we must see the writing on the wall. No more is to be gained by our willfulness in refusing to work. It's time to hoist some rock."

This shocking news ricocheted down the steps and across the lawn. Some cheered; some jeered. Finally, Redeemer managed to get the crowd quiet.

"I'm not any happier about it than you are, but we have to face reality. The Company can go on indefinitely without our work. I'm sure you've seen the scabs coming in by the trainload to take our places. If we don't claim our rightful positions, and surrender union cards, we're done for. The Company isn't looking for old friends. It's looking for men willing to hoist rock." He stopped to raise a hand and hush the crowd.

"I know, I encouraged you to stay out, and I think in the end the strike will prove to win us some gains. Maybe not immediately, but things will change." He paused. "Look men, I know you're hungry. I know your kids are. Winter is here. And Christmas is coming. Isn't it time you brought home some bacon?"

The men left disgruntled, but some went back to work. Redeemer gave many such speeches in the next few weeks. Each time he grew in confidence. He was amazed to realize the power he had.

CHAPTER EIGHTEEN

The women were gathered for another meeting.

Val was speaking. "It's been such a dreary fall, with so many men out of work, and many families struggling to keep mouths fed. And now with Christmas only a month away—"

"The children, at least, need some merry-making. We ought to do something for them," Annie said.

The other women on her auxiliary committee overwhelmingly approved.

"A party. We'll give them a party!" Annie said.

"If we put out the word, I'm sure we'll get some donations for presents."

"If we could just give each child one gift."

"That would be wonderful."

"We could arrange some games."

"Let's put a Mother Goose play together for them," Annie said.

"And we'll get someone to play Father Christmas."

The ladies left the meeting excited. It would be wonderful to see happy smiles again.

For the next several weeks they knit mittens and scarves.

So sparse were their funds that the Christmas tree could be decorated with only ten cents worth of tinsel and paper cutouts.

The party was planned for the afternoon of Christmas Eve. Because of the hostility between union and non-union men, it was decided to have one of the men stationed at the bottom of the stairs to make sure that anyone who entered was from a union family.

"I want to be there to help," Betsy told Annie.

"Oh, you can't do that!" Annie said. "Your husband would never permit it."

"I will come and I will bring my daughter, AnnaBeth. She can help, too. You will make sure they let us in, won't you, Annie?"

The afternoon of the party over five hundred people arrived at the Italian Hall, got checked by the security guard, and marched or ran upstairs to the hall. Most were children, from all ethnic groups. Miss Sawyer sat at the piano, and Christmas carols were sung in five different languages.

Val had brought all of her five children. She put the oldest, Louise, in charge of watching her younger ones, as she helped to manage the party. Some of the parents were there, but most had just dropped their children off for a happy afternoon.

It was noisy and chaotic, but everyone was deliriously happy. The women were ready to put on the play, but the children were eagerly awaiting their gifts.

"Oh, let's give them their presents now."

Louise came running up to Val. "I can't find Sammy!"

"Go back to the others before you lose them all!" Val said.

AnnaBeth tried hopelessly to corral the exuberant children into a line. They pushed past her and crowded up to the stage. Delighted squeals filled the room as little ones ripped off wrappings and discovered a new top or puzzle. Those who had their presents sought out places to enjoy them, or share with a friend. Others still clamored with excitement waiting for Santa to present a gift to them.

Suddenly, through the noise and confusion, a loud cry of "Fire!" rang out.

Laughter turned to screams and shouts. Fear choked everyone.

Children made for the stairs, stumbled and tumbled on top of each other. Presents flew in the air.

"Let go of me!"

"I've got to get to the door— let me by!"

"You're pushing me!"

The mayhem continued. Frightened children dashed for the stairway. Frightened adults tried to bring them back. In an effort to reclaim their children pandemonium parents too, were dragged into the swarm of bodies.

On the stairs, children tripped, were pushed from behind, and down they cascaded, an avalanche of humanity rolling over each other, clawing their way to the door.

Boots came down on a child's head, broke an arm or smashed a breast.

Like lemmings they raced, colliding headlong at the exit. The door could not be opened. Screams were heard throughout the building.

Annie realized that there was no fire, that this was some kind of cruel prank. She shouted to others, but could not be heard above the cacophony of screams and cries in the room.

Annie, Val and other parents ran to join hands to form a barricade near the stairwell, preventing more children from diving to their destruction.

A stricken Betsy came running up to Annie. "Have you seen AnnaBeth?"

"No, no, I haven't."

Betsy joined the line. She didn't know if AnnaBeth was still in the room, or below her on the stairs. Neither did the other parents.

Someone yelled, "I saw him! He was wearing a Citizen's Alliance white button on his coat!"

"I did too!"

"He had his coat collar turned way up— I couldn't see his face."

Two who saw him were clubbed unconscious before they could report anything.

The screaming at the bottom of the stairs stopped. They were crushed together. There was no air for breath.

Whistles pierced the darkness of late afternoon. Firemen and others— some of them Alliance Members— arrived to save the living and to remove the bodies.

When the firemen got to the door they were sickened by what they saw. The bodies were so tightly crushed together, they couldn't be separated. They were stacked five high.

The firemen raised ladders in the back of the building to help the living to safety. Then they used the ladders to remove bodies— from the top downward.

Annie tried to revive a dying boy with water. She sat with him, willing him to come back, but nothing she could do revitalized him. Timmy Brodsky was dead.

Val ran around like a crazed person calling for her children. None responded.

Outside, men on horseback tried to hold the crowd back.

A woman screamed, "My son's in there! Let me in."

"Nobody's going in."

"I have to get him!"

The bodies were taken by motor cars to the Red Jacket Town Hall, used as a temporary morgue.

No one had been able to identify the guilty party for sure.

The line stretched out a mile into the winter darkness of Red Jacket, as parents, relatives and friends came to identify the dead. There were seventy-four bodies. All but eleven were children. Even with all their experience of the accidents and deaths in the mines, never had anything so shocking happened to this community.

Val, supported by her husband, finally climbed the steps of the Town Hall. One by one, they identified their children. At the end she fainted. Only Sammy had escaped. He'd been playing on a partial fire escape with other boys.

In a daze of pain and disbelief, Val wandered the streets for days calling for her children.

Betsy was one who stood in the long line of parents to look for her daughter. She prayed and prayed that somehow AnnaBeth had survived. Many children had been led down the ladders erected by the firemen. Perhaps she should be looking at these first. But as she stood beside other parents choking, screaming and gasping in horror, her feet led her into the tomb of the dead. Betsy felt a great tightening in her belly. Row upon row of children lay next to each other, covered with white sheets. They looked asleep, as if at a slumber party.

There she was, her dear, sweet AnnaBeth. Betsy stared at her a few moments, trying to take it in, make herself believe it— that her daughter was dead, would never speak to her or offer her sweet smile again.

She turned away and numbly left the building. Somehow she found her way home, though she didn't remember even leaving the hall.

At home, Jeremy roared out his frustration and anger.

"What the hell was she doing there?" he bellowed at his wife. "You took my daughter to a party for union families?"

She fell near the stairs in a faint.

Later, she had all she could do not to shout out her secret. Often she had imagined what it would be like to tell him. Feelings of shame, vengeance or relief would fill her, depending on the mood she was in— whether she wanted to punish him or find absolution, which she doubted he would offer.

His ranting didn't let up for three days. There seemed little point in answering him. She seldom did, lest it provoke an apoplectic fit.

It was difficult to tell which bothered him most— AnnaBeth's death or the public disgrace that his daughter had been at the union party.

For the most part Betsy stayed in her room, removing herself as best she could from the clamor of this domestic scene.

She would allow only Cal to come in and talk to her. Just his presence was a comfort.

Then Annie came. Cal ushered her upstairs to his mother's room. The women held each other, cried together, and said little for the first hour.

Cal was so shocked at his sister's death that he forswore any thought of joining the alliance. He didn't know what he was going to do, only that he wanted nothing more to do with management. He buried his head in the little book of Shakespeare sonnets AnnaBeth had given him. He didn't know what he was reading half the time, but it didn't matter; it was his tangible tie to his beloved sister.

The horror of the day brought many together. People of different ethnic groups, who didn't even know each other, hugged and prayed in their own languages as thousands mourned the dead.

The entire community was shocked and grief-stricken by the tragedy.

The Citizen's Alliance denied any responsibility, but the Union was sure it was one of them who had called out the fatal word. The Alliance collected twenty-five thousand dollars for the victims' families. When it was presented to the president of the WMF, who had come from Denver, he refused it.

"It's blood money. We will bury our own."

Going door to door, the Alliance members encountered repeated refusals when they tried to distribute money to members of the union.

"Don't take anything from them!" they shouted to their neighbors, up and down the streets.

Members of the Alliance, who had gathered most of the money, were offended. These were the children of the community. Didn't they have a right to mourn them too, to reach out and help? The culprit who'd instigated the terrible avalanche of children down the stairs was only one person. How could the mine workers blame everyone in the alliance for this misdeed?

Fathers made the little coffins for their children. Sometimes strangers came to offer assistance. Wherever hammering and sawing were heard that week, they were sure signs that the little boxes were being made. Though they often worked in silence, a deep bond developed between them.

Two of Dennis Tory's mates came to help him. Then a German strode into Tory's yard with tools and some boards. It was obvious why he was there.

Dennis Tory could only nod as his chin quivered with profound astonishment and emotion.

The man introduced himself as Johann, and Dennis showed the stranger where he could work.

Johann gestured with his arms asking how long the box should be.

Tory gestured with arms giving him the answer. It need only be three feet long.

It seemed the German knew little or no English. The foursome worked in total silence.

As each coffin was finished, it was painted white.

They finished this most heartbreaking of tasks as the sun fell from the blustery, darkening sky. Denny's mates left first, and only the German was there, the last to finish painting.

Johann completed his offering, brushed himself off, and collected his tools. He looked up at Tory. Their eyes spoke to each other in the language of shared sorrow that no spoken language could have expressed better.

Just as Johann turned to leave, Tory reached out his hand and said, "*Danka.*" It was one of the few German words he knew. The German took it in a firm grip.

That night under a cold, clear canopy of stars, Dennis Tory carried the little coffins to the cold shed. The bodies lay on blankets from their beds. Four times he lifted child and blanket together and lovingly placed it in the proper coffin. Two boys, two girls. He kissed each and mumbled a prayer learned in childhood: *If I should die before I wake, I pray the Lord, my soul to take.* He stood looking at them, burning their faces into his memory. Finally, he closed the coffin lids and nailed them down.

On December 28th, the funerals were held at five different churches in their native tongues. A thick blanket of snow had fallen since Christmas Eve. But no amount of the clean white icing could cleanse the town of the recent carnage. Horse-driven hearses carried the coffins of the adults. Fathers and brothers carried the little coffins of the children down the street.

Jeremy wrestled for days with his conflicting emotions. His daughter was to be buried, but goddammit, why was she at the fucking party for union members? He couldn't forgive Betsy for taking her there.

Maybe she wasn't his daughter at all. Certain things he'd long wondered about— she didn't look like the rest of the family, she didn't act like any of them. He knew that before he met her Betsy had been engaged to a young man. There were those letters her parents had handed over to him, but he hadn't read them. Although he'd been tempted, he couldn't bring himself to invade her privacy. But he didn't give them to her either.

A couple of times he thought Betsy was about to say something. Well, he didn't know, wasn't at all sure he wanted to. If she'd told him the girl wasn't his, he couldn't be responsible for his behavior.

But he'd be damned if he'd march along with the very people he'd been fighting against. He just couldn't go.

But then he felt guilty. Not to go to your child's funeral? The torment was such that he couldn't stand to stay home, either.

He decided to take a walk. Actually he knew where he was going, but he didn't want to admit it. There was only one way he could get some relief. He approached her porch, passed it up, and circled back. Finally he mounted the steps and knocked on the door.

She came to the door in a Japanese kimono, and stared at him.

"What are you doing here?"

"What do you think?"

"I mean—"

He pushed past her, and climbed the stairs to her room. It was a familiar room; he'd been here many times before. Yellow Bird followed him.

He motioned for her to undress. She slipped out of her kimono and undergarments and sat on her bed. Jeremy was still towering above her when she said, "Why are you here now?"

"What do you mean?"

She dropped her eyes. "I heard about your daughter."

"You leave her out of it."

"I thought the funeral was going on now."

"It is," he answered curtly.

"Well, why aren't you there?"

"Stop!" he ordered.

"Jesus!" she said. "What kind of father are you?"

"I said 'stop! Enough!"

"Well, maybe I won't stop."

He'd been in the process of removing his belt. Suddenly, the fury he'd been feeling all week was unleashed. He swung the belt, striking her across the breast.

She screamed and turned over to protect her breasts. He continued lashing her, across the back and buttocks. He held her down by the hair, as she scrambled to escape the blows. Finally he realized what he was doing. She peeked up at him from the floor on the opposite side of the bed. He saw in her the frightened face of the little girl who'd been his AnnaBeth. Tossing the belt to the ground, he flung himself on her settee and sobbed. It was twenty minutes before he sat up, and got dressed.

"I'm sorry." He threw some bills on the bed and left.

Cal and Betsy walked behind AnnaBeth's hearse. The tears she shed for her daughter mixed with the shame and pain she felt that Jeremy had refused to attend the funeral.

Cal had made his sister's coffin by himself. When it was finished he tucked the poem he'd written to her for Christmas inside. Somehow, he hoped in some way it would comfort her. He hoped she could still feel the words through the tears that covered them.

Val and Denny Tory were helped by Denny's mates to carry the four little coffins of their family. Two of these men had helped make the rough-cut pine boxes in the days before.

When the services were over, a procession was held from the churches to the cemetery, where most bodies were buried in a common grave dug by the strikers. More than fifty thousand mourners took part in the five mile hike through the snow from the churches to the cemetery. Many of the mourners were members of the Citizens' Alliance.

Hoisting the heavy flag she'd carried so many times before, Annie led the procession with tears streaming down her face.

More tears were shed and prayers said at the cemetery. More hugs, too.

Some fainted at the mere sight of the long trenches, and some from the long trek through the snow to get there.

Finally, like a defeated army, the trudge home began, quiet groups turning off to different villages in the silence of the night.

Such a tragedy would never be forgotten. The wound was too deep. The parades stopped.

CHAPTER NINETEEN

It had been a dismal winter, but Jenny was smiling one evening, and Cal wanted to know what was on her mind.

"You have a secret," he prodded.

"Yes, that's true," she teased.

"Well, aren't you going to tell me?"

"If it will make you happy."

"How do I know if you don't tell me?" Cal prodded.

"I— we are going to have a baby."

Cal looked stunned at first, trying to grasp what she'd said.

"Well," Jenny asked, "are you happy about it or not?"

He broke into a big smile. "Of course, I am. Oh, Jenny, that's splendid!"

He took her in his arms. "When?"

"This summer— June."

"We will be a family! That's grand, my darling."

Jeremy's former high spirits deserted him. Business was slow, with the miners out of work. Invitations to important social functions had ceased, he felt, because of Betsy's behavior. Everyone knew she had been at the party for the miners; and that reminded them of that awful display at the Fund Raiser. Then there was AnnaBeth— he hadn't even gone to her funeral. And Roy— where the hell was he? Was he even alive, this son he'd placed all his hopes in?

Something close to despair overcame him.

For weeks he tried to win back his wife's affections. He complimented her meals. He bought her gifts. She remained distant. At night if he approached her, she'd have none of it.

One night he ran out of patience. She lay on her back, her legs tightly together. He rose over her and spread her arms wide to each side, where he held them tightly.

"Our preacher tells us," he said between his teeth, "that each must bear a cross in this life. Well, woman, you are my cross!"

Jeremy pressed her arms down hard and held them there for several moments. Then he rose and left the room. He never slept there again.

The strike did not end— not yet. More men went back to work. They had to feed their families. Others packed up and left the Upper

Peninsula. Their hopes withered by disappointment, many headed south to Detroit, where Henry Ford was paying five dollars a day.

"I'm fed up with mining— the whole thing. I want to get out of here," Cal told his wife.

Jenny wasn't surprised. He'd been open with her about his feelings.

"I hate the position I'm in. I'm supposed to be with management, but I couldn't join the Alliance. I feel for those laborers. I care about the union men and their families. There is no happy medium."

She nodded.

"And Pa not going to his own daughter's funeral, because his loyalty is so deep-rooted in management. The whole thing stinks."

"Where would we go?"

"Downstate. The auto industry is up-and-coming. Maybe I can get into engineering or something."

"When were you thinking of leaving?"

"Not until the baby comes. What do you think? Do you agree with me?"

"Yes, if it's for the best."

"I believe it is."

"What's wrong, Jenny?"

They lay together in bed. Cal had tried to arouse his wife, but Jenny had been putting him off for days.

"Nothing."

"Don't say that. Please tell me."

"I'm with child, Cal"

"I know that."

"I think the desire leaves a woman when she's with child."

Cal wasn't sure how to respond to that. He figured it made sense from nature's point of view. If the purpose of sex was procreation, and his seed had taken, then there was no further need for intimacy at this time.

But he wasn't at all sure that Jenny's explanation was the real reason for her withdrawing. She was pleasant and supportive during the day, but at night he saw more of her back than he cared to.

He thought about the change— how uninhibited she'd been on their trip to Chicago. But that was before the explosion, before Roy had disappeared.

Roy wanted out. Oh, God, how he wanted out. At first he'd known it as a sanctuary, an underground cathedral. The depths of the mine were home to Roy.

But then it had become a prison, and he its prisoner.

He knew it had been winter for a long time, but then winters were always long in the Upper Peninsula.

Roy had traveled far along one of the drifts. And taken a branch to the left. When that split off, he'd taken the path to the right. He knew this drift extended under Lake Superior. He could hear the waves during a storm. He depended on the fresh water that trickled down the walls for drinking, and for an occasional wash of his clothes and himself.

The temperature in most of the mine was in the nineties. But near Lake Superior, where a lot of water dripped down, it formed icicles on the ground— ice stalagmites— sticking straight up from the ground, several feet high and close together. When it got warm, they'd melt. Roy didn't stay in this freezing cave, but it was a good source of water; he'd take a couple of them back to his lair and let them melt. He'd established his habitat mid-way between the choking heat and the icicles.

The mine was a maze— every drift crazily following the vein of copper— never in a straight line.

He'd brought blankets, and he was skilled at making a fire. He had with him two knives— a hunting knife and a pocket knife. With all the timbers holding up the walls, there was no shortage of wood. He cut shavings from them to start the fire, and larger pieces to keep it going. He'd brought candles— lots of them. When the carbide helmet lamp gave out, he'd need something for light. He'd brought one change of clothing, for he expected to be here for a while.

He had also brought a supply of dried venison, which he knew would only last a couple of weeks. What he would live on after that he hadn't wanted to think about. When the meat was gone, he endured three days of hunger before he brought himself to do it— kill and eat a rat. The first few times he puked. But in the weeks to come he got used to it.

If he were lucky he'd trap the baby ones. Sometimes he caught a bat. Numerous mushrooms grew in the caves, and he knew the ones that were safe to eat. So that was his diet. However it disgusted him, it kept him alive.

He was never warm enough. Sometimes he'd shake and shiver. A few times he had chills and a fever. Was this the result of the climate, or was his disease advancing?

He had come down here to get away from prying eyes, from the prospect of being arrested, to hide away with his illness. But now, none of that seemed to make sense. He wanted to get out of here. He'd tried for months to find the fissure that had allowed him to descend into this drift in the first place. But wandering down one winding path leading to another that split off in different directions always ended in frustration and a sense of madness.

Vehicles of all kinds were plentiful in Red Jacket. But some pedestrians had not learned to take precautions when crossing in front of them. If an automobile moved along too slowly, it likely would stall, which would require the driver to get out in front of it and crank up the starter again. They did not like to slow down too much. In bad weather, the brakes were of little use, the tires being likely to slip on the ice.

For that reason, many automobile owners put their cars up for the winter months, but others slid down the slippery streets. Trucks were numerous too, and often expected right of way as they barreled down the streets at high velocity.

Such was the case on a Monday morning in January of 1914, when Jeremy Willis stepped out in front of a large logging truck with a full load. Reports of witnesses were conflicting. Some said the driver honked as Mr. Willis started out in the street, and others said he did not. Some said Willis walked right out in the street knowing full well that a truck was coming down on him.

The question remained open. Was the victim too distracted to notice the car? Did he assume the driver would slow down or was able to stop? Did he think he had time to cross the street safely? Or did he, in fact, walk out in front of that truck deliberately?

The newspapers did not mention the last possibility. Neither did the Methodist preacher at the funeral. The paper did note that the stoic widow, on the arm of her son Calvin, did not shed a tear.

With too much death on her mind, Betsy turned her thoughts back to happier times. She thought about those early days with Peter Follett, the young man who she'd been madly in love with. Peter was going east to prepare to become a doctor, and when he finished at the university they would marry.

She had been on the wild side then, and so in love with him that they'd been foolish, and she had become pregnant. She suspected it before he left for college, but wasn't sure. Within weeks after he'd gone she was certain, and waited desperately for his letters. He'd promised to write to her, but week after week no letter came. She had no way of reaching him.

Betsy couldn't understand it. He'd shown her his love, he'd made promises. Her mother told her to forget him— it would be years before he'd be in a position to marry. Not only all the years of schooling, but time to pay back the loans incurred for that purpose. Panic set in as she waited. Perhaps she could get an abortion, but who could she find to do such a thing?

She hadn't told her parents. Looking back, she realized that had been a mistake. They would have contacted Peter's parents and insisted that Peter come home and 'do the right thing'.

Meanwhile, Jeremy Willis had proposed to her. Her parents urged her to accept. He had a good business running the Company grocery store. He was well established in the community. He would certainly be able to provide well for her. It seemed the only solution.

When she accepted, there was still the question: should she tell him? Now? Later, or not at all?

He was delighted that she wanted an early wedding— "While the weather's still nice," she'd said.

And so she'd dried her tears, married this man, and determined to make the best of it. She had decided not to tell her husband, and he believed that the baby just came early— or tried to, anyway.

He did provide well for her. They were one of the first families in Red Jacket to have electricity, own a phone and a washing machine.

"Why do you think Pa died?" Cal asked her one night.

"What do you mean?"

"Do you think it was an accident, or—"

"Or what? That he took his own life?"

"Well, do you? I mean what do you think?"

"I don't think about it much." She surprised him by adding, "I'm not sure it matters."

Cal was shocked at her response, but when he thought about it, it made sense. He'd always taken his parents for granted, but upon contemplation realized he had never seen much affection between them. He'd just figured older folks didn't feel it, or at least didn't show it. And his parents argued a lot.

Now that her husband was gone, Betsy felt she'd been released from a tight corset— free and unsuppressed. She could now indulge in grieving all she wanted to for AnnaBeth, for poor Roy, and for all the children who'd died at the Italian Hall. She could join the Women's Auxiliary, and she did.

She and Annie could comfort each other— she could even go to Annie's house. She didn't have to care what others gossiped about. Many evenings they sat together reliving the tragedy. Perhaps they hoped that by doing so, the horror and the nightmares would dissipate.

For Annie, it was almost impossible to shed her feeling of responsibility. She talked to Frank as well.

"I feel responsible, I'm the one who planned it."

"You're not responsible, you know you're not."

He was holding her quietly in her bed, as he had for many nights since the tragedy. There had been no love-making, but his gentle touch and holding her was very comforting. He rocked her back and forth, and let her tears slip once again onto his shoulder.

It was January, and Annie decided it was time to serve her ten days in jail for assaulting a non-union member.

On the other side of her cell she heard someone banging something against the floor. It sounded like the iron bed was being raised and thrown down.

When it was otherwise quiet, she heard crunching in the walls, and realized it must be termites. The single window had probably never been cleaned. A collage of cobwebs from different time-periods filtered the light. The smell of old tobacco polluted the air. When she lay on the bed the smell of urine and feces assaulted her nose. But she was so miserable, it mattered little to her where she spent her days and nights.

Frank visited her every day, offering his brand of sunshine to her life.

To her surprise, Judge Foster visited her on the second day. He looked embarrassed.

Annie motioned him to the single chair. She sat on the cot.

"It's chilly in here," he commented.

She nodded, wondering why he'd come.

"How are you getting on?"

"All right." She put on a brave smile.

"I'm sorry you're in here. I felt obliged—"

"It's a good time to reflect on all that's happened."

She looked thinner to him. "Are you getting enough to eat?"

"Yes."

"Is there anything I can get you?"

"If you could spare an extra blanket—"

"Yes, of course."

They sat in silence for a time. Finally, Earl rose to go.

"I just want you to know . . ." He cleared his throat in a way indicating he wanted to say something, but he swallowed it. He finished with, "I respect you a great deal, and all you stand for."

He left.

His words were such a shock to her that again the tears ran down her face. Being in this cell and despised by so many, Annie had felt utterly alone. His kind words cracked a hard shell that had formed around her heart.

Within an hour a blanket was brought to her cell.

When she was released from jail, Annie offered what help she could to the families in need.

Frank said, "I must go back to Chicago, to work. Please come with me."

"I can't. Not now. I have to see this thing through."

He wanted to tell her how useless it was, but he knew it was the only thing that kept her going. She was driven.

He waited another week, and tried hopelessly to persuade her to join him.

"I want to marry you. You know that, don't you?"

She hugged him. "Yes, I think I do."

"You'll apply for a divorce?"

"Yes, I will do that."

"It shouldn't be too hard to get. After all, he abandoned you."

She nodded.

"Then will you— marry me?"

"I will, someday. But I can't stop— not just yet. You do understand, don't you, Frank?"

He nodded, and wrapped her in his arms.

The night before he left, they made love as they never had before, and the first time since the massacre. As if trying to pour all her pent-up frustration and anger into this one night, she took the initiative, mounted Frank and rode him to exhaustion. She had conquered something; she didn't know what, but at least for the moment it felt as though she'd been triumphant in some way. When it was over they lay quietly together. She was grateful to this man for permitting her this victory.

Then, arousing her again, Frank stroked her lightly in the places she liked to be caressed. He applied pressure where he'd learned she enjoyed it. She obeyed him, be it verbal or physical command. Just as she loved the role of leader during the day, she enjoyed being submissive in these ventures of the night. It left her feeling that every note in her body was aligned, in tune. This was hard for her to understand, but she came to accept it. She needn't do anything but lie in the serenity of love.

CHAPTER TWENTY

The strike dragged on through the cold and blustery spring. It finally ended on Easter, with a snivel. Beleaguered miners, who hadn't enjoyed a decent meal in months, realized they weren't getting anywhere. Even Redeemer, the man they'd put so much faith in, had capitulated. What was the point in fighting the battle now?

It seemed ironic to Annie that the worst of it happened at Christmas time, and the end came at Easter, April 13th. She tried to find some connection between Easter and the end of their struggles. What had risen, besides their rage? There had to have been some gains.

It was spring, according to the calendar, but the snow was coming down so thickly that April evening, he couldn't see across the street. That suited Redeemer just fine. He wanted to get out in the fresh air, and not be seen by anyone in this white-out. He strolled out of town. He tilted his head up and caught some of the flakes on his tongue. How new and clean it felt. And how cool on his eyelids. No wind, just large flakes falling slowly.

His ears had been trained to hear any extraneous sounds. A couple of times he thought he heard footsteps— the crush of boots in the snow, but when he checked, he saw nothing but more snow. Maybe one of his *eyes* following him— probably Flem, his barnacle, as he called him. He didn't remember asking anyone, but maybe he had. God, they were a loyal bunch.

So the strike had finally ended today. He could relax. He wouldn't have to give any more speeches. He'd made an impression with the Company, though, and he was sure they'd find him some important work to do. Hopefully, it wouldn't be as stressful or dangerous as persuading the men first to strike, and then to go back to work.

He reached in his pocket and felt a prick on his finger, pulled it out and saw a drop of blood. He sucked it off, reached back in his pocket, grasped the offending white pin and threw it into a snow bank. It had practically given him away. Maybe he should leave this place, get out of town, before fingers began to point.

Suddenly, he felt the crush of his windpipe as he was grabbed from behind. At the same time he felt the prick of a blade on his chest. He made a fierce effort to turn around but he was held in a vise grip.

"Don't speak."

Redeemer recognized the voice.

"You've betrayed me. You betrayed us all. Collected our union dues, then turned coat and worked for the Company. Snake in the grass."

"There was no—"

"Shut up."

"—point in—" he choked out.

"I said shut up."

"What do you want?"

"You're gonna die. You got that, Walter?"

"No, no, let me explain—"

Walter felt a deep, sharp pain in his chest. Incredulous, he turned sideways, and clinging to his assailant, dropped slowly to the ground. The blood gushed freely, in sharp contrast to the newly fallen snow. Walter lay on his side, focusing on the scarlet flow carving a stream in the deepening whiteness. As his lights dimmed he saw the crimson rivulet, but the white stuff seemed to be trying to conceal it. Then, just as fast, Walter's blood carved through the falling snow. He tried to speak but couldn't.

He died with a question on his face.

The new sheriff didn't do much to discover the killer. The sheriff was still trying to figure out who shot the Jane brothers in Painesdale. Was it men from the Union, or the Alliance trying to make it look like Union members killed them?

There were many faithful followers at Redeemer's funeral who still believed in him. But there were also many who felt betrayed, and stayed away.

Cora Foster poured maple syrup over her pancakes. "Did they ever solve Walter Radcliff's murder, Earl? I never heard you say,"

"No one was arrested," Earl answered.

"That's so queer," Cora said. "The Redeemer turning out to be Walter."

"He had a lot of people fooled."

"But you knew who he was."

"Yes."

"Why do you suppose he was murdered?"

"He was a turncoat. The union was paying him big money, and then he started working for the Company."

"Oh, God bless Mary, and Jesus to boot!" She held her fork in midair, while syrup dripped off her pancake and ran down her arm.

"Do you know who killed him?"

"No. Just got a hunch." Earl poured himself more coffee, and filled Cora's cup.

"Then why don't you get him arrested?"

"That's not my job, anymore, Cora." A sly grin crossed his face. "Some would say that whoever did it performed a real community service."

"Is that true?" Cora wiped the syrup off her arm.

"A lot of miners felt betrayed." He stuffed half a sausage in his mouth. "Good breakfast, Cora."

James McNeary sipped his brandy with the newspaper man.

"It's finally over. The goddamn strike is finally over."

"You held out, James. Got to give you credit."

"Well, I'll make some improvements, but the one-man drill is here to stay."

"Then you're satisfied," Able said.

"I did not give in to these changes as concessions to the union. But as a generous and concerned employer, I will take the paternal role as I always have, and provide 'betterments' when and where necessary."

The reporter nodded in strong agreement.

"Have some more brandy, Able."

Another favorable article would surely be coming out. The brandy was good. And so was life.

A congressional committee was sent to the Copper Country. Hearings were held, and people from all sides testified. It included Harry Berglund's report from the company that had sent him to the mine. In the end, the Keweenaw was blamed for most of the violence, and the committee declared working conditions unsafe.

After all was said and done, the chairman of the committee told a reporter he felt the Copper Country was a feudal fiefdom in which King James ruled over his serfs.

The union had failed to get the two-man drill back, or be recognized as a union. But with government pressure, Keweenaw did offer an eight hour day and three dollars a day wage. There had been gains.

Frank called. "Will you come now?"

"Soon," she replied. "I am not going to let the fight for just labor practices die."

"What now?"

"First of all, you'll be happy to know that I've filed for divorce. I'm told there's a very good chance that it will go through unchallenged."

"I'm very glad to hear that."

"And in the meantime, I'm going on a tour of the mid-west to speak for organized labor."

"Annie, I want you *now*."

"Patience, my dear. Please? I must finish my work."

In May she set off for a tour of the mid-west, determined to raise funds for the families of the Italian Hall tragedy, and to spur interest in the common cause of labor. At the train station she was given a beautiful feathered hat by her supporters.

As the train pulled away midst tears, cheers and good wishes she shouted, "We would rather die than give up!"

Betsy had put off the distasteful task of going through Jeremy's things. When she finally did, she found a bundle of letters under an old stack of papers in his desk drawer. She was amazed to see that they were addressed to her. They were from Peter! What were they doing here? She saw they were sent to her at her parents' home, and dated before she married Jeremy.

That could only mean her parents had withheld them from her! And how did Jeremy get them? Her parents must have passed them on to him, perhaps suggesting that at some time in the future, if he felt it appropriate, he could present them to her. But he never had. They had been opened and read— by her parents, Jeremy, or all. She didn't know.

Fury rose in her. What right did any of them have to keep these precious letters from her?

She took them downstairs, made herself a cup of tea. Shaking, she sat down to read them.

But first she held the bundle against her breast, and let her mind travel back to the days they'd been together. Happy in the sunshine, happy in the fog, they had not noticed a single fault in the other. They had been passionately aroused by nature, by poetry, by each other.

In the spring, when they first starting seeing each other, they'd hike into the woods with a picnic lunch. Just delighted in each other's company, they marveled at the many wild flowers. They inhaled the unforgettable arbutus which filled the woods with its sweet musky fragrance. And kissed. Oh, yes, how they'd kissed. She could even now relive the moist warmth of his lips against hers.

She remembered the summer of their wild madness, and the settings of these ardent interludes. When hot, humid days bore down on them, the forest with its parasol of verdant leaves provided a cool respite. The floor of the woodland, covered with pine needles and moss, added to the intimacy. Here they made love for the first time. The infamous mosquitoes found their sweet flesh. For the most part they ignored them, batting at only a few of the most tenacious. When they got home, Betsy had so many bites folks wondered if she had the measles. Peter, who escaped this insult, decided the insects didn't care for the flavor of his flesh.

Betsy smiled, remembering.

Another time, before they learned to take a blanket, they brought back with them another souvenir of their ardor: poison ivy. Peter had it on his elbows, and she on her shoulders. What an itchy time they'd had for three weeks! Later, they could laugh about it, and wonder that they'd been able to conceal it.

Once, they were in the bottom of a wooden canoe, where the ribs of the boat pressed up against her back as Peter pressed down upon her body. She hadn't complained. It was so heavenly to be locked together with the man she loved. The song of their love-making had been louder than the discomfort of the canoe ribs.

Oh, the discomforts they'd suffered in the fervor of their love.

Betsy squeezed the letters in her hand as she remembered the feel of his hand— the little depression between his thumb and forefinger. She could bring back his touch caressing the back of her neck and all the way down her back. She could re-know the warmth of his breath in her ear, the taste of his salty skin. And she could relive the tumultuous sensations of his mouth in the place where her legs met.

For more than an hour she savored the sweetness and heat of that time.

It was clear from the first letter that Peter had not broken it off with Betsy at all. In fact, his many amorous remarks only verified his affection for her. As painful as it was, Betsy forced herself to continue reading right up through the last one. His letters became more and more anxious, asking again and again why he hadn't heard from her. Did she no longer care for him? Had she met someone else? Perhaps his address was not clear, so he printed it very clearly in the body of the letter.

Reading these missives was like walking through the broken pieces of her past.

The last letter was dated September 5, 1886. This was after she was promised to Jeremy. What gave parents the right to manipulate their children's lives? No doubt they had her best interest in mind. She was nevertheless very angry.

Those letters had been written so very long ago. There was no way of resurrecting the past.

Peter Follett had finished his studies out east and come back to Red Jacket to practice medicine. Betsy knew he was there. But in all these years she'd refused to go to him, professionally or personally. Although they lived only a few miles apart, they had not spoken in all these years.

Bitter tears rolling down her cheeks mixed with sobs of joy as she realized this man had not abandoned her. He had loved her deeply.

Then a shadow of resentment brushed by as she thought of all the spilled years. It was too late now.

CHAPTER TWENTY-ONE

Annie finished her mid-west tour in a joyous spirit of success. People had heard of her before her arrival. She'd been in newsreels, and they looked forward to her appearance in their towns and cities. She had collected thousands of dollars for the survivors of the Italian Hall tragedy, and convinced many of the value of organized labor.

She was ready to come home. In the spring of 1914 she appeared before the court, and Judge Earl Foster granted her a divorce. She was so happy that when the business was finished, she just stood there smiling.

Finally he said, "Is there something else?

"Sir, if I may be so bold, I was wondering if you would officiate at my wedding."

Earl broke out a broad grin. "Ah, you mean the newspaper man who seems most devoted to you?"

"I do."

"I'd be glad to, Annie. When's the happy event to be?"

"We haven't set a date yet."

"Well, when you do, let me know. I'd be most delighted to see you a smiling bride."

"Thank you, sir."

"I've never known anyone so brave, so determined in my life. This is the least I can do to pay my respects."

Betsy was taking Annie to the best women's shop in town. Although Annie had refused the offer twice, Mrs. Willis had insisted on buying the wedding gown for her.

They had lunch afterwards at Linden's Tea House. Betsy told her friend about the letters. In fact she told her the whole story about Peter. She had never told anyone before.

"But I shouldn't be talking about this. Not when it's your special, happy time."

Annie ignored the apology. "What will you do? Will you see him now?"

"I don't know. He's married."

The day finally arrived. Frank had come north, and all was ready. Judge Foster would be presiding. Betsy was to be matron of honor, and Cal best man, with his wife close by.

Cal was nervous that Jenny might have her baby that day. She was already a week overdue. But that concern faded as the day progressed.

No others were at the ceremony itself, but Betsy had gotten the word out that all Annie's friends and followers were invited to an outdoor reception afterwards. When she stepped out on the porch in her fancy gown and the feathered hat her followers had given her, cheers and whistles rose that could be heard around the block.

Betsy had furnished lemonade and wedding cake. Some of the men brought their own flasks of whiskey. Someone played a mouth organ and another a fiddle, while several danced to the tunes. Frenchie put on his own little show, miming a happy couple— first as the bride, then as the groom. He could make himself look like two people, with his back to the audience and his arms around his neck or chest.

Sean Sullivan sang the Irish love song, *Love Thee Dearest, Love Thee?* The answer was, "Yes, 'til death I'm thine".

Annie went up to him to give her thanks.

He peered at her closely. "Is that the little pin we gave you?"

"It is, and I wear it every day."

Sean could hardly believe it. "You don't, now."

"Oh, but I do. It reminds me that if a bumblebee can work against gravity and lift his weight with those tiny wings, then so can I."

It brought tears to Sean's eyes. He shook her hand gratefully in his. When she'd left he turned to Michael Leary and said brightly, "Right fancy shindig."

Flowers were thrown at the couple, and flowers were handed to them. They were showered with baskets of fruits and vegetables from the well-wishers' gardens. Even hand-embroidered pillow cases and napkins were given to them. Annie was so touched that once more tears flowed down her cheeks.

"Settling down now, are you, Mrs. Shavs?" asked Sean.

Mrs. Shavs. She had to smile. She'd have to get used to this new name.

It was a joyous occasion. The men imbibed and joked and the women chatted. No one wanted to leave. The sun was finding its way to bed before the guests found theirs.

Jenny had a very long labor, over thirty hours. When the baby finally came, it was a girl.

"Is she healthy?" asked Cal, who had been pacing in and out of the house.

"Seems to be perfect, to my eyes. Or were you meaning your wife?" replied the midwife.

"Well, both, actually. Can I see them?" Cal wiped sweat from his neck and face.

"Your wife is resting. It was a long haul for her."

"But she's all right?"

"Oh, yes. She's worn out, poor soul. She had to do most of the work, the baby being a bit lazy." She laughed. "Just give her a bit of time, eh?"

When he was finally allowed to see Jenny and the baby, he took off his shoes and crept into the room. He thought he'd never seen a sweeter picture of mother and child. The baby had fallen asleep at Jenny's breast, and Jenny's eyes were closed too. She opened them when Cal tiptoed in.

"Jenny," he whispered, "How are you feeling?"

"I'm happy, now that it's over. Isn't she beautiful?"

"Absolutely. I'm sorry you had to suffer so long." He bent over and kissed her.

"It was worth it." She motioned him to sit on the bed.

Soon he was resting on his elbow. Gently, he moved closer to his wife and child. As Jenny's eyes were closing, he pulled his feet up beside hers. Cal was still in awe at this picture of mother and child in repose. It wasn't long before he joined them— the three of them lying close together asleep in peace, after Jenny's long struggle.

Surely, this baby, if nothing else, would bring them into the deep intimacy he longed for.

Cal and Jenny made Betsy's life a bit cheerier by bringing the baby over. Indeed it seemed that Betsy forgot her grief, delighted by the smiles, sweet sounds and movements of her granddaughter. She quite enjoyed her daughter-in-law too. A sweet and caring girl, Betsy felt she made Cal the perfect wife.

But she was disturbed that they wanted to go south to Detroit.

"I told you, Ma, we'll take you with us. You can help with Alice."

"I just can't see myself in a big noisy city, after living in North Country so long."

"You must try it out, Ma. You're a survivor."

She gave them a wry smile. "We'll see."

Two days after the wedding, Annie and Frank left for Chicago. Annie was exhilarated.

They were on the southbound train. This would be a brand new life for her. She was with a man who was devoted to her, and she in turn loved him.

She leaned into her husband. "What's it like— Chicago?"

"Big."

"Tell me more."

"Well, there's gangsters, murderers, thieves," he teased.

She looked up at him. "And what else?"

"I said it as a joke. But it is true. That's not all, though. Chicago has art museums I think you'll like, and theatres for film as well as legitimate theatre. And when I get an auto, we can go see all the parks and beautiful parts of the city."

"You're going to get an auto?" She looked at him in surprise.

"I aim to get one as soon as I can afford to. We'll go for rides on Lake Shore Drive."

"I should like that," Annie said.

She snuggled up to him. What happy days lay ahead.

Frank's apartment was not what she was expecting. She didn't think it would be so small, for one thing. There was a sitting room and a bedroom. Both were undersized, she thought. And the dark, grimy kitchen seemed to Annie to be carved out of the hall wall. It smelled of garlic and rancid cooking oil. Well, she could clean it up. She'd make new light colored curtains and bright colored slip covers for the worn sofa and chair.

"I know it's not much, but as I get on with the paper, we'll move to a bigger place, in a better neighborhood."

After cleaning up the kitchen, Annie tackled the windows on the inside. But most of the dirt was on the outside. Years of city street grime had accumulated there. They were on the fifth floor. The obvious solution, as she saw it, was to hang out the window with a wet rag over one shoulder, and a dry one over the other.

She was clinging to the window frame, with one foot hooked on the inside, and the other braced against the outside wall when Frank walked in. He saw her at the window and let out a shout.

"My God, Annie! What are you doing?" He rushed to the window.

If she had fallen, it would have been because of Frank's outburst.

She finished drying the window, and lowered herself back inside. Frank gave her a gratuitous assist.

"You scared the life out of me," he said.

"Darling, do you think it took less bravery to march before the militia and the goons?" She kissed him.

The morning sun could now pierce the glass and illumine the room.

Frank was proud of all the things she did to brighten up the apartment. "I should have hired you years ago," he teased.

But when the improvements were nearly finished— as much as they could afford— Annie grew restless. She was not used to being inactive.

A letter from Betsy arrived. Oh, how glad she was to hear from her old friend. In it, Betsy was encouraging her to write letters to the editor, as she herself was doing.

"We must develop a coterie of women all over the country to convince our citizens to see that justice prevails for the working element of our society. Annie, you could do it. You've given speeches; surely you can say the same in writing, and send them to the people all over. Ask the folks you met on your trip to do the same." She went on to tell her about life in Detroit, and what a joy it was to watch dear little Alice.

The seed grew in Annie.

She talked to Frank. "I want to write. I didn't do all that work to fight for labor only to drop it now. I have to keep it alive. I want to write for the newspapers."

Frank expressed some qualms about the opportunities she would find, but Annie was determined.

"Don't you have some connections, Frank? Someone you know at your paper, or another paper?"

"I'll do what I can."

But he was not able to provide much help.

Finally, Annie wrote letters to the editorial sections of the papers, signing them A.R. Robal. She was thrilled when the first was printed in a small neighborhood weekly. Then came more.

With these small victories, she decided she was ready for bigger presses. She wrote to the *Chicago Tribune*, the Detroit Free Press and other Midwestern dailies.

"Why don't you use your real name?" Frank asked. "You've established quite a reputation as 'Big Annie'."

She grinned. "I'll do that."

When she signed off as *Big Annie,* responses began to pour in. She was overjoyed that her writing was getting some attention.

"It's time you had a by-line," Frank said.

Why not?

Annie was jubilant about her life in Chicago. Frank was doing well, and her by-line was being accepted at more and more papers.

When finally it appeared in the coveted Chicago Times, she was ecstatic.

She wrote to Betsy, sharing her success with the newspapers and her life in Chicago.

"And, dear Betsy, the biggest news of all. We have a baby on the way!"

As much as possible, Annie put aside the pain of what had happened in the Italian Hall. She focused on what was ahead— a loving husband, a baby in the making, and a career in writing. She learned to say yes to new life, yes to forging ahead and yes to joy.

No one had been arrested for the death of Redeemer. His real name was publicized, and a reward had been offered for any information regarding the killer. Three months had gone by. Although there had been accusations, and many had been questioned, nothing was offered to back up the claims.

So far, Flem had gone unnoticed. He was thought to be Redeemer's best friend and protector. Flem was passionate about what he'd done, afraid and proud. He wanted to talk about it, to brag, in fact. He realized one night after having a few pints at his local saloon that he'd almost spilled the tale to a pal of his. He decided that very night that it was not safe for him to drink. Liquor was known to loose a man's tongue, and Flem couldn't take that chance. So, as hard as it would be, he was determined to tipple no more.

Lest his sudden abstinence cause remarks, even suspicion among his fellows, he decided to join the local temperance society. Now, he reasoned, he could put his behavior where his mouth was. Yes, he had the perfect solution.

Roy had tried to find the base of the shaft, and climb up the old ladders. After days of pointless and exhausting staggering, he did find it, but he knew he wasn't strong enough to make that long ascent. He'd have to eat more to gain strength, and get more rest.

But if he got to grass, where could he go? He could imagine only one place.

Then it hit him. What was he thinking? Even if he could make the climb, he could never push away the eight hundred pound cap that would be bolted over it.

Numbly, he'd tried to find the fissure in the earth that had allowed him to find his way below in the first place. From the top he knew exactly how to locate it. Not that it was easy— very few had discovered it. But once found, years ago, he'd made careful notes of its surroundings—the bushes, rocks and an old beech tree— scarred on one side by lightning. In the past, he had never descended more than a few feet.

He traversed one conduit after another looking for the marks he'd made on the timbers on his way in. The place was a warren of passages, and without adequate light, he lost sight of the markings. When all the trails started looking alike, he began to believe that madness had indeed claimed him.

He thought his disease was progressing. From the painless sores he had in the beginning, he now had muscle aches, sore throats and rashes. Most of these symptoms could be ascribed to the life he was leading, but the doctor had warned him that signs like these were indications of the second stage of the illness. And he was tired, so very tired.

What was he doing down here? Had his sickness so rapidly advanced that he was already insane? He had to get out. Even if he got arrested, which no doubt he would.

Exhausted and shaking, he sat down and cried. What if he never saw another human being? Or the sunlight? What if he just died down here? It wasn't the first time he'd given in to dark thoughts, but it was the first time he'd cried.

He pulled out the worn and dirty handkerchief Jenny had given him on the evening of their engagement. He had tried to wash it a few times, but it was grey and torn. He could just make out the perfect initials she'd embroidered on it. The sight of that careful stitching and the love she'd put into them brought on more sobs.

He fell asleep then, and woke to what he thought were footsteps. The sound didn't last long; he must have imagined it. His hearing was keen; he listened carefully to everything. Mostly what he was used to were the rats scurrying around in this maze, alarming wind surges and the diabolical air blasts that he knew to be the caving in of an abandoned shaft. He was in such a shaft. The same could happen here.

Again he heard the steps. His heart began to beat faster. Was it fear or anticipation? He didn't know whether to be afraid or joyful. The soft thud of the steps came closer.

He rose to his feet and unsheathed his hunting knife. His instinct was to take on whoever was here.

Even with a torch, in the near darkness it was impossible to tell who it was. Roy did not recognize the intruder. The scarred face in front of him confirmed his delusional state. Was this man or beast? He'd never seen a person with a countenance so distorted. He must be imagining things. His heart thumped against his chest.

The apparition stepped near him— then backed away. Roy couldn't see him. A gust of wind made his candle flicker twice. Then it died.

An adversary he couldn't see? What chance did he have?

In the total darkness he smelled, rather than heard the creature approach. Foul and acrid, it could only be steps away. Who, what was it?

Flem was surprised to see some of his old pals at the first meeting he attended. They were quite sincere about the evils of drink, and embraced Flem into their fold. He discovered the society was also involved in women's rights and had been active in the abolition of slavery. For a while the speeches only made him wish for drink the more. But after being sober for a while, he could think more clearly than he ever had before, and that made him feel good.

He had learned a lot under Walter's tutelage— learned how to talk to men, get them convinced. Before long he was using his new skills to give speeches on temperance in the saloons. At the end of the year he was toasted at the annual potluck for bringing in more new members than anyone else.

CHAPTER TWENTY-TWO

"**M**r. Willis?"

Roy caught his breath. The voice was almost human.

"Mr. Roy Willis?"

"Who wants to know?"

Please, sir, I h'am not 'ere to 'arm you. I h'am Twister Trewella. My brother was killed h'in the h'explosion. The No.9."

Roy was so stunned he couldn't speak.

"I've come to get you."

"What? Why?" Some of his words didn't come out. Had he lost his vocal chords?

"You can tell by my face what 'appened to me h'in the h'explosion, and my brother Fred, 'e was killed. I thought maybe you was, too."

"Why did you come back here?" The last two words bore no sound.

"To get you," the man repeated.

"How did you—" He stopped to clear his throat. "How did you know where to find me?"

"Well, I looked h'all over for you h'in town. Your brother's been looking for you, too— h'even running h'ads in the paper. I figured you 'ad to be down here— dead h'or h'alive."

Roy was silent.

Twister said, "What did you come down 'ere for?"

"Never mind."

"If you're looking for the way h'out, sir, I can 'elp you. I'll show you. It h'ain't too far from 'ere." Twister sat down. "Need to rest a bit first. I got some water— want some?"

Roy took the water and quenched his thirst. He was puzzled and confused. An angel in the form of a devil had appeared out of nowhere and was offering to shepherd him back to civilization.

They retraced the way Roy had come, and Twister took a hook to the right that Roy had overlooked. They had trudged about half a mile when Roy noticed a tiny shaft of light coming through a narrow break in the ground above.

Thank God! This was exactly the spot he'd been hunting for. How could he have missed the turn?

The way out was treacherous. It was not a man-made shaft, but a series of cracks and crevices that turned and twisted, eventually coming out on top. Ascending the climb was an arduous task for both of them, but more so for Roy. It took three hours with several rest breaks against outcroppings that supported their weight.

When they got to grass Roy was blinded by the light. He feared he'd lost his sight.

"Let's rest a spell," Twister said.

They flopped on the ground. Roy closed his eyes. Periodically, he'd open them. The light was so bright he had to close his eyes again. Gradually he was able to tolerate more light, but he couldn't see clearly. He reckoned he'd have to wait until dark to navigate his way out of here. He was used to moving about in minimum light. He picked a blade of grass, chewed it, smelled it. How wonderful to finally be on top of the ground.

He was thinking of a lot of things, wondering if he should report to the sheriff straight away, or try to hide out some place above ground. He was barely listening to the man beside him, when suddenly he caught the last words.

"I never expected to kill h'anybody with that h'explosion— east of h'all my brother. Maybe Mr. Rhodes— I wouldn't 'ave been sorry to see the last of 'im. And then you couldn't be found nowhere, I thought I'd killed you too. I had to come down 'ere h'and find h'out."

Roy's mouth went dry, and his heart started pounding.

Finally, he said it. "Are you telling me that you caused the explosion?"

"Well, I guess I h'am. But nobody h'else knows. You're the h'only one. I figured I h'owed you that much. I figured maybe you thought they'd blame you, and that's why you were hiding h'out in the mine. Is that right, sir?"

Roy couldn't speak. He had to make his mind go elsewhere so as not to kill the man. His eyes had begun to focus. Roy realized this was the exact place from which he'd descended. He focused on a tree nearby. The tree had leaves, rustling in the wind. At least, half of it did. The other half seemed dead. He hadn't seen a tree with leaves since he'd gone below. He just couldn't think of the name of the tree.

But his mind couldn't stay away from what he'd just learned. This man had just saved his life, and he'd felt most grateful. But then this man had revealed a terrible truth. Roy's head was in a spin. Did this mean he, Roy, wasn't wanted, wasn't suspected? That he'd hidden out for nothing? Roy tried to clear his head.

No, it didn't mean that. The man had said no one else knew.

As he lay on the grass, Roy knew that somehow he'd have to get this Twister to go to the authorities and tell the truth. Would that be possible? The fellow seemed a little dim-witted, but Roy wasn't sure. He couldn't deal with all that now. He didn't feel the man was any threat to him, so he thanked him, and sent him on his way. Roy said he'd stay and rest a while.

He lay there exhausted, with his mind reeling. Finally, the smell of sweet grass and the evening breezes sang him to sleep.

When he awoke it was dark. Just as well. He had a vague idea what he looked like, and it wasn't pretty. His hair hadn't been cut in months, nor had his beard. And he wasn't all that clean. He didn't want to see anybody, let alone be recognized by any of the town folk. He knew where he was going. He was hoping that she was still there, and would let him in.

It must have been about four o'clock in the morning, Roy figured, when he stumbled onto the land that held her little cabin. There were no lights, but there was a trail of smoke coming from the chimney.

He was so tired he could barely stand. But if he didn't do something soon, he would drop to the ground. He knocked on the door. No one answered. He knocked again.

Finally, he called, "Carlene!"

She came to the door, huddled up in her bear rug, and opened it a squeak.

"Is it you?"

"Will you let me in, woman?"

She opened the door so he could enter. He staggered in and fell on to the chair.

"What a sight you are! Thin as a fence post."

He had not the strength to respond.

"I had a feeling you'd be coming. What took you so long?"

He held up his hand to stop her questions. She brought him a blanket, studied his face. Now she could see how totally exhausted he was.

"We'll talk in the morning," she said, and returned to her mattress.

Soon after sunrise she was up and made her strong coffee. This time she'd wait for him to speak before she questioned him.

When his eyes opened, she handed it to him.

He nodded his thanks, and blew on it. In quick gulps he drank it.

"I haven't had coffee since. . ."

"There's more."

He handed her his empty cup.

When the second cup was gone, he began to take in his surroundings.

"Must be spring," he said.

"June."

He looked at her. Her stomach was flat. "Where's the babe?"

"I lost it. Still born."

He frowned, and sat thinking about this. He didn't know whether to say he was sorry or not. Perhaps it was for the best. What if it had been born sick?

"Are you OK?"

She shrugged. "As well as expected. Tired a lot. Rashes, sometimes sore throats."

"Same as me," he muttered.

They were silent for a long time, as she rocked in her chair.

Finally, she said, "I'll fix you something to eat."

"I'd be obliged."

She returned with fried bread, thick bacon, and more coffee.

Roy grunted his appreciation several times. When he had finished, he said, "What have you heard about me? Am I a wanted man?"

"Wanted for questioning, anyway. They've come a couple of times looking for you."

"Then I am a suspect for the explosion."

"I'm not sure."

Carlene sniffed the air. "Maybe you could go down to the river and wash yourself, and your hair."

"Yeah. I must smell like an old grizzly bear."

She didn't contradict him. She smiled and gave him an old towel and some soap. The woman was almost as big as he; she offered him a clean pair of her trousers and a shirt.

His legs were stiff from all the climbing and walking he'd done yesterday. Still, he enjoyed being outside, strolling through the swaying grass and cattails down to the river.

Half-way there, he threw up. He guessed human food was too rich for him. Ironic to think his innards would have done better with a morsel of rodent. He'd have to break in easy to normal food.

The water was still icy cold, but refreshing too. He washed his long hair three times.

When he got back to the cabin she had a fire going, sat him in the rocker near it and covered him with a blanket.

"Shall I cut it?" she said, combing the snarls out of his hair.

"Maybe it's just as well I look like this. No one will recognize me. What do you think?"

It was the first time he'd asked her opinion on anything.

"Well, as long as I can see your eyes, I guess it will be all right."

"Are you asking me to stay?"

"Do you want to stay, Roy Willis?"

He looked at her a long time. It seemed a reasonable choice to him. They could help each other. They could comfort each other, and offer company.

"We can try it out," he said, "if you're willing."

"Just don't call me 'woman'."

"Carlene, eh?"

Within a week Roy began to feel stronger. Gradually, he got used to the food she prepared. In the days to come he chopped wood for her and brought in buckets of water from the creek.

Roy was ignorant of all that had happened while he was underground. Little by little Carlene filled him in on the strike, the tragedy at the Italian Hall, and the death of his sister. Finally, she told him of his father's death.

If he asked, she filled him in on the details. She knew it was a lot for him to take in. Carlene was careful how she parceled it out for him. It would take a long time for him to digest it all. If there was grieving to be done, she knew he'd do it when he was alone.

When she told him about the strike he said, "I could see that coming."

One day she said, "You're white as a ghost, Roy Willis. You need to be out in the sun more."

He started a vegetable garden. It was good to be outdoors, and sometimes he'd spread himself out on the ground, just to soak up the sun.

Carlene cooked hearty soups and stews and kept the cabin cleaner than it had ever been before. She made a kind of distilled brew he'd never tasted before. It was strong and bitter. He had trouble getting used to it, but like the rodents, in time he did.

They sat in the evenings with the fire crackling, passing a cigar between them and drinking the pungent concoction. There was very little conversation. When they tired, they lay side by side under the bearskin cover, but there was no coupling.

As they lay in bed one night, Carlene was studying Roy's face. A bit of light shone through the glass, highlighting his scars. She traced each one gently with her finger.

"What are you doing?"

"I put these here."

"Enough of that, Carlene. It is what it is." He squeezed her hand. "Let's just move on."

He turned and twisted that night. In the morning he said, "I'm too old to sleep on the floor. What do you say to a real bed?"

"If it would please you," she smiled.

So Roy got to work making a rough-hewn pine bed two feet off the floor, with slats of wood going from side to side. Carlene sewed old flour sacks together, and they stuffed it with straw. On top of that they put the old mattress.

"We'll have to get a better mattress," Roy noted.

"Some day."

But they enjoyed their new bed, and laughed when the straw crunched beneath them.

Jenny was concerned about the baby's weight. Only five pounds at birth, she'd lost some, which Jenny was told was natural. Finally, the baby began to gain, but very little. She slept more than most babies, and had some trouble breathing. She began to cough— harshly and often— a heartbreaking sound to Jenny. She took little Alice to the doctor's.

Dr. Follett was not alarmed. "I know the cough sounds bad, but it's probably just the croup, and will go away in a few days."

Jenny nodded uncertainly.

"Is your milk coming in all right?"

"Oh, yes. But she takes little of it."

"Call me if she isn't better in a few days."

Jenny left with small consolation.

Roy was out in back chopping kindling when a figure appeared around the corner of the cabin. He knew instinctively that it wasn't Carlene. On guard, he looked up and faced the man. Identifying his brother immediately, he hoped Cal didn't recognize him. With a long beard and great mop of hair, he knew he looked very different than the last time Cal had seen him. And skinny as a fence pole, as Carlene had said.

But Cal was not to be fooled. "Hello, Roy."

Roy said nothing, just looked at his brother.

"Thought I might find you here," Cal said.

"What made you think that?" Roy continued chopping up the hemlock.

"I've turned over about every other stone around here, and some— not around here."

Roy nodded cautiously.

"Look, rumors get around. Somebody told me there was a man staying out here. I figured it might be you."

"Ball in the pocket," Roy said.

Cal hadn't expected much of a welcome. At least he hadn't been chased off the land— not yet, anyway. But he did hope to break through to Roy.

Finally, he blurted out, "You're an uncle now," and immediately regretted it.

"So the fair Jenny has given you a kid."

Cal nodded weakly. "But she's sick— the baby, that is. Coughs all the time. More like a bark."

Roy put down the ax and stared at his brother until Cal was uncomfortable. Finally, Roy nodded thoughtfully. "Bring her by. Maybe Carlene can do something for her."

As pleased as he was that his brother invited them to come, he didn't think Carlene was the answer to the baby's cough. He almost refused the offer, but realized that if he did, it would probably kill any chance of reuniting with his brother.

"Are you sure she wouldn't mind?"

"I'll tell her you're coming."

"Tomorrow, then," Cal added.

Roy turned away then, strode toward the cabin. Cal stood paralyzed for a moment until it struck him that the encounter was over. He'd imagined the meeting going several different ways, but this hadn't been one of them.

Roy had been feeling very horny for some time. He hadn't had any contact with a woman since last with Carlene.

"What would you think of us having a poke?" he said into the darkness.

"What— you and me?"

"You see anybody else? I mean we've both got the pox now. What harm could it do?"

"I don't see as it would make us any worse."

"I don't either."

That was all the permission he needed. He turned toward her and ran his hands through her hair. She placed her hands over his shoulders and worked her way down his spine. He'd never felt this kind of tingle, from his shoulders to his tailbone, and then some.

In the past he hadn't wasted much time trying to arouse her. This time he caressed her, gently, as he never had before. And she responded as she never had in the past. They joined in a way that startled them both. Neither had ever been pulled into the world of pleasure so completely.

A loud knock on the door startled them both.

Before he could put clothes on, a second knock, louder than the first rattled the cinders in the fireplace.

"Hold your horses!" he yelled to whoever the intruder might be.

Roy pulled on his pants and crossed to the door, opening it cautiously.

"What do you want?"

"You Roy Willis?"

"Who wants to know?"

"We're the sheriff's deputies, and here to arrest you for the explosion in the No.9."

Roy took a deep breath. So they'd finally come for him. He wondered dimly who'd reported him. Would Cal have betrayed him once again?

He nodded, said, "Let me get dressed."

They followed him back into the cabin, and watched while he finished dressing. He told Carlene in quiet tones who it was and why he had to leave.

"There'll be a trial, I reckon. Maybe I can clear this thing up."

He could see her concern, and thought he saw her lips tighten.

He tried to lighten up. "You can come into town and check up on me."

Slowly she shook her head. "I'll know."

He said good-bye to her and left with the deputies.

They had come in an automobile. He'd only ridden in one a few times. He tried to focus on the particular features of the vehicle he was in, rather than the situation.

When Cal heard that Roy had been arrested, he decided not to take the baby to the Tallfeather place. He couldn't— not yet, anyway. He didn't want to face Carlene without Roy there. And he wasn't sure he could get Jenny to go. He was very upset that Roy was in jail, but not entirely surprised. Roy going into hiding wasn't going to help his case.

Earl Foster had thought a lot about the explosion in the mine, and Roy Willis running off and hiding himself somewhere. He knew it made Roy look guilty, but Earl still couldn't make himself believe that Roy was guilty. Perhaps Roy was so sure he'd be found guilty, he didn't want to take the chance of being charged. Or maybe his mind had been affected by his disease.

In any case, he decided to pay a visit to Roy in jail. As judge, he probably shouldn't be doing this, but once an investigator always one, and he had to talk to Roy alone, not wait for a courtroom trial.

He found Roy lying awake on his cot. He didn't look so awfully different from when Earl had last seen him. Except he was so very white. And thinner too. The sheriff had insisted that "all that hair" be cut off. So Roy had lost his beard, and most of the hair on his head.

"Remember me, Roy?" Earl asked.

Roy sat up and squinted. "You're the sheriff, right?"

"I used to be. The citizens of our county demoted me to judge."

His attempt at humor didn't go over.

"Watcha doing here? Are we going to have the trial right here in my cell?"

"No. I just wanted to talk to you."

"Well, you won't believe anything I have to say."

"Why don't you let me decide for myself?"

Roy shrugged.

"Is it true that Twister Trewella found you in the old No.2? And unearthed you?"

"Where did you hear that?"

"He's been bragging about it."

"Yeah, it's true.

"How did he get in?"

"Same way I did. Through a natural fissure. It's covered with brambles and bushes. Not easy to find."

Judge Foster nodded thoughtfully. "Why do you suppose he came after you?"

"Said he didn't want me to take the blame for the explosion."

"Why would he say that?"

Roy shook his head. "If I told you, you'd never think it true."

"Try me."

"Twister said he did it."

Much to Roy's surprise, the judge did not laugh; he did not even look surprised.

Roy went on. "I don't know if he did or didn't, but he told me no one knew except me."

Earl nodded. "Twister is foolish, you know. He started a fire last year and got caught. I thought all along he might be the cause of the explosion. But his brother was killed, and he was maimed. It was a head scratcher all right. It didn't make sense that he'd— "

"I know. He didn't want that. But his grudge against the Company has spun way out of line."

"He shouldn't have been hired back again after the first incident," Foster said.

"But what made you think the explosion was his fault?" Roy asked.

"Because even though you looked guilty— running off— I just didn't figure you'd do something like that. Always responsible, you were. And Rhodes? Well, he can be a snake in the grass— like tampering with the angle of the cut— but he's trying to improve his situation, not jeopardize it."

"So you never believed I was guilty?"

"No. But my hunches aren't going to get you out of this mess. There will be a trial."

Armed with a bottle of liquor, Earl drove to the other side of town where Twister Trewella lived. He was still a bit skittish about driving, but the retired Judge McKinney had convinced him that any self-respecting judge had to own an automobile. Besides, his old horse Bigot had succumbed to old age. Earl surrendered to the newfangled motor car.

Driving at night was an additional challenge. With so little road in view it would be easy to hit a deer or other animal. Still, it was too damn far to walk. Fortunately, the roads weren't slippery tonight, just wet from all the recent rain. The Tin Lizzy rattled right along without a hitch all the way to Twister's place.

"Whoa, Lizzie," he called, as he put the brakes on his new Model T.

Twister was so surprised to be paid a visit by the judge, he just stood there, saying over and over, "I'll be damned, I'll be damned."

"Can I come in?" Earl Foster finally said.

"Oh, sure, sir. Come right in."

Earl hadn't planned to drink, but it was so cold, he had a fast one to warm his belly. He was wishing he'd brought firewood, too.

"Just thought we might have a little chat."

"Sure."

He handed the whiskey to Twister, who took a deep swallow. Some slurped off his warped face. He licked it off his hand.

"Do you have a job now, or work of any kind?"

"Naw, not really. I do the mucking h'out h'over to the smelting plant when they need me, but that h'ain't regular. Can't depend on h'it."

Besides his Cornish accent, his twisted face made it even more difficult for Earl to understand him.

"How's that?"

Twister repeated himself.

"What do you do for food?"

"You'd be surprised what the restaurants throw h'out. I do pretty good, cleaning h'out their throw-h'outs at night."

"You make the rounds, do you?"

"Yeah, and well, there's certain places that save a little back for me, if they 'ave left-hovers."

"I see."

They sat in silence for a time. Twister knocked back a second slug, and handed the bottle back to Earl.

"Is it true you helped Roy Willis get out of the mine?"

Twister sat up straighter. "Yes, sir, I did. He'd a never gotten h'out by 'isself. But I been h'in and h'out a there for years. I know my way through h'all those twists and turns like I know my nose." Then he slapped his ghoulish countenance and turned away.

"Well, I guess he owes his life to you, Twister."

"Yes, sir, I think you could say that."

"There's all kinds of dangers down there."

"No truer word said."

"Say, how'd you get that name— Twister?"

The man squirmed in his seat. "Well, sir, folks used to say I twisted their words." He laughed in a nervous kind of way. "Some folks said that— not h'everybody."

Earl saw Twister reach up, involuntarily slap his face again, then lower that arm with the other.

Twister asked, "How's 'e doing now— Mr. Willis?"

"He's been arrested for that explosion in the No. 9."

"No. Sorry to hear that." His knee started jumping up and down. With his hand he pressed it down.

Earl handed the bottle to him. "What made you go down there to save him?"

Twister stirred in his seat and took his third gulp before answering.

"Well, nobody ever found 'im. And I was wondering if he was moldering away down there. I wanted to find h'out if 'e were dead down there, living down there, or what. Know what I mean?"

"I guess we've all wondered that."

"Say, do you suppose I could visit him h'over to the jail?"

"I don't see why not."

"I feel for the bloke."

"Why don't you come by tomorrow afternoon?"

Earl rose to leave.

"I'd h'appreciate that, sir." He held the bottle of whiskey out to Earl.

"No, you keep it, Twister. You've been real helpful."

Earl Foster arranged with the sheriff and the turnkey to notify him as soon as Twister Trewella appeared at the jail.

Twister arrived about two o'clock in the afternoon, and the judge was dutifully notified. There was a vent between Roy's cell and a small room used for cleaning supplies next to it. It would not be too difficult to hear the conversation between Roy and his visitor from this space.

The three men crept into the room, crowded together. Twister was already talking to the prisoner.

"I'm real sorry, Roy, to see where you landed yourself. I was hoping that was h'all blown over by now, and nobody would bother you."

"How did you know I was here?"

"The judge— I can 'ardly believe it— paid me a visit last night. Brought me some 'ooch, too. Next, the president will be coming by." He laughed heartily at his joke. "Anyway, he told me h'about you being h'arrested on the sheriff's h'orders, and said I'd be welcome to visit you."

"That's good of you," Roy said.

"Well, h'it's the least I can do, considering."

"Considering what?" Roy asked.

"You know. What we talked h'about before."

"What was that?"

"Well," Twister looked around to make sure no one was listening. "'bout 'ow I know it wasn't you who done the deed."

"Which deed is that?"

"Like we said."

"Maybe it's cuz I was in down below so long, but sometimes my mind doesn't seem to work right. I forget things."

"I know what you mean. Same thing 'appens to me. I mean the h'explosion in the No.9 last year."

"Oh, right. You told me you did it, right?"

Twister coughed. "And I told you that you was the h'only one who knew. I h'ain't told nobody else."

"Tell me again, Twister. Why did you do it?"

"Damn Company. They never gave me credit for nothing. But I didn't mean to kill nobody— 'cept maybe Rhodes. 'E was a slave driver."

Twister started to tear up. "I still feel terrible, h'about Fred's— my brother. I didn't come h'out too good, either." He rubbed the side of his face.

"How did you do it?"

"Oh, it weren't hard. Just fired h'off a hell of a lot of h'ammunition. Fred, 'e was busy drillin' holes— didn't see me. Trouble is I didn't make the fuse long h'enough. Thought I did. But I didn't get my figures right."

"Were you trying to ruin the Company?"

"At least slow it down."

"How do you feel about it now?"

"H'ain't sorry 'bout the mine, if that's what you mean."

The turnkey stepped in front of the cell. "That's all the time I can give you, Trewella. Visiting time is over."

"OK. You take care 'o yerself, Mr. Roy. I'll come visit you next week."

The turnkey opened the door and ushered Twister Trewella out.

The sheriff stepped forward and spoke to him.

"If you'll just step in here."

Twister was guided into a cell two doors down.

"'Ey, watcha doin?"

"We'll explain."

"Let me h'outa here. I h'ain't the prisoner."

"You are now," the sheriff said. "We couldn't have dreamed up a cleaner confession."

"Hey, that h'ain't fair. Willis squeal h'on me?"

"You told us yourself— just now."

It took Twister a minute to comprehend.

"You listened h'in?"

"You could say that."

"You gotta 'ave witnesses. Not just yourself."

"We have three."

"Bloody 'ell!"

"We ought to get you for prosecuting attorney," Earl told Roy. "You did a fine job getting all that information out of him. Couldn't ask for more."

"It felt pretty sly. You know he's got a few cards missing. Always has. He walked right into the trap."

"Would you rather spend your life in prison for what he did?"

"Nope."

"Well then, be free and be glad."

"You letting me go?"

"Yeah, unless you've become attached to the place."

"What will become of Twister?"

"He'll get a fair trial. Listen, he'll be better off incarcerated than on his own. He's half starved, can't get work, and as you know, he's playing with less than a full deck. I think confinement will be his savior. Probably go downstate to Ionia."

"What's there?"

"Hospital for the criminally insane."

Roy nodded. He shook hands with the judge, free at last of the cloud that had hung over him for so long. He strode back to the cabin, where Carlene was waiting for him with a warm meal.

He had gotten used to her knowing things before they happened.

She took him in her arms. He began weeping, quietly at first, and then in huge blubbering sobs. It was over— the hiding, the fear.

They lay down together, and she just held him. She knew he needed this outburst, that he was opening the floodgates of his anger, his sadness of loss, his relief. And the freedom that now lay ahead.

When at last he calmed down, he fell asleep in her arms.

CHAPTER TWENTY-THREE

"I don't see how I can face him," Jenny protested. "But I have to see him before we leave, and that was what he offered— that Carlene see the baby."

"She can't help Alice."

"Probably not. But she won't harm her, and we have to make the call."

"Oh, Cal, don't you see how hard that would be for Roy, and me?"

"I do."

"And you still think I should go, and take Alice?"

"Yes."

The baby continued to cough.

Cal's look was so earnest that Jenny finally gave in.

"Tomorrow, then."

Cal nodded. In the morning Jenny didn't think about why, but she put the baby in her best dress.

When they arrived at the cabin, Jenny's heart was beating so hard, she wondered if she could walk to the door.

"You'll be all right. I'll be right beside you," Cal said.

Roy heard the auto's engine and came out to meet them. He avoided looking at Jenny; he was gazing at the child. Jenny didn't know what to expect from him. She only knew she felt an awful shame, but that didn't feel right either.

At last he glanced at her, and then looked down at the baby again.

"Come on in. She's expecting you."

As soon as they entered, Carlene said, "Give me the child," holding out her arms.

Jenny was aghast at being expected to hand her baby over to this stranger, with not so much as an introduction.

Cal nudged her. "It will be all right."

After several moments, and an encouraging smile from the strange woman, Jenny hesitantly placed Alice in Carlene's arms. Cal had to support his wife as she was shaking so.

Carlene sat in her rocker, humming a tune unfamiliar to Cal and Jenny, as she gently swayed back and forth.

A rough-cut wooden seat, large enough for two, sat across the room. Probably something Roy had made. Cal couldn't remember there being any place to sit when he was here before. He guided his wife to the bench. He sat beside Jenny while she clutched his hand until it turned white. He withdrew it, placing it over hers.

Carlene began mumbling things over the child— spells, Jenny supposed. The baby held her head up, and showed keen attention. After a while she even smiled at Carlene.

To herself Jenny thought, these spells are probably harmless. But if they're powerful, they could do harm as well as good. Perhaps this woman sought to punish the couple, for Roy's sake?

Finally Carlene spoke. "She has the croup. Does she cough worse at night?"

The couple nodded.

Cal and Jenny looked at each other. No one had told the woman Alice's condition, and Alice hadn't coughed once since they arrived.

"Yes," Cal stammered. "How do you know?"

The woman smiled and shook her head.

Carlene rose. She handed the baby back to her mother. Then she took a small cotton bag from a drawer. "This herb will make it easier for her to breathe."

Jenny took the bag cautiously. "Then it's not serious?"

"No. She should be well in a few days, probably sooner."

"Thank you so much."

As she turned to go, Jenny knew the hardest part was still ahead. She needed to say good-bye to Roy. She handed the child to Cal and made herself cross the room to her old beau.

"Thank you for inviting us. Thank you. And . . ." she stammered. She could feel the color in her face a vivid shade of scarlet. "I'm truly sorry about . . . everything."

He shoved his hands in his pockets, and looked at her. "Me too."

Then she took a daring step and held out her hand.

As he took it in his, Jenny could feel both of their hands shaking. He looked at her with his deep sad eyes. They held each other's gaze for several moments. When her lips began to quiver, she nodded good-bye to him, reclaimed the baby from her husband and stumbled to the car.

She knew Cal wanted to speak with his brother privately. She was glad for this opportunity to be alone with the tears she could no longer hold back.

Cal walked outside with his brother.

"Let me show you the garden," Roy offered.

Surprised, Cal was grateful for the offer. Grateful that his brother was willing to talk.

"What are you growing?"

"All sorts of thing. Tomatoes, asparagus, peas. And root vegetables that will keep."

"That's wonderful."

Carlene is canning some, so we'll have food for the winter."

Finally, Cal said, "We're leaving for Detroit soon. I can't work for the mining company anymore, so we've decided to go downstate. Will you go with us, Roy? This isn't an idle offer. We both would like to heal old wounds and take you with us."

Roy looked away and ran his hand through his hair.

When he finally looked back at Cal, he said, "Thanks, but my place is here with Carlene now. And mining is all I know. It's too late to learn a new trade."

Cal started to say something, but Roy waved him off.

"Parker offered me a job— not sure what I'll be doing. But I'll work as long as . . ." he shrugged.

Cal nodded. "I understand, but if you change your mind— I'll send you our address when we get settled."

"I appreciate the offer."

"And—" Cal hesitated. "There's one more thing. There's a new medication out, I don't know if you've heard of it. It's supposed to cure—"

Roy shook his head. "Mercury is poison, Carlene says. She won't let us take it."

"She's right— that's the old stuff. No, this is new, Roy—"

Roy cut him off. "I'm doing just fine with Carlene's remedies."

Cal looked suspicious. "You don't think she can cure you—"

"I didn't say that."

Cal kicked a stone with his boot. Finally, he said, "Let's stay in touch."

"Yeah. That would be good."

"Well, I'm glad to finally know you're alive. And have a life, brother."

Good luck with the child."

"Thanks for all the help. And thank Carlene, too."

They shook hands.

Roy worked his mouth in a way Cal recognized. His brother had something else to say. He waited.

Finally it came out. "It's OK— you being with Jenny."

A lump rose in Cal's throat and a catch in his breath.

Unspoken thoughts passed between them. Their eyes expressed a mixture of pain, forgiveness and blessing. For brothers who had long known the bond of love, it was enough.

Cal was quiet as they drove home, and Jenny respected his silence. She knew he was thinking about his brother, and would tell her about their conversation when he was ready.

Jenny wasn't sure why, but she trusted the half-breed. Maybe it was the compassion she saw in the woman's eyes. She gave the baby the medicine as Carlene had directed, and by morning the child had stopped coughing. Jenny didn't know whether, as the doctor said, the cough would be gone in a few days, or it was Carlene's herb. But she felt a humble gratitude to the woman who knew so much and cared enough to offer her aid. She was so very thankful that her baby was finally well.

The encounter with Roy had been very healing for her— and for their marriage. She knew that she had distanced herself from her husband because of a misguided loyalty to his brother. She'd permitted Cal to make love to her, but she had never given herself completely.

Gradually, Jenny began to feel an internal balance and peace she hadn't felt before. Worries faded about the whereabouts of Roy, and how he was faring. Roy had a partner. He and Carlene were with their problem together, and they would face it together. She, Jenny, belonged to Cal.

Within a week after their visit to the cabin, Jenny felt strong desires for her husband. She even initiated some of their love making. In turn, Cal got more aroused and did more to excite his wife. Their coupling led to happier times during the daytime, too. They were more determined than ever to make their marriage joyful.

As soon as Betsy found out that the baby was ill, she lost no time in deciding she would go downstate. She'd do what she could to take care of the child, and give the babe's parents her support.

"Oh, Ma, you'll be loads of help."

"And we can keep you company. We don't want you alone up here."

Betsy was looking very pensive.

"What is it, Ma?"

"I must see Roy before we go," Betsy said solemnly.

"Of course," Cal said.

On a cloudy morning that week, he drove his mother out to the cabin. They rode in silence most of the way. Then Betsy twisted in her seat, and Cal knew she was anxious about the visit. "What'll I say to him?'"

Cal didn't have any ready answers.

Betsy continued. "You know it is I who put him in this jam—sending him there to get herbs for Patty. Oh, how I blame myself—"

"Ma, please. You can't do that. You didn't send him to do what he did. He had a choice. That's all his responsibility. And he knows it."

"Still, you can't imagine how I regret it." She looked up sharply. "Oh, I'm sorry, Cal! I'm not wishing you don't have Jenny. Or little Alice. Oh, I don't know what I'm saying."

"Well, we're here. You'll be fine. Just don't go apologizing for what you didn't do. Wish him well, and be nice to Carlene. She may have saved Alice's life. Anyway, she's a good person.

Betsy gave her son a brave smile.

"I'll stay in the car. You go in, Ma."

She looked hesitant. "Perhaps it's best."

Cal walked around the car, and opened the door for her.

She took a deep breath and got out.

"Here, don't forget the sour-cream cake you made for them." Cal handed her the box.

She was inside longer than he'd thought she'd be. When she came out she looked upset.

Then she smiled. "They seem happy together. I guess that's the best we can hope for." She sat up straight, ready for the ride home.

"That's right, Ma. I think they are."

Betsy read Peter's letters over and over. There were times when she felt bitter, and times when she was just sad how her life had turned out.

Finally, she decided she owed Peter a visit. Three times she picked up the telephone before she dared put through the call.

"I'm Betsy Willis. I'd like to make an appointment with Dr. Follett," she told the receptionist.

It was even harder to approach his office. She had to marshal all her courage to go through that door. While she waited, she wondered once again if she should tell him of their child. She had fought this battle with herself for years. Well, if the time were ever right, it had passed. AnnaBeth was gone. He could never see his daughter now. What could it bring but sadness to tell him?

She didn't have to wait long to see him. His entrance stopped her breath for a moment. He was still tall, straight-backed with a full head of brown hair. Not a single grey strand.

Peter broke all tension by grasping both her hands in his. "Betsy!" He looked overjoyed.

When she was seated, and he'd given her an encouraging smile, she said, "I'm not here for medical reasons."

Peter nodded. She searched his face for some sign as to how to proceed.

"I'll come right to the point. I thought you should know why I never answered your letters," she blurted out.

She produced the bundle. "I only discovered these among my husband's papers after he died. I never saw them before."

He stared at them for a long time, finally taking a jagged breath. At last his eyes met hers.

"I thought that might have happened. But that was my fantasy. It seemed more likely you'd given up on me."

"How could you think that? And if it were true, surely I'd have written you."

Peter dropped his head and nodded.

"I'll be moving downstate with my son Cal and his family. I didn't come here to start up anything, Peter."

He nodded. "I'm married."

"Yes. I came because I wanted you to know that I finally understand why I never heard from you."

"And now I understand why I didn't hear from you."

Their eyes expressed the sadness of all those lost years. They sat still, hearing only the ticking of the grandfather clock. For a moment it seemed to reverse itself.

She noticed that he still had that little depression between his thumb and forefinger. She wondered if his skin would still taste salty if . . .

She forced herself back to the present, and ventured a question. "I wondered why you came back here, Peter."

She thought he blushed. "Well, at first I was hoping— but then I heard . . . " He tossed his hands up.

"But you stayed on."

"I love the North Country," he said. "It's home for me. Didn't care much for all the hustle and bustle out east. Here you have time to listen to your own thoughts. I like the slower pace."

Betsy smiled.

"And you, Betsy, have you been happy?"

He reddened as soon as the words were out.

"I shouldn't have said that. You've lost your husband and your daughter. You've had a hard row to hoe."

Betsy nodded briefly.

"And your son Roy," he shook his head remembering. "Whatever became of him?"

She'd forgotten that he'd been Roy's doctor.

"He's re-surfaced. Oh!" She stopped herself. She hadn't meant to make a pun. But Peter didn't know where Roy had been.

Peter smiled, putting them at ease.

"He's making a life for himself out in the country."

"Good. That's good to hear."

They were silent for a few moments.

"I was so sorry to read of your daughter's death in the Italian Hall disaster."

She took a quick intake of breath. *Our* daughter. Her hand shook. He had mentioned AnnaBeth twice. But he showed no sign of knowing. Again her resolve wavered. She decided it was time to leave. She nodded, and rose.

"Thank you very much for coming in. I'm very glad that you did." He took her hands in his.

She looked straight into those soft grey eyes. "Are you— really?"

The embrace he held her in was unexpected. She let him hold her for a few moments. Then she broke away before she lost all decorum and burst into tears. She turned to the door.

"Good-bye, Peter."

She didn't suppose she'd ever see him again, but she felt a great burden slipping away, and a sense of relief and joy for having brought a peaceful close to all those years of sadness and resentment.

And she would remember that embrace for a long time.

CHAPTER TWENTY-FOUR

Plans to travel south were falling in place. Some things were shipped ahead to a storage facility until they found a place to live. Betsy would leave the sale of her home and the guest house in the hands of a broker.

She missed Annie. They had become the best of friends; it had been hard to see her leave for Chicago. But now they'd be a little closer, with both of them living in the Lower Peninsula. They had exchanged letters, and would continue to do so. Both hoped that one day they'd be able to visit again, face to face. In the meantime she let Annie know that she would not let the role of a doting grandmother keep her from writing to the newspapers. There could not be too many people fighting for fair labor practices!

Cal and Jenny were in bed in the little guest house for their last night. They were lying wide-awake, side by side, in silence.

Finally Jenny asked, "Are you sad to be leaving Red Jacket?"

"In a way, yes. Are you?"

She nodded. "I know I'll miss it."

"It's been home my whole life— yours too."

"I've never even been downstate. Have you?"

"Once," he said

"Did you like it?" She grasped his hand.

Cal took a while to answer. "Well, it's warmer. Shorter winters."

Jenny swallowed. "Very noisy around Detroit, isn't it?"

"I suppose so. Busy."

They could hear a fly buzzing about the room.

"Well, it will be exciting to see another part of the world," Jenny said.

"Yes."

Again they were silent.

"We can always come back if it doesn't work out, can't we?" Jenny said.

He reached over and brought her into his arms. "Sweetheart, we're just being scared. It will be fine." He held her against him.

In the morning, dressed and ready to leave, little Alice was laughing and flopping her arms up and down.

"She's ready to go," Cal laughed.

"And so are we." Jenny said.

He led her out the door. "And so are we."

Earl leaned back in his office chair. It was as squeaky as the one in the sheriff's office. Well, there was something comforting about this familiar sound.

On his way home, he reflected on all that had gone on in the last eighteen months. What a torrential initiation he'd had into the judicial side of Copper Country law! At least the strike was over, and everybody could breathe a little easier. The riots had stopped. Most men had gone back to work, or left the North Country, while others came to replace them. A watchful quiet had settled over the community.

It was even safe to take a stroll at night and look up at those wonderful stars. Earl decided he'd ask Cora to do just that.

He slowed his pace to take in the beauty of the autumn scene. Why was it, he wondered, that leaves looked their most splendid just before their downfall, whereas with people it was the opposite? The colors of maple and birch waved in the breeze, showing off their glory. The sky was casting that passionate shade of blue it proffered only in the autumn. Low clouds chased each other across the western horizon.

This was God's country, and he loved it. Even in the long bitter winters— what was more glorious than waking after a snowfall when the sun's alchemy had transformed every tree into a sparkling ice sculpture?

But it was autumn itself that he appreciated the most, when whole hillsides blushed with opulent magentas, yellows and tangerines, and the smell of burning wood fires made you want to curl up with a good book and a cup of cocoa.

After supper he pulled his napkin off his chest and wiped his mouth.

He said to his wife, "Lovely evening, Cora. Unusually warm. Let's go for a breath of air."

She looked amazed. It had been a long time since her husband had suggested anything so leisurely. He'd been too busy. She stared at him.

"A stroll, a walk?" he teased.

Cora was overjoyed.

Outdoors, the moon was peeking through the leaves. It was a quarter moon, but Earl wasn't sure if it was waxing or waning. Now, with a little more time, maybe he could keep track of the cycles better. Yes, he meant to do that, he told Cora.

"You'll be spending more time at home now, eh? Now that the Trouble's over."

"That's the plan," he said as he put his arm around her and led her home. "Maybe tonight we can catch the early bed."

QUESTIONS FOR GROUP DISCUSSION

1. Why do you think Betsy was driven to write letters to the editor?
2. Did you understand how Redeemer 'took care of'' Big Annie?
3. Why do you think Roy chose to go underground after the explosion?
4. When did you realize Betsy and Dr. Follett had a past?
5. Was the terminology of the mining industry clear to you?
6. What arguments can you present on the behalf of Management?
7. As you read the book were your sympathies always with Labor?
8. In what ways is the issue of Management vs. Labor relevant today?
9. What characters in the book do you think are purely fictitious?
10. Which characters do you think are real, perhaps with changed names?
11. Who was your favorite character? Why?
12. Were there any aspects of the book that you found confusing?
13. Would you recommend this book to others? Why or why not?

REFERENCES

CRADLE TO GRAVE, *Life, Work and Death at Lake Superior Copper Mines,* by Larry Lankton, Oxford University Press Inc. New York, 1991

STRANGERS and SOJOURNERS, *A History of Michigan's Keweenaw Peninsula, by* Arthur W. Thurner, Wayne State University Press, Detroit Michigan, 1994

BIG ANNIE OF CALUMET, *A True Story of Industrial Revolution,* by Jerry Stanley, Crown Publishers, Inc. New York, 1996

A MOST SUPERIOR LAND, *Life in the Upper Peninsula of Michigan,* Two Peninsula Press, Michigan Department of Natural Resources, Lansing, Michigan, 1983

AND IN WHOSE HILLS YOU SHALL MINE COPPER, *Historic Diaries of the Copper Country,* Keweenaw Press, Calumet MI, 1994

20007355R00132

Made in the USA
Charleston, SC
22 June 2013